DIRTY BUSINESS MYSTERY SERIES

DEATH at the DENTIST

A Sonja Hovland Adventure

SUE BERG

LITTLE CREEK PRESS
MINERAL POINT, WISCONSIN

Copyright © 2025 Sue Berg

All rights reserved. No part of this publication may be reproduced, distributed, or transmitted in any form or by any means, including photocopying, recording, digital scanning, or other electronic or mechanical methods, without the prior written permission of the publisher, except in the case of brief quotations embodied in critical reviews and certain other noncommercial uses permitted by copyright law. For permission requests or other information, please send correspondence to the following address:

Little Creek Press
5341 Sunny Ridge Road
Mineral Point, WI 53565

ORDERING INFORMATION
Quantity sales. Special discounts are available on quantity purchases by corporations, associations, and others. For details, contact info@littlecreekpress.com

Orders by US trade bookstores and wholesalers.
Please contact Little Creek Press or Ingram for details.

Printed in the United States of America

Cataloging-in-Publication Data
Names: Sue Berg, author
Title: Death at the Dentist
Description: Mineral Point, WI Little Creek Press, 2025
Identifiers: LCCN: 2025907477 | ISBN: 978-1-967311-02-6
Classification: FICTION / Mystery & Detective / Women Sleuths
FICTION / Mystery & Detective / Amateur Sleuth
FICTION / Thrillers / Domestic

Book design by Little Creek Press

ACKNOWLEDGMENTS

This book is for all the blue-collar people.
Thank you for all that you do for others every day

For Alan—thanks for the memories!

MONDAY, MAY 25

CHAPTER 1 • SONJA
Down and Dirty

My name is Sonja Hovland, and I am married to Trygve (pronounced Trig-Vee for those of you who are not of Norwegian American descent). By the way, if you don't have Norwegian heritage, then you don't know what you're missing—blessings like rommegrot, lefse, fattigman, lutefisk, sandbakkels, strul, anything salmon, and oyster stew, which is always served on Christmas Eve. Sorry, I got off on a tangent there, but after twenty-three years of marriage to a dyed-in-the-wool Norwegian American, you learn what's important in a relationship.

I own a cleaning agency called Dirty Business Cleaning Services in La Crosse, Wisconsin, which doubles as a cover for the private detective inquiries I do for some of my customers. The parallel between the two occupations can be striking; the dirty business of cleaning up other people's messy houses is not unlike the tangled affairs people get into in their personal lives. Although most of my customers have no idea that I'm a private detective on the side, there's nothing wrong with killing two birds with one stone, is there?

My detective work includes adultery, embezzlement, the terms of a will, or DNA tests to determine parentage. The dilemmas confronting some of my clients have been eye-opening and, at times, shocking. I try to counsel them through their decisions when difficult topics like divorce or unfaithfulness arise, but my biggest challenge is helping my clients resolve their anger issues. I have a couple of therapists on speed dial, so when I notice a client who can't let things go or can't accept the results of my investigations, I suggest a visit to a qualified therapist. My clients make wise decisions most of the time, but I've had a few disappointments along the way.

My husband, bless him, has worked for the La Crosse Parks and Streets Department of La Crosse for over twenty-five years. We live on a small farm in the unincorporated community of Barre Mills in La Crosse County. Most people call this area the Driftless, which is a fancy way of describing the geography of a place where the glaciers never went. The stuff left behind by a glacier is called drift, and since we don't have any here, it's called the Driftless Region. Make sense? Anyway, it's been a wonderful place to live. The beauty of the gently rolling hills, spectacular sandstone bluffs, clear creeks and streams, and the mighty Mississippi River create a unique landscape. In addition, Barre Mills is the home of the Freethinkers Society. Being able to discuss ideas and issues in our culture is a much-needed skill in a democratic enterprise like ours.

Throughout my experience as a house cleaner, I've learned that people who work in blue-collar occupations such as janitorial and cleaning staff, night security, short-order cooks, licensed practical nurses, waitresses and bartenders, carpenters and plumbers, road construction workers, hotel/motel receptionists, and other similar jobs are grossly underappreciated in our society. You might say the blue-collar crowd is all but invisible to the average consumer. But what these people see, hear, and observe is not irrelevant by any means. When you hunt down and root out the nasty tendencies in society—lying, unfaithfulness, fraud, deception, and a host of other immoral behaviors— the services and observations of these ordinary working people are invaluable. As Garth Brooks once sang: *I've got friends in low places*, thank you very much. And I've found in my profession, my most valuable asset is the relationships I've built in the service industry. These are my people. We help each other.

On the morning of May 25, I woke early and spent time on my deck, sitting in my fuzzy bathrobe, sipping a cup of coffee, watching the deer browse at the edge of the woods in the gently rolling countryside on our fifteen-acre farm northeast of La Crosse. Sonny and Cher, our two mules, were watching the deer, too, from their spacious enclosure next to our iconic red barn. My chickens, too numerous to mention here by name, were pecking happily in the gravel next to the fenced-in chicken coop. Foxes, raccoons, skunks, and other varmints cannot resist a meal of tender chicken, which explains the protective fence. Coco, our little black poodle, sat at my feet chewing on a rubber banana. He seemed especially proud of himself this morning, having made it through the night without leaving a puddle of pee on my kitchen floor, which is his frequent overnight routine. Coco stopped chewing briefly when the screen door slid open and Trygve walked over and plopped down next to me in the other Adirondack chair. He was still in his T-shirt and pajama pants.

"Mornin', love," he said quietly, sipping a Cherry Coke.

I cringed at his choice of morning beverage—my disapproval usually ended in a lecture about the importance of controlling his blood sugar—but I bit my tongue and gently squeezed his hand. Reminding him about the extra fifteen pounds he was carrying on his large frame or his genetic predisposition for developing early-onset diabetes wasn't a good way to start the day. He was here next to me enjoying a beautiful May morning. *Don't get on your high horse at six in the morning. Just shut up and appreciate the little blessings in life,* I thought. I harrumphed to myself. *Those words may come back to haunt you when Trygve has a heart attack without warning and drops dead in the street.*

"What's on your agenda this morning?" Trygve asked quietly as he reveled in the beauty of the waking world. "Any bizarre cases you're working on?"

When I didn't answer, he continued.

"What prominent citizen are you snooping on now?" He slurped some more Coke.

I watched him swallow the syrupy soda and wondered what his blood sugar levels might be.

"Nothing earth-shattering, just cleaning today," I said. "I'm off to the new dental office downtown, that shiny, new building on Copeland Avenue. Who designs these buildings anyway? The thing is made of glass, for Pete's sake. God help them if anyone ever feels inclined to throw rocks. Those windows will be toast." I paused and looked over to see if Trygve was listening, because frequently he nods and says he's listening, but then ten minutes later he's lost the gist of the conversation, and that's when you know he was never listening in the first place.

Trygve looked confused, so I continued my explanation. "The dentist on the third floor of the building is a new customer of mine, and his office is in that big new monstrosity with the green-tinted windows that sits next to the big blue bridge over the Mississippi River on your way to La Crescent."

He thought for a moment, finally tuning in to what I was saying. "Oh, yeah, I remember now," he finally said. "The guy who only does implants, right? Dr. Diangelo or somethin' like that. I've seen his commercials on TV."

"That's right, honey," I commented. "His secretary called me last week. The cleaning agency they originally hired charged outlandish fees, but their work was very shoddy, not up to par. The gal on the phone told me they were looking for other options, so I quoted my fee and told her what it would include, and she hired me on the spot. She said I came highly recommended. What about you? Anything exciting at work?"

"Naw. Same old thing," Trygve said, crinkling his nose. He rubbed his hand along the whiskers that had sprouted on his face overnight. "Same ol' people. Same white truck. Same potholed streets. I could do my job with my eyes closed."

"That might not be a good idea," I said, envisioning my husband with his eyes closed, his white city truck weaving haphazardly through traffic up on the sidewalk, barely missing a pedestrian. Trygve gave me a wry look, took another sip of Coke, and continued staring at the distant rolling hills, his mind on who knows what.

"You sound like you need a shot in the arm. Something to boost your mood and outlook on life," I continued, watching his rugged profile. There was a moment of silence.

"Well, there is one thing you could do..." he said looking at me sideways with a grin, wriggling his eyebrows in my direction.

"Uh-uh, not happening today," I said. "Not this early. If you wanted that, you should have lured me into your arms before I showered and put on my makeup."

He smiled widely, his eyes sparkling. "Worth a try, though," he said.

I gave him a playful tap on the arm, got up from my deck chair, grabbed my coffee cup, and walked into the kitchen. Trygve slipped on his high-top rubber boots and casually strolled down to the barn, where he had a conversation with the mules and chickens as he fed them grain and hay.

I retreated to the bedroom and pulled on my comfy cleaning clothes: stretch pants, a medium-weight Dirty Business T-shirt, socks, and my Skechers. In the bathroom, I ran a brush through my brunette bob and checked my image in the mirror. Leaning closer, I tipped my head to the side, noticing a few strands of gray hair at my temples. I clucked my tongue, curled my lip, and shrugged. My hairstylist and I had already discussed whether to color my hair when the gray showed up. The discussion ended when I told her I'd earned every gray hair on my head and had no intention of disguising the passage of time. She didn't push the issue. The gray hairs are still there, but I'm getting used to it. Sighing, I turned off the light and walked back into the kitchen.

Trygve had returned to his chair on the deck. I peeked my head around the frame of the patio door.

"I'm leaving, hon," I said. "I'll see you tonight for dinner, okay?"

Trygve touched his fingers to his lips and blew me a kiss. "Sounds good. See you then."

Little did I know that my day was about to explode into a chaotic chain of events that would have the entire city of La Crosse buzzing with horror by nightfall.

CHAPTER 2
Death to the Capitalists

The morning sun had barely eclipsed the horizon over Grandad Bluff in La Crosse. The temperature was cool now, but balmy skies overhead promised a day of sunshine and early summer heat. The bluffs rising above the city glowed in the morning sunlight. A red fox, its tail luxurious and full, crossed the path and stopped briefly to watch the runner coming toward him. He sniffed the air, blinked a few times, and disappeared into the thick brush along the path. Birds were singing raucously at the start of a new day. Somewhere in a low bush, a cardinal sang out—*cheer, cheer, purty, purty, purty*—and then glided across the hiking trail in a flash of ruddy color.

Tina Diangelo, wife of Dr. Tony Diangelo, huffed along Wilder Way Trail directly below Grandad Bluff Road, oblivious to the beauty of nature that surrounded her. Tina was a petite size two who barely weighed one hundred pounds soaking wet. She was a fitness freak who regularly pontificated about the obese, unfit masses of U.S. citizens who could hardly lean over to tie their own shoes. Disgraceful. Pathetic. Outrageous. Her zeal in the quest for good health propelled her into a constant state of hypervigilance focused on proper weight management, nutrition, and positive mental attitude—and, of course, massive amounts of exercise in all forms. Richard Simmons would be thrilled to have Tina as his poster child—the perfect example of a forty-year-old healthy, athletic middle-aged woman with strong bones (thanks to a weightlifting regimen). Fit as a fiddle. Hale and hearty. As people in the business liked to say—fighting fit.

As Tina ran, she thought about her husband, Tony. He'd left early this morning to meet a client who was having a problem with an implant. Tina had always been impressed by Tony's laser-focused care of his patients. He went above and beyond to meet their needs. His office wall was plastered with patents for many cutting-edge tools used in the dental and oral surgery fields. In addition, his dental implant techniques were featured in several medical journals and publications. He took great pride in his reputation, earned through innovation, dedication, and professionalism.

Tina rounded the final corner on the gravel trail, stopped, and leaned over, resting her hands on her knees, panting hard. She stood like that for a moment, alarm bells ringing inside her head. *Am I normally this winded?* she thought. *Is there something wrong with me? I've been so tired lately. Hmm ... I'll have to put an extra dose of beetroot powder in my smoothie when I get back to the house. That'll shore up my system and fend off any problems.*

Tina stood up straight and began slowly walking back to the parking lot on 29th Street below the bluff, cooling down, feeling the heat of the run dissipating from her body.

A slight chill from her sweat-soaked running clothes caused goosebumps to break out on her skin.

She thought about the day stretching before her—the people whose lives she would change. The health spa she owned on the outskirts of Onalaska, Fitness Forever, had been successful beyond anything she could have predicted. Exercise classes were filled to overflowing, and the three personal trainers she'd hired were doing a bang-up job of enrolling new clients thanks to her weekly exercise blog on Instagram and Facebook. In addition, the sauna and beauty salon attached to the spa were constantly scheduling new clients who were anxious to change their image into something more socially acceptable—permanently inked eyebrows, a new frosted hairdo designed to minimize the gray, makeup to match aging skin, astringents to tone and tighten pores in the face and neck. All of this in a desperate effort to maintain the illusion of youth and vitality which gets incrementally more difficult beyond the age of thirty.

Tina sighed loudly. Everyone was so needy these days, always chasing after a more youthful appearance. And the drama never ended. Everyone wanted a makeover *today*, and she didn't have the staff to accommodate the fickle desires of her clients. Due to an increased demand for services, new clients had to wait for an appointment for at least two weeks. She'd have to hire more people soon. In another month, Fitness Forever II was scheduled to break ground on the south side of La Crosse. Her heart raced when she thought of the money she'd make reshaping and rearranging the lumps and fatty bumps of the forty-somethings flocking to her facility.

As Tina continued strolling down the trail toward her car,

she noticed a distinct throbbing in her left arm, which grew in intensity until she was grimacing in pain. The discomfort spread to her chest. She stumbled and clutched a low branch on a small birch tree next to the trail. Her breathing became erratic, and the pain in her chest increased to excruciating levels. A crushing weight between her breasts was squeezing the air from her lungs, making her feel like she was suffocating. Tina's knees crumbled beneath her. She fell against the birch tree, then unceremoniously slid down the trunk. Her thoughts became confused, but despite the pain she was in, she noticed the leaves of the trees above her, such a beautiful green, their shape lovely and distinct against the background of the powder blue sky. She felt herself drifting in and out of consciousness. Her breathing stopped. Her heart continued to beat sporadically for a few moments, but it finally stopped, too. Tina Diangelo, the most fit woman in the city of La Crosse, was dead.

At the same time across town on Copeland Avenue, Sonja Hovland arrived at the parking lot of the five-story green glass structure called Midwest Medical Services. In the misty morning light, the new sleek building dominated the skyline next to the big blue bridge over the Mississippi River. Sonja got out of her car, unloaded her cleaning tote from the back of her SUV, and walked across the lot to the building's back service entrance, swiping her ID card through the security scanner. The door clicked loudly, she pulled the handle, and stepped inside the cool, darkened hallway. Sonja walked to the service elevator, her cleaning tote rolling along behind her. She stepped into the elevator and pushed the button to the third floor. The elevator rose slowly, dinged after a few moments, and the door slid open. As far as Sonja knew, she was the only one on the third floor of the building.

When she stepped off the elevator, a feeling of unease came over her, and a shiver ran down her spine. She stood in silence for a full minute, which is a long time when you're just listening. Sonja had learned to pay attention to the warning signals—the physical sensations, smells, premonitions, and subconscious red flags she picked up about her environment. Some people called it situational awareness; Sonja called it being tuned into your immediate surroundings. It was what had protected her in college when she found herself in some dicey situations after a night of partying with people she barely knew. Now, it was what made her quite effective as a private detective. She picked up clues that others missed.

Gradually, the tension she felt as she stood by the elevator on the third floor evaporated like mist over the river when the sun began to burn off the fog in the early morning hours. The uneasiness in her brain retreated; the tension vanished. She shrugged her shoulders, grabbed her rolling tote, and headed for the large janitorial closet on the other end of the dental suite, chalking up her nervousness to the demands of a new cleaning job.

Sonja opened the closet with her key and stood there for a moment, assessing what she needed. She stocked her cleaning supplies and solutions on the rolling cart and began her cleaning tasks. The first order of business was to develop a routine for cleaning the area. She decided to work her way down the west side of the floor, which included the reception area, exam rooms, and public restrooms. Once that side was done, she would head back along the east side, where a suite of rooms equipped for implant procedures lined the hallway. There were toilets to clean and disinfect, sinks and countertops to wipe down, mirrors to shine, carpets to vacuum, and floors to mop. *Whoever said cleaning was for wimps and the feeble-minded didn't know what they were talking about,* thought Sonja. Organization and muscle power combined with a sense of competence and pride in a job well done was what had made Dirty Business Cleaning Services so successful. She was a one-woman show and proud of it.

After an hour of vigorous work, Sonja was ready to begin cleaning the actual rooms where Dr. Diangelo performed implant procedures. She glanced at the clock on the wall. It was 7:10. The staff would begin arriving at about 9:00. Sonja stood in front of the door to Suite One across the hallway from the reception area, the first of the three implant suites. Opening the door quietly, she walked in, and immediately a sense of alarm came over her. There was a slight scent in the air—something sweet yet vaguely putrid. Chemicals? Aftershave? Air freshener? Garbage? Her nostrils flared as she stood stock-still in the sterile room. At the same time, she thought she heard the elevator ding. That was strange. She paused momentarily, filing the sound away in her memory. Then her eyes traveled to the hydraulic chair where the patients underwent their procedures. *Why was someone lying in the dental chair at this time of the morning when no one else was here? Was this some kind of sick joke?*

Sonja swallowed hard and tiptoed up to the examination chair. She could feel her heart beginning to pound. A mustached man was lying in the chair, perfectly still, his eyes closed, his hands folded across his waist. His fingernails were impeccably clean and trimmed, his hair styled and perfectly coiffed, but his skin had a slight grayish pallor. He wore an expensive navy suit, a luxurious light pink dress shirt, and a perfectly knotted baby blue silk tie imprinted with tiny white teeth. Sonja thought he looked like a corpse in a coffin. She stood next to the chair and cautiously lifted the tie with her gloved fingers, turning it over to read the label—Forzieri. She recognized the man from his commercials on local television stations—this was Dr. Diangelo. His reputation for wearing the finest quality Italian suits, handmade leather shoes, and Florentine ties was apparently true.

Sonja gently shook his arm. A chill raced up her spine to the nape of her neck and across the top of her head. She shook his arm again, a little more vigorously this time. There was no response. The quiet in the room was suffocating, and she took a deep breath and held it. *Was this really happening?* she thought. *What are the chances I'd discover a dead person on my first day of a new cleaning job?*

"Dr. Diangelo?" Sonja said. Her voice sounded hollow and loud in the deadly quiet of the room. She repeated herself, this time a little louder. "Dr. Diangelo?" Sonja turned her head away from the man and swallowed the bile that had crept into her throat. Fighting the tendency to run out in the hall to escape the unsettling situation, she leaned over the chair and placed her ear on the man's chest. Nothing. No respiration, no heartbeat. Sonja struggled to maintain her composure. She felt like throwing her head back and letting loose with a blood-curdling scream. Instead, she slowly backed away from the chair.

Dapper, confident Dr. Diangelo was dead. It was then Sonja noticed a note sticking out of the pocket of his very expensive suit. She took a few steps back toward the edge of the dental chair. Carefully she plucked the note between her gloved thumb and index finger and pulled it out of the jacket pocket. Her hands shook unsteadily as she unfolded the note and read it. It said:

DEATH TO THE CAPITALISTS

Sonja slipped the note back into the pocket, reached for her phone tucked in her stretch pants, and dialed 911. "Hello," she began in a soft voice, "I'd like to report a suspicious death at the Midwest Medical Services building on Copeland Avenue."

CHAPTER 3 • SONJA

You've Come a Long Way, Baby

I've had an interesting life since I left the little town of Stickley, Wisconsin, on the shore of Lake Superior, where I grew up. Stickley was once known as a stronghold of Swedish descendants who established the little coastal town in 1874. The town's residents engaged in fishing, lumbering, farming, and mining. My father was a commercial fisherman there, and my mother was a schoolteacher. My blue-collar roots run deep. Both my parents are deceased now. I have a sister, Darlene, who lives in Lake Elmo, Minnesota, and another sister I haven't seen for decades. There's a backstory about my missing sister, but that's another story for another time. For now, you've got the gist of my humble Wisconsin beginnings.

After high school, I attended UW–La Crosse and majored in partying and fun. Though I didn't earn a degree, I did meet a lot of great people who are still my friends. I clean some of their houses now—doctors, lawyers, accountants, artists, dentists, corporate executives—successful, forward-looking people who are focused on the accumulation of money, possessions, and reputations. In other words, rich people. My efforts to keep their houses clean and organized have given me a certain degree of financial freedom. My services are not cheap. A verse in the Good Book applies directly to my business: "The laborer is worthy of his hire." It's somewhere in the New Testament, although I don't recall the book or verse offhand. Dirty Business Cleaning Service has given me some great money-making opportunities. I set my own hours, maintain my independence, and it has allowed me to own a debt-free small farm with my husband. I've furnished our home with the comfortable trappings of modern life, and we take a vacation to the Caribbean every year in February when the winter doldrums, gray skies, and slushy snowbanks in Wisconsin overstay their welcome. I have a little black dress and diamond necklace that I take on our trips to the Caribbean every year.

You can learn a lot about people when you clean their homes. I should, however, clarify a couple of things at this juncture of the story: First, I do not snoop on people when I clean their homes. Second, whatever I discover about my clients' personal habits, preferences, or histories during the process of straightening and cleaning their homes is strictly confidential. Privacy is one of the touchstones of my business. I'm very good at keeping my mouth shut.

I met my husband, Trygve, in a most unconventional way. During a snowstorm in December 2001, I was cleaning a client's home on Bainbridge Street on French Island near the La Crosse airport. A driver, who had passed out in his car after spending the better part of the previous evening until closing time at the Frog and Toad tavern down the street, woke up after his binge and decided to head home. Unfortunately, in his inebriated condition, he overshot his driveway and plowed into the south wall of Mrs. Kravitz's living room. Fortunately, I was at the other end of the house vacuuming a bedroom when the accident occurred, but the crash got my attention in a big way.

Trygve was plowing the street at the time and witnessed the entire incident. He stopped, called the police, and hurried into the house to check on the people inside. While he was describing the incident to the local police, I was checking him out. He seemed honest, almost detached about the whole thing, but intent on telling the truth. I admire a man who tells the truth. We began chatting when our interrogations with the police were finished. He asked me out to dinner, I accepted, and I found a gem in the rough who was an employee of the City of La Crosse doing street and park maintenance. Not bad looking, either. Go figure. I guess God does work in mysterious ways. Trygve has blessed my life in ways I can't even begin to explain.

Up to this point in my life, my inquiries for my clients have been pretty innocuous—a visit to the courthouse, a clandestine meeting with a wayward spouse, or a family meeting to discuss financial concerns. But when I found Dr. Diangelo dead in his dental chair with a cryptic note tucked in the pocket of his suitcoat, I knew my investigations were headed in a different direction—my life was about to change. When I entered Midwest Medical Services with its gleaming glass walls and attractive interior design to perform a cleaning job for a new client, little did I know I'd entered new territory. Standing next to the dead body of

Dr. Diangelo, I felt like I was clipped to a zipline whizzing through a landscape I didn't recognize—a full-blown murder investigation.

CHAPTER 4
Stayin' Alive

At 7:47 on the morning of May 25, La Crosse Chief of Police Tanya Pedretti arrived at the scene on Copeland Avenue via a flotilla of police squad cars, their whining sirens and flashing red and blue lights alerting the neighborhood to the event.

Nothin' like blowin' your horn from the rooftops and lettin' the whole city know something's up, Sonja thought, watching from a window on the east side of the building as the vehicles screeched to a halt along the curb. A large woman with a hefty middle-aged spread stepped out onto the curb from the back seat of the lead police cruiser. She briefly tilted her head backward and squinted up at the third-floor windows. Sonja had been waiting for the arrival of the police, and now that they had come, she stepped back from the window and walked swiftly to the elevator, where she stood impatiently waiting for the police chief to appear.

In less than a minute, the elevator door swished open on the third floor, and Chief Pedretti stepped out accompanied by two male police officers who stood next to her, one on each side.

Pedretti wore a pair of navy dress pants and a matching navy blazer with her police badge pinned conspicuously to the front pocket. Underneath the jacket was a pale yellow silk blouse, adding a touch of elegance to the business attire. Around her neck was a string of pearls, and tiny pearl earrings peeked through her dark brown hair, which was styled in a neat, efficient bob. Although impassive, her face was pretty in a disarming kind of way—tastefully applied foundation and blush, a hint of light pink lipstick, and gray eyeshadow. Sonja thought Pedretti looked like a college professor, not the leader of one hundred police officers and an administrative staff of over twenty. *She's used to pressure and demanding situations. She looks as cool as a cucumber*, Sonja thought, observing Pedretti's calm demeanor.

Sonja stepped forward. "I'm Sonja Hovland from Dirty Business Cleaning Service. I called 911 about a body I found in there," she said, pointing in the direction of the implant procedure room where Dr. Diangelo lay dead.

When Sonja introduced herself to Chief Pedretti, the woman cop gazed directly into her eyes with a neutral expression that betrayed none of the angst one might feel when a dead person has been discovered in somewhat suspicious circumstances. Sonja was impressed and immediately thought, *She's a tough cookie.* She felt an instant camaraderie with the commander of the police force, which was hard to explain. Perhaps it was Chief Pedretti's calm demeanor and unruffled self-assurance in the face of the daunting task before her that impressed Sonja. Or maybe it was the frank, unperturbed gaze that caused Sonja to feel comforted and safe like a child whose mother just walked in the door after a long day at work. Sonja breathed a sigh of relief. Someone else was in charge now. She was off the hook. The heavy, stifling weight of responsibility that had dragged her down a few minutes ago seemed to melt away.

"Thank you for calling in about the body you found," Chief Pedretti began.

"I just wanted to tell you—" Sonja interrupted.

Pedretti held up her index finger. "Hold that thought for a moment, Ms. Hovland." She turned to the two accompanying officers who were standing a short distance behind her. Her voice took on an authoritarian edge as she addressed the two men. "Secure the entire building. No one leaves, and no one gets in except police personnel. When the building is secured, we'll meet here on the third floor and conduct a more thorough search. As soon as the coroner arrives, send him up, please. Ms. Hovland will remain with me. We'll find a place to sit down and talk," she said. The two policemen nodded, turned, and began executing Pedretti's orders. The police chief laid her hand on Sonja's shoulder. "Let's go over here by the window and find a seat," she suggested, her voice returning to the soothing tone she'd used earlier.

One of the policemen left to secure the building, while the other began to move efficiently and calmly throughout the third floor checking every room, closet, and bathroom for anyone who might be hiding, although Sonja could have told him no one was there.

Chief Pedretti and Sonja settled into two chairs in the reception area to discuss the situation. Outside, the view of the Mississippi River flowing south, dark and deep, imparted a sense of permanence and familiarity. Once the officer had searched the third floor, he took the elevator down to the entrance of the building to prepare to meet the workers arriving at the building within the hour.

"Aren't you going to look at the body?" Sonja asked.

"He's not going anywhere, is he?" Chief Pedretti remarked, one eyebrow cocked upward.

Sonja shook her head, folded her hands in her lap, and sat quietly, waiting for Pedretti to start the interview.

"I understand this whole situation can be rather unsettling, Ms. Hovland, but let's start with what happened when you arrived at the building this morning," Chief Pedretti said. She reached inside her blazer and pulled out a small memo pad and mechanical pencil. She sat poised to listen, her hazel eyes patient and calm, waiting for Sonja to begin.

"I arrived about six o'clock," Sonja began. "I entered the back service entrance with my ID card and took the elevator to the third floor." She paused, wondering if she should mention the discomfort she'd felt when she first stepped from the elevator. "I got a funny feeling when I arrived, but I just chalked it up to nerves." Chief Pedretti was an excellent listener, and when she heard this statement, she looked rather alarmed.

"Did you see or hear something that made you anxious?" she asked.

Sonja crinkled her nose and shook her head. "No ... not really. Sometimes when I start a job for a new client, I get sort of nervous. That must have been what it was. I pride myself on doing a great job."

Chief Pedretti nodded casually, but she was clearly

interested in what the cleaning woman had seen and heard.

Sonja continued her account. "I shrugged off the uneasy feeling I had and began cleaning the west side of the suite, the reception area, and exam rooms, and then I moved to the surgical rooms, which are on the east side facing the bluffs. That's where I found Dr. Diangelo—in Room One." Sonja pointed in the direction of the room. "I haven't seen too many dead people in my life, but he's certainly dead, although I have no idea what killed him. He's laid out in his Sunday best. He looks like he's lying in a casket ready for viewing."

"We'll examine the body and the room shortly to try to determine what could have happened to him," Pedretti said. "What else did you notice after you found Dr. Diangelo?"

Sonja briefly stared out of the window and then suddenly remembered the ding of the elevator. She turned quickly to Chief Pedretti and snapped her fingers. "There was something," she said.

"Okay. Tell me about it." Pedretti leaned forward, her interest piqued by another detail that might help solve the mystery of the dentist's death.

"I heard the ding of the elevator—either somebody was coming or going, but I'm not sure which one it was because I didn't actually see anyone."

"And you were standing next to Dr. Diangelo in Room One when you heard the elevator ding?"

"Yeah. I was pretty upset, and I was trying to figure out what to do next, and then I heard the ding."

"You're sure it was the elevator?"

"Yes, it was. It was the ding of the elevator," Sonja said confidently. She waited for the police chief to say something, but she was furiously writing in her notebook. She flipped to the next page impatiently, then looked up at Sonja. At that moment, Lt. Brousard strode out of the elevator and walked over to the chief.

"Sorry to interrupt, ma'am, but several officers are downstairs, and more are on their way over. Should we meet in the lobby and get organized?" Chief Pedretti held up a hand to the officer, then looked at Sonja.

"I'd like you to stay for a little bit longer," Pedretti said.

Sonja swallowed hard. *Buck up, girl. You're in the big leagues now*, she thought. "Yeah, I guess I could do that," she said.

"Good. I want you to rethink everything you did this morning when you arrived at the building, and we'll go through it again to make sure we've gotten it all down accurately," Chief Pedretti said.

Pedretti stood up and addressed Lt. Brousard. "I want everyone who works in this building, especially Diangelo's staff, to be questioned. Find his secretary and ask her to cancel all of Dr. Diangelo's appointments. Have someone call Dr. Diangelo's family and inform them about his death. Find a couple of rooms downstairs to do the interviews."

"What are you looking for specifically, Chief?" Brousard asked.

Pedretti looked irritated. "Ask them what they do in the building, their jobs, their start and leave times, people they may know who are on Dr. Diangelo's staff—that type of thing. Also review the security procedures with the appropriate people. I want to know how everyone gets in and out of this building, especially during off hours when no one else is around. I want a thorough record of every person who works here whether that's a Monday through Friday nine-to-five job, or whether it's cleaning staff or security personnel during the week or on weekends," Pedretti said. "Understand?" The officer nodded. Pedretti pointed her index finger at the ceiling again. "And get someone to look at the security footage on the CCTV cameras. I'm sure they have them. They'll know where the cameras are positioned," Pedretti ordered. "Secure the tapes so we can start going through them."

"Yes, ma'am. I'll see to it," Brousard said. He turned and walked quickly to the elevator.

Chief Pedretti turned back to Sonja. "Now, let's go back over what you saw one more time. I want to be sure you haven't forgotten anything that might be important." She sat down again and used her notes to review the moment Sonja had discovered the dentist's body. Pedretti stopped her frequently to confirm the facts. "I'm concerned about the elevator ding. Did you see any evidence of someone other than yourself being on the floor when you arrived?"

"No, I didn't think anyone else was here," Sonja said. "But I did feel uneasy for some reason, so maybe I surprised someone, and they stayed out of sight until I began cleaning the rooms, and then they slipped into the elevator to get out of the building." She shrugged her shoulders, looking doubtful. "That's just an idea off the top of my head. But if someone was in the building and they left, wouldn't that show up on one of the surveillance cameras?"

Pedretti nodded. "Probably, although someone could have studied where the cameras are located and avoided a direct shot of their face. Or they may have used a disguise of some kind so they weren't easily recognized. We won't know until we look at all the footage."

Sonja suddenly remembered the note. She lifted her hand to her mouth, and her eyes widened.

"What's the matter? Did you remember something else?" Pedretti asked, noticing the change in Sonja's expression. "What is it?"

"Be sure to check the pocket of Dr. Diangelo's suit coat," Sonja said. "There's a little note folded up in it."

"There is?"

"Yeah. I didn't notice it right away. But it was sticking out a little bit, and I pulled it out and read it. Don't worry. I was still wearing my cleaning gloves. It said 'Death to the Capitalists.'"

"Excuse me?" Chief Pedretti said, leaning toward Sonja, her eyes widening in alarm. "Death to the capitalists? What's that supposed to mean?"

"I have no idea, ma'am, but that's what the note says, 'Death to the Capitalists.'"

CHAPTER 5
Nothin' but the Truth

By the time the news of Dr. Diangelo's death hit the streets of La Crosse, a group of bystanders and reporters had formed on the sidewalk in front of the glass building. People milled around holding their coffees and lattes, chattering and exchanging opinions about events that had occurred inside.

After Sonja's interrogation by Chief Pedretti, she was permitted to leave the building. Chief Pedretti and Sonja rode the elevator together down to the lobby.

"You're free to go, Ms. Hovland," Pedretti began, "but don't leave town. You are, after all, a witness in this unfortunate event … and a possible suspect."

Sonja swallowed hard, blinking rapidly. "What? Me? I'm a suspect? You've got to be kidding!"

Chief Pedretti stared at Sonja, watching her reaction carefully. If she had any qualms about her announcement, she remained calm and in control. "No, I'm not kidding. It's unfortunate you are the only witness so far in this terrible tragedy, but just for your peace of mind, I seriously doubt you're involved. However, I have an obligation to the public to cover my bases and keep you on my radar. I hope you understand," Pedretti said reasonably.

Sonja was shocked at the allegation. "Well, frankly, ma'am, I don't understand that at all," she said angrily. "Without my discovery and call to your department, you'd be in the dark right now. You'd have very little to go on. I reported a suspicious death and the circumstances surrounding it, and this is how you treat citizens who discover a crime that's been committed in their community? Really?" Sonja's face was red with frustration. Her attitude halted any reasonable, productive dialogue.

Chief Pedretti held up her hands, palms outward in a gesture of conciliation. "I know. It seems totally unfair, but it's really just a precautionary procedure. I don't believe for a minute that you had anything to do with this, but I hold my department to a high standard, especially if this turns into a murder investigation. I appreciate everything you've told us. We have some good facts, thanks to you. Please don't take this personally. Like I said, it's just precautionary."

Sonja huffed loudly, frustrated with the procedure. "Precautionary? Really? I don't think it's fair to consider me a suspect in a murder—especially when I had nothing to do with it."

Chief Pedretti continued calmly, staring at Sonja. Then she said, "We don't know if it's a murder yet. Like I said, this is just precautionary."

Eventually, Sonja toned down her argumentative stance. She let out a big sigh. "Well, I guess I can understand your need to have some kind of protocol. After all, it is a little chaotic around here right now."

Sonja looked around the lobby of the Midwest Medical Services building. Employees were milling about, checking their phones for messages, shaking their heads at the inconvenience of being interviewed when they were supposed to be at work. Their expressions reflected a combination of surprise, disgust, and skepticism. A few employees were teary and showed signs of regret and sorrow. "Nobody looks too happy about your procedure, Chief," Sonja commented caustically, raising her eyebrows. "In fact, most of them look pretty pissed off."

"That's understandable, but I can assure you it's all quite normal when we find a body in a suspicious situation in a public building," Pedretti said reasonably.

"Yeah, well, good luck with that. Since you said I was free to go, I'm leaving. My husband is going to find all of this very hard to believe."

Tanya Pedretti nodded sadly. "I'm sure he will. Listen, if you think of anything else that might be relevant, don't hesitate to call me or one of my officers," Pedretti said as she handed her business card to Sonja. "And take care. We really appreciate what you've done." She smiled sadly.

Sonja thought she looked tired already, and the investigation into the death of Dr. Diangelo was just getting started.

"By the way, I'm aware of your private inquiries on behalf of some of your clients, so if you discover anything about this incident, can I count on you to contact me?"

Sonja waited a moment before answering. Frowning, she glanced at Pedretti, and suddenly she felt sorry for her. Somehow over the last few minutes, some of the police chief's authoritative mojo seemed to have evaporated. "Yeah, I'll contact you if I find out anything interesting. I've got your card, and I'll let you know," Sonja said brusquely.

She turned and walked through the crowd, spoke briefly to the police officer at the entrance of the building, and then tramped to her car, pulling her cleaning tote behind her. Opening her hatchback, she loaded the cart, then went around and got in the driver's seat. She sat there for a minute rethinking everything she'd told Pedretti. *The truth, the whole truth, and nothing but the truth,* she thought. *But if you consider me a suspect, Ms. Pedretti, then I have some work to do to prove to you how wrong you really are.*

CHAPTER 6
That's What Friends Are For

Wally Leatherberry, proprietor of Windows on the World, a window-washing service, sat at his rickety desk in the corner of his small office in a strip mall on Jackson Street in La Crosse. He only had five employees, but they were in high demand. Apparently, clean, sparkling windows were becoming the new trend in office maintenance. *Good thing for me,* he thought. *I was almost bankrupt two months ago until everyone started calling to have their windows cleaned.*

Since the sudden influx of customers who were anxious to increase the curb appeal of their businesses with sparkling clean windows, he'd had to invest in more equipment: telescoping squeegees, microfiber scrub pads, extendable razor blades, and vacuums to suck up the mayflies, Japanese beetles, and other crawling insects who liked to defecate on the windows and hide along the cracks of the windowsills. In addition, he'd spent big bucks on a bucket truck with a scissor lift that could reach the upper windows of multi-story buildings with complex setbacks and forms.

The truck elevated his window washers as high as three stories. He'd fretted about the cost of the lift and wondered how he would pay for it, but in just two months he'd paid back over half the loan he took out to buy the truck. He shook his head in disbelief. Who knew you could actually make money cleaning windows? Huh, go figure. He never saw it coming. So much for his business plan.

Wally was a high school graduate, but just barely. He did, however, have better-than-average math skills, and believe it or not, his favorite class his senior year was bookkeeping and accounting. He loved everything about it—accounts receivable, balance sheets, assets and liabilities, profits and losses. Mrs. La Vonne Budwright, the accounting teacher at Central High School, was a pain in the backside, but she did know her stuff, and better yet, she could communicate it to her students. Lucky for Wally. He found the whole accounting landscape fascinating. And it was a good thing he did, because his business was growing by leaps and bounds. Pretty soon he might even be able to hire a full-time secretary so he could concentrate on his profit and loss profile.

The office was quiet this morning. Wally had dispatched his five employees to various sites around the city, promising he would check on them later in the day. He flipped through his list of clients, noticing several repeat customers. He made a call to a guy in Trempealeau inquiring about another truck for his business. Then he started working on an advertising budget, comparing the estimates for radio and television ads he thought he might purchase. He was still unsure how to develop an advertising budget. He was of the persuasion that the best advertising a business could have was a satisfied customer. Weren't windows cleaned with an attitude of excellence and cheerfulness the best way to build his business and make his customers happy? His eyes traveled to the small sign that hung above his desk: "Always render more and better service than is expected of you, no matter what your task may be." *Yeah, that includes window washers,* he thought. Some guy named Og Mandino said that. He'd written a lot of books about salesmanship, but Wally wasn't a reader. However, he tried to instill Mandino's service philosophy in his small crew of window washers. So far, it seemed to be working.

As he sat contemplating his next advertising move, the door to his small office blew open, and Sonja Hovland strode briskly across the room and abruptly stopped at Wally's desk. *Uh oh*, he thought as he looked at Sonja. *Something's up.* She had a strange expression on her face, but Wally was used to her brash communication style. He wondered what had brought her here this morning. She looked like she was on some kind of mission.

"So, Wally, what's the dirt at Midwest Medical Services over on Copeland? Have you heard what's going on over there?" she asked brusquely. Her eyes were jumping in her head, and her whole body was as tight as a fiddle string.

"Good morning to you, too, Sonja," Wally said laconically, trying to ease the tension. He leaned back in his cheap office chair covered in imitation leather and casually took in Sonja's persona—good-looking, trim, and athletic with a bigger-than-average ego. Her good traits aside, she was more than willing to admit her mistakes when they were pointed out to her. Still, when all was said and done, Wally couldn't quite figure her out. She was always asking questions about people and events that had nothing to do with her cleaning business. What was up with that?

"Sorry, but I'm in kind of a hurry," Sonja started to explain, "and I just wondered if you'd heard anything about all the cop cars over on Copeland. The place is lit up like a Christmas tree—sirens, lights, the morgue truck, the whole nine yards. Something must be going on." When Wally didn't respond immediately, she rushed on. "I just drove by, and there must be at least a hundred people milling around in front of the building. That's a little unusual, don't you think?"

Wally shrugged nonchalantly. "Maybe they're having a medical convention or something," he said, smiling. His attempt at humor fell flat.

"Doubt it," Sonja said crisply. Wally's smile disappeared. "Your people are out and about, right?" she asked, her voice clattering like an old-fashioned typewriter.

"That's a foregone conclusion, Sonja." Wally sat up straighter. "Of course they're out around the city. This is a prime window-washing day—sunshine, perfect temps.

Just then, Wally's cell rang. He picked up his phone from his desk and looked at the screen. A frown appeared on his narrow forehead.

"Osmat? Do you need something?" Wally asked when he answered. As he listened, his eyes grew wide. "What? Where are you?" He listened some more. Whoever was on the line was talking loudly and rapidly. "Okay, okay. Slow down. You're talking about the Midwest Medical building on Copeland?"

At the mention of the building, Sonja took a few steps closer to Wally and leaned down to eavesdrop on the conversation. Wally leaned away from her, but she persisted, bending toward him, turning her ear toward the phone.

"I think I saw a murder," Osmat said again rather loudly.

"Now, listen, Osmat, you're not making any sense," Wally said patronizingly, as if he were talking to a small child. Sonja grabbed the phone. Wally sputtered and jumped out of his chair. "What do you think you're doing, Sonja? You can't walk in here and grab my phone!"

Sonja held up her hand toward Wally. "Osmat, this is Sonja Hovland. Tell me what you saw over on Copeland," she demanded.

"Put Wally back on the line," Osmat said loudly. "I have to talk to him."

"No, I won't put Wally back on the phone," Sonja said forcefully. "I need to hear what you have to say because I'm the one who found Dr. Diangelo dead in his dentist chair this morning when I came to work at the Midwest building." *Desperate times require desperate measures*, she thought.

Suddenly the line went quiet. "You found Diangelo?" Osmat whispered.

"You found Diangelo?" Wally repeated, frowning. "Well then … Wait a minute, if you knew about it already, then why did you ask me all those questions?" Wally echoed.

Sonja waved at him trying to shush him up. "I'll explain all this in a minute," she whispered to Wally.

Then she spoke to Osmat again. "Yes, I found Dr. Diangelo when I was cleaning his office. He was dead in his dentist chair," Sonja reiterated firmly. She changed her demanding tone to something softer and gentler, a tone a mother might use with a frightened child. "Now listen, Osmat, I need you to tell me what you saw. Take your time. It might be crucial in solving some ... issues." Sonja touched the speaker icon on Wally's phone and laid it on his desk. She looked over at Wally and said, "Sorry."

"Okay, we're on speaker now," Sonja said. "Just tell us what you saw, Osmat."

"Wally, are you there?" Osmat asked gruffly.

"Yep. I'm here. Go ahead, Osmat. We're both listening," Wally said, giving Sonja a dirty look.

"I arrived at the Midwest building at five-thirty. I set up my truck, loaded the bucket with my squeegees and other stuff I needed, and started washing the first-floor windows on the east side of the building. When I finished that, I moved up to the second floor. A little after six, I was ready to move the bucket up another story to the third floor. I had just passed the floor line and was hanging about a quarter of the way up the third-floor windows when a bright light came on inside one of the rooms. I stopped the bucket and hung there midair, peeking through the very bottom of the windows. Dr. Diangelo walked into the room with another person."

"Did you recognize the other person?" Sonja asked.

"No, he had a nylon stocking pulled over his head. That's why I couldn't identify him. I only recognized Dr. Diangelo because he gave me a tip one day after I cleaned his windows," Osmat said. "He told me I did great work."

"I understand. Keep going. What happened next?" Sonja asked.

"Dr. Diangelo sat in his dentist chair and reclined. The other person was watching him very carefully, which was pretty weird. I got really frightened that the stocking man would see me hanging outside the building and come after me. So, I lowered myself to the ground, climbed out of the bucket, and got into the cab of the truck. I was totally confused by what I saw and didn't know what to do. Obviously, something was wrong," Osmat explained. "After sitting across the street from the building for a couple of minutes, I got nervous and went to my next job."

"So, you never saw this guy actually do anything to Dr. Diangelo, right?" Sonja asked.

"That's right, and I have no idea who he was, but who walks around with a nylon stocking over their head unless they're up to no good?" Osmat responded. It was quiet for a very long moment.

"That's very true, Osmat. Did you see the nylon stocking man leave the building?" Sonja asked.

"If he left, I didn't see him leave, but I did see a lady arrive at the building to clean—that must have been you. Once you arrived, I left to go to my next job."

"What happens now?" Wally asked.

Sonja grew thoughtful for a moment, then said, "Let's keep this between ourselves until I can find out a little more about the whole situation. Thanks for the info, Osmat. Try and have a good day. I may contact you again later." She disconnected and handed the phone to Wally. He took his phone and shoved it in his pants pocket. He was still fuming at the high-handed attitude of this common cleaning lady who burst into his office uninvited and proceeded to derail his calm, peaceful morning. He turned toward Sonja, his body tense, his face dark with frustration.

"Look, Sonja, you can't just walk in here and—" he started to say, but Sonja interrupted him.

She laid a hand on his arm, patting it gently, and she

began to feel the tension between them dissolving.

"I'm very sorry about this, Wally. I apologize, but the fact remains: Dr. Diangelo is dead. I saw him lying in his dental chair, all decked out in his suit and tie, and he was very, very dead." Sonja swallowed and made a face like she'd just eaten a frog. "I know I was out of line barging in here, but it's not every day you come across someone who's been murdered."

"Murdered?" Wally responded, his eyes searching Sonja's face as if she were joking. "Don't be dramatic, Sonja. Maybe the doc was having a medical issue of some kind, or maybe he committed suicide."

Sonja dipped her head to the side, thinking. Her eyes drifted out to the traffic on Jackson Street, but her mind was envisioning the moment she'd discovered Dr. Diangelo in his dental chair. It all came back in living technicolor. Slowly, she brought herself back into the present and took a deep, cleansing breath. She locked eyes with Wally again. "Suicide is a possibility, but I didn't get that vibe from the whole situation." Wally continued to stare. "You had to be there, Wally. Then you'd understand my desperation."

"What I don't get is why should you care? You were just cleanin' the joint."

"I care because the police consider me a prime suspect."

Wally's mouth fell open in amazement, the shock written on his face. Finally, he spoke. "Man, I hate to say it, Sonja, but you are in some very deep shit."

Sonja looked sad. "I'd say you hit the nail on the head, Wally."

CHAPTER 7
Just the Facts, Ma'am

Chief Pedretti stood beside the dental chair in Room One on the third floor of Midwest Medical Services. She looked down at the corpse reclining there. *He was certainly a smart dresser,* she thought. *Clean hair and well-manicured fingernails, neatly shaven, a precisely clipped mustache, trim and fit, expensive clothing of the finest materials. A man of meticulous habits.*

Her police procedural questions kicked in. What would cause a healthy, strong middle-aged man to lie down in a dental chair and die? Did he do it of his own free will, or was he coerced into the chair by an unknown combatant? Did he experience a medical emergency? Was he murdered? If so, by whom? Was he murdered by someone who knew him, or was it a complete stranger? The other possibility was suicide. What was going on in his personal life that might cause him to end it all? And then the biggest question of all: How did he die? There seemed to be no wounds—no entry wounds from a gunshot, no punctures from a knife stabbing, no bashed in brains from a blunt force object. No blood at all. So, what killed him?

The small procedure room was crowded with personnel trying to be polite and step around each other, including the coroner, the crime scene people, Pedretti's second-in-command, Lieutenant Hank (Hatchet) Brousard, and Pedretti. The air, although scrubbed clean by the HVAC system, was laden with suspicion and the turmoil of an unexpected death. Everyone was carrying out their duties efficiently, seemingly devoid of human emotion, although Pedretti knew from experience that their hearts were beating a little more rapidly than normal, and their thoughts were probably similar to hers. *What in the world happened here? If this was murder, it was the most sterile killing any of them had probably ever encountered.*

"What are you thinking, Chief?" Lieutenant Brousard asked, getting straight to the point. He stood next to her, their jacket sleeves barely touching.

"Lots of things, none of them pleasant topics of conversation," Pedretti commented dryly. "But..." her blue gloved index finger popped up, "off the top of my head, I'd say Dr. Diangelo is a victim of foul play. The note suggests some kind of political agenda, although that's a shot in the dark right now. We're going to need to begin an extensive investigation into groups that are on the fringe of society, particularly any who are active in our immediate area."

"Yeah, that note makes you wonder, doesn't it?" remarked Brousard. 'Death to the capitalists.' Any ideas about that?"

"For starters, there are a lot of left- and right-wing groups hiding in the shadows these days," Pedretti reflected. "With AI on the loose, political discord and misinformation are at an all-time high. The national scene is chaotic and ripe with groups who are determined to create political and social upheaval at the hint of any perceived insult or injustice, so who knows? Did Diangelo malign some group on social media, and they took offense and vowed to get even?" Pedretti shrugged. "We don't know yet. Was he a member of some fringe group who decided to eliminate him for some weird reason? Those are possible theories, but without any real hard facts, we're only guessing."

"Maybe some of his staff can shed a light on his activities," Hatchet said.

Pedretti and Brousard stepped away from the body and watched the coroner place Dr. Diangelo in a black bag for the trip to the city morgue. As they rolled the body out of the room, Pedretti could feel Brousard studying her profile, trying to anticipate her next move in the investigation.

"I'll get some people on the social media thing," Brousard commented. "They can go through Diangelo's Facebook and Instagram and his email accounts, check out his online associations. We'll go to his home and look at his personal computer. Maybe something will pop up. I'll get some people to research the slogan, if that's what it is." He stopped momentarily thinking about the phrase. "A capitalist?" he continued. "Isn't that just another name for someone who makes money?"

Pedretti pulled her phone from inside her jacket, typed rapidly with her thumbs, then scrolled with her index finger. She stopped and read the definition. "According to the Merriam-Webster dictionary, a capitalist is a wealthy person who uses money to invest in trade and industry for profit in accordance with the principles of capitalism. A broader definition just says a capitalist is a person of wealth." She looked over at Brousard and locked eyes with him. "There you go, Hatchet. Does that answer your question?" She lifted her eyebrows slightly, feeling her heart trip a little when she looked into his green eyes.

"Yep. Sure does," he said with a deadpan expression. "Gives us a starting point anyway."

Pedretti's phone jingled. She walked to the window and looked out.

"Chief Pedretti." Tanya listened for a moment and then said, "What? No way. How is that even possible?" More listening. "Okay, I've got it. We all need to meet downtown at headquarters—say one o'clock?" She disconnected, shaking her head.

"What now?" Brousard asked, stepping toward her.

"Dr. Diangelo's wife died this morning on a trail below Grandad Bluff while she was on her morning run."

"What? Are you serious? That's unbelievable!" Brousard rasped, his eyes widening. "Does it look like foul play?"

"I don't know, but this case is going to challenge us like no other case we've ever encountered in recent memory." Pedretti turned away from the window, talked briefly to the crime scene people, then left the room. She stopped suddenly by the elevator. "Let's get some people on Diangelo's wife: medical history, personal stuff. You know the drill. We'll have to determine if these two deaths are related or just a crazy coincidence." She stepped into the elevator accompanied by Brousard. On the way down to the first floor, Hatchet asked, "Everything okay at home, Chief?"

Tanya sighed loudly. "I miss my mom every day. Didn't expect her to die so suddenly, especially when she seemed to be in good health. We were looking forward to doing so many things together this summer. Roy does his best to be attentive, but when you work from home as a CPA as he does, well, most of the time you're distracted. Working from home is way overrated in my book. You never really leave the office, do you?"

Hatchet looked at her face and saw the sadness there. His heart went out to her.

She continued. "The kids, they're sad about their grandma, but you know kids. They're resilient. Besides, everyone's so busy, I don't think we hardly spend fifteen minutes a day in adult conversations. Just another symptom of modern-day culture taking its toll, I guess."

"Wow. That's quite the description," Hatchet said as the elevator door slid open. "You always were good at verbalizing your thoughts."

"It is what it is. Right now, that's my life in a nutshell," Tanya said, the sadness permeating her pretty features.

"Look, if you need anything, just holler," Brousard said, lowering his voice. "You know, a soft shoulder to cry on?"

Tanya shook her head. "What I need, you can't give, or at least you shouldn't offer if you're the gentleman I think you are," she said.

Hatchet hung his head, waiting for his boss to say something.

"Come on. We've got work to do. It's going to be a long haul, so we better get started," Tanya said as she strolled to the front entrance of the building. When she opened the door, a mob of reporters and videographers swarmed around her. Hatchet led the way through the crowd and held his arm in front of her in a protective gesture. Questions flew through the air like a volley of arrows. What happened in there, Chief? Did someone get hurt? Is somebody dead? Tanya walked to the curb and crawled into the back seat of the black and white cruiser. Hatchet got behind the steering wheel and pulled out from the curb, slowly driving past the crowd gathered in front of the building.

"This town sure has changed since we were kids, huh?" Hatchet said.

"Very true. The world seems to be skidding to the edge, and we're just spectators with our heels dug in the dirt, trying to avoid going over the cliff," Tanya said.

She thought about her husband, about the indifference he seemed to feel toward her lately. Was it just stress, or was there something else going on? Another woman? Didn't seem likely. He worked from home. How many women did he meet each day? Not many, but then, it only took one. Tanya had a better-than-average understanding of the ways couples could cheat on each other. Her surveillance work as a cop had taught her that. Still, she dismissed it for the time being, refusing to believe her marriage was in trouble. *We love each other; we're just too damned busy to show it,* she rationalized.

What about financial issues? As far as she knew, they lived well under their incomes and had a hefty savings account. They were careful with their credit cards, paying them off monthly. They both had good retirement plans and adequate insurance coverage. Fortunately, she'd never been seriously injured or disabled in her work as a cop, and they'd had no serious accidents. She wasn't a whiz-banger when it came to finances, but she had a decent understanding of their money landscape, and it was better than the average couple. Not to worry.

Boredom? That's what really scared her—that her husband of almost twenty-three years found her boring. Of course, she had to admit she hadn't been the most passionate, happy wife lately. Fighting crime seemed to drain her of any romantic inclinations, but she wasn't about to go off the deep end and go on a crash diet, walk three miles after work every night, or cut and color her hair in some crazy new style just to get the attention she wanted and needed from her husband. But she was perceptive and knew if something didn't change soon, her relationship with Roy would be on the rocks.

She sighed again, which garnered the attention of her partner in the front seat. He stared at her for a few moments in the rearview mirror, then flicked his eyes back to the road and drove silently to the police headquarters on Ranger Road next to Logan High School.

CHAPTER 8 • SONJA
The Devil's in the Details

I tried everything I could think of on the morning of Dr. Diangelo's death to manage my thumping heart, my clammy hands, my racing thoughts, but nothing helped. After devouring an apple pie at McDonald's and drinking several cups of black coffee, my hands were still shaking with the magnitude of my morning discovery. Nothing could erase the fact that I had inadvertently found a dead dentist under questionable circumstances, and I was now a suspect in a possible murder investigation. If someone had told me this was a possibility in my line of work as a private detective, I would have said they were nuts. However, the fact remained: I was the one who found a dentist dead in his chair. No one else had been at the scene or had been on the third floor of the building that morning. I remembered Chief Pedretti's intense stare as she broke the news to me that I was a suspect—in theory, anyway. *Well then*, I thought, *two can play that game. I guess I'll have to show her where the bear shits in the woods, as we Midwesterners like to say.* My one saving grace was the investigation was in the early stages, and I had time to get my ducks in a row.

I left Wally at the Windows on the World office on Jackson Street after my conversation with Osmat and hopped in my 2022 Subaru Forester. Pulling out my phone, I began working my contacts in the service industry around the city. I talked to Janelle at the Midwest Motor Lodge, Tory at Olson's Vac & Sew, Lolita at the Mexican Hacienda restaurant on the south side, and Blaine, who was the facilities manager of the law firm Huntley, Blake & Shasta down on Pearl Street. Always a good idea to have a foot in the legal world. After informing them of Diangelo's death, I asked them to keep their ears to the ground and let me know about any scuttlebutt they might hear through the grapevine. In addition, Scott from Barnes & Noble and Marie from Sephora out at the mall called to ask me what I knew about the incident at the new Midwest glass building. I filled them in. My people came through for me. They were behind me all the way.

After an hour of phone conversations, I dialed Trygve's cell.

"Hey. What's up?" he asked. I heard some rattling and banging and the whining of the city truck engine in the background.

"Have you heard the news?" I asked.

"No. What news?" Trygve asked. "What are you talking about?"

When I heard his calm, deep voice over the line, an intense wave of emotion washed over me, and I felt a deep abiding calm settle over my soul. This was my man, my love, my husband. If anybody understood what I was feeling, it would be Trygve. We'd been through a lot together.

"I found Dr. Diangelo dead in his dentist chair this morning when I went to Midwest Medical to clean." The silence that followed was unnerving. "Tryg? Did you get that?"

"Let me pull over here. Hang on," he said. I could hear the truck engine winding down and then the rustling of the phone as he picked it up from the seat again.

"Now, let's start over," Trygve began when he got back on the phone. "Did you say you found somebody dead?"

"Yeah. Dr. Diangelo, the implant guy. When I went into one of the procedure rooms to clean, there he was, laid out like a gobbler on Thanksgiving Day. Dressed in his Sunday finest. Deader than a doornail."

"Was he shot, or what?"

"No. There were no obvious signs of trauma," I explained.

"Suicide?"

"Maybe, but Chief Pedretti is skeptical."

"She said that?" Trygve asked.

"Well, not in so many words, but she implied it," I responded. "There was a weird note in his pocket that said, 'Death to the Capitalists.'"

"Death to the capitalists? Whoa, that is weird. Somebody must have come unhinged over politics or the economy. That's pretty radical. So, what now?" Trygve asked.

"I'm not sure, but could you meet me for lunch at Subway—the one up in the strip mall next to Red Wing Shoes?" About twelve?"

"Yeah, I guess that'll work. See you then." My husband is a man of few words. Can you tell? But just remember, still waters run deep.

I put my phone back in the front pocket of my purse,

then headed to Equity Care over on the south side of the city. Dr. Tom Nielson is a client of mine and a good friend. I needed to ask him a few questions.

Equity Care is a private, pay-as-you-go clinic that serves low-income families with minimal or no health insurance coverage. Dr. Tom is supposed to be retired, but he can't keep himself on the sidelines of the medical profession. His heart hurts for those who receive only the very basic medical care. He is a real swell guy. I guess you'd say he's a humanitarian to the lower-income population of La Crosse. I met him in college, and now I clean his modest home on Mississippi Street every other Wednesday.

I rolled up to the small, yellow brick building on Mormon Coulee Road that served as his clinic, which was right next to the south side Walmart. A row of bright red geraniums lined the sidewalk leading to the front entrance. I walked in and approached the receptionist's desk.

"Hey, Sheila," I said. "Dr. Tom in?"

"Absolutely, but his schedule is crazy. You need to see him today?" she asked, looking over her pair of reading glasses.

"Yeah, like in the next fifteen minutes, if possible," I said.

She looked over the edge of the desk at my feet and legs. "Don't see any blood or broken bones. What's the problem? Sounds like an emergency."

"It is, but not of the medical kind."

Sheila's eyebrows knitted together in a frown. "Okay. Have a seat, and I'll fit you in," she said, pointing me to a molded plastic chair. I sat down and picked up a magazine, flipping through it absentmindedly.

Sheila called my name twenty minutes later and led me

back to the examination room. When the nurse came in to check my vitals, I shooed her out the door, explaining that my appointment was not for a medical concern.

Five minutes later, Dr. Tom burst into the room. His wiry, red hair stood up in every direction, and his thick glasses hung precariously on the end of his nose. He was wearing a pair of well-worn blue jeans, and his feet were decked out in a very expensive pair of cowboy boots. I was surprised he wasn't wearing chaps, a bandanna, and a cowboy hat. He gave me an intense stare, his legendary impatience on full display.

"If you're here about Diangelo, then you're barkin' up the wrong tree," he said gruffly.

Social niceties have never been Dr. Tom's strong suit, but he usually mellows out after a couple of whiskey sours.

"Come on, Doc. I need your help. Chief Pedretti has me on her radar, and I don't like being a suspect in a possible murder investigation," I whined. "Have you heard anything from the coroner?"

"Why would I?" he barked loudly. The guy could be irritating sometimes.

"Because you play golf with him every Thursday at Forest Hills, and you go to the same church. That's why," I reminded him. "And he's one of your best friends."

Dr. Tom leaned his lanky frame against the exam table and took a deep breath. "The whole deal stinks like—never mind," he said, shaking his head. "There's something wrong with that whole scenario—the way Diangelo died. I'd be very surprised if it's suicide."

"I thought you said you hadn't talked to Phillips," I said in an accusing tone.

"News travels fast, and bad news travels even faster. Unfortunately, most of the time it's more gossip than fact," Tom sermonized.

When I continued to stare him down, he confessed.

"Okay, okay. I talked very briefly to Phillips—literally two minutes. What can you find out in two minutes? Not much," he finished grumpily.

"But? You found out something?"

"He noticed a spot of blood on the waistband of Diangelo's underwear, and when he looked closer, he found a needle puncture."

"So, it's drugs?"

"Possibly. Blood tests weren't back from the lab yet when I talked to him. They might be back by now."

I jumped out of the chair, kissed him quickly on his dry, whiskered cheek, and stepped into the hall. "I appreciate this," I said, walking rapidly down the hall.

"Is it worth a couple of free house cleanings?" he yelled, leaning around the door frame, finally smiling.

"Maybe. We'll see," I yelled back, waving goodbye.

I was ten minutes late getting to Subway near the mall. I whipped into the parking lot and jumped out of my car. Trygve's white city truck was parked a few spaces down from me, and when I walked into the sandwich shop, he was already chomping on a BLT. I twiddled my fingers at him, ordered my sandwich, and got a drink.

I sat down in the booth opposite my husband and unwrapped my turkey bacon ranch sandwich.

Trygve leaned over the table and whispered, "The whole town is talkin' about this deal. It's all over Facebook and

Instagram," he rasped, pointing to his phone. "How did you get yourself in this jam anyway?" he hissed. His nostrils flared, and his face was dark with anger.

"Well, thank you very much for all the overwhelming support," I hissed back. "I was just doing my job, bud." Trygve leaned back in an effort to cool off. He held up his large hand.

"Sorry, babe, but I worry about you sometimes. One of these days, you're gonna get yourself in a pickle you can't get out of."

"And if something happened to me, you couldn't live without me, right?" I said with a grin.

"This is not funny," he said, firing up again, pushing his half-eaten sandwich away.

It was my turn to tone down the rhetoric. "I know, I know. You're right; it's not funny. This is a serious matter, and I'm smack dab in the middle of it—through no fault of my own, I might add."

"So, tell me. Come out with it. I want an explanation of this whole deal from the beginning, please," my husband said.

Trygve is not a hard-nosed authority figure, but sometimes he gets a certain look on his face that tells me the buck and the bullshit stop here. This was one of those moments.

I began explaining what happened from the time I arrived in the parking lot of the Midwest Medical building until I left at about nine-thirty after being interrogated by Chief Pedretti. I told him what I'd found out at Windows on the World from Osmat and what Dr. Tom told me at his office. When I finished, Trygve crossed his arms over his big chest and looked out the window of Subway. He stayed that way for several moments, studying the traffic buzzing by on Highway 16. When he finally met my gaze, he seemed to have made some kind of decision.

"Okay, I think I've got the picture," he said. He leaned forward and placed his elbows on the table. "Listen, here's the deal. From now on, you will keep me informed about your movements around town. Carry your cell at all times, and look in the back seat of the car before you get in. You've got your handgun in the cubbyhole of your—"

"Trygve, honey," I interrupted, "step back for a minute. I think you're getting carried away here."

"*I'm* getting carried away?" he asked, pointing to his chest, his eyes wide with indignation.

"Yeah, I think you are," I said, reaching for his hand.

He grasped it firmly, leaned over the table and kissed me on the lips, gathered his trash and threw in the wastebasket, and walked toward the door. He had his hand on the handle when he turned around and walked back to the table. Leaning down toward me, he said very softly, "You need to have a conversation this afternoon with Chief Pedretti. Tell her about the window washer, what he saw, and anything else that might help her. I don't want to have to come down to jail and bail you out for withholding evidence in a murder investigation." His eyebrows flipped up. "Got it?" His hazel eyes sparkled with determination and a hint of anger.

"Yes, that was my plan, dear," I said meekly.

"I'll see you at home tonight," he said. He kissed my cheek, walked out of Subway, got into his city truck, and drove out of the parking lot.

I sat in the booth for a long time after I'd finished my

sandwich, sipping my lemonade and thinking. I recalled the story of Jonah and the whale. Like Jonah, who didn't want to go to Nineveh, I didn't want to go to the police chief's office, but if I didn't come clean about what I knew, then a great big whale was going to swallow me and eat me alive. Somehow it seemed as if I had no choice in the matter. I gathered my purse, exited Subway, and drove to the La Crosse City Police Headquarters on Ranger Road.

CHAPTER 9
A Watched Pot Never Boils

The classroom on the second floor of the police station on Ranger Road was packed with city police officers, Ed Phillips the coroner, the crime scene investigation team, Lieutenant Brousard, and Chief Tanya Pedretti. The loud buzz in the room reminded Pedretti of a swarm of angry insects, but then she reminded herself that everyone in the room was a highly trained professional intimately acquainted with shocking crimes committed by desperate renegades. That's what they were taught, and their time in the city had confirmed the theory in hard-fought street experience. Pedretti reminded herself that most of the officers sitting at tables or standing at the back of the room were seasoned veterans; a few were newly graduated with a degree in criminal justice from the Law Enforcement Academy, a division of Western Technical College in La Crosse. Many of the city's off-duty police officers were on hand to get the latest dirt on this puzzling crime that was sending shockwaves throughout the city.

Pedretti locked eyes with Ed Phillips, who was standing next to the whiteboard at the front of the room. He fidgeted with a marker, dropped it, picked it up again, and gave her a nod. Hatchet, her right-hand man, straightened up from his casual pose against the wall and stood attentively, his back ramrod straight. Time to get this meeting started. Pedretti strode purposely to the podium near the whiteboard, raised her hand, and said loudly, "May I have your attention, please? Let's get started." The room quieted down quickly.

Tanya felt the stares of the thirty officers and specialists in the room. A chill ran up her spine even though the classroom was quite warm. She could feel a familiar tightness across her forehead and temples—another rotten headache was brewing. *Maybe it's just a caffeine low.*

"This morning, Dr. Tony Diangelo, a dental implant specialist at Midwest Medical on Copeland Avenue, was found dead in his dental chair at his office," Pedretti began. "His body was discovered by one of the cleaning staff who was performing her duties on the third floor of the building. She called us when she found him unresponsive in his chair. This meeting is to discuss our initial findings into what we are calling, at this point, a suspicious death." Looking at Ed Phillips, she said, "The coroner will give his report, but remember, it's early in the process. We're just getting started."

Ed Phillips was an unassuming man—small in stature, meek in personality, quiet and thoughtful—but he frequently wowed his colleagues with his astute medical knowledge and analysis of injuries to the human body. Ed looked out at the officers in front of him, turned and nodded to Pedretti, and began his report.

"Dr. Tony Diangelo, a white, forty-seven-year-old male, was found dead reclined in a dental chair in his clinic this morning. There were no gunshots or knife wounds, no trauma injury to the body at all. However, when I examined him, I found a tiny bloodstain on the waistband of his underwear, and upon closer inspection, I found a needle puncture on the left side of his body. Blood draws are still being analyzed in the lab. At this point, an overdose of drugs may be one explanation for the man's death, but other medical possibilities, such as a heart attack, stroke, or aneurysm, could also explain his demise. We simply do not have enough information to go on at this time. I will keep Chief Pedretti informed as I learn more when the autopsy is completed." Phillips closed his manila folder and stepped away from the podium.

Tanya walked back to the podium. "Thanks, Ed. There is one other thing of interest in this case. It's really the only other clue at the scene that might give us a good lead—" Tanya was interrupted by a commotion at the classroom door. She looked toward the door and noticed Sonja Hovland standing there with another officer. "Umm, just a minute while I talk to this lady," she finished.

The eyes of the officers followed Pedretti as she walked to the classroom door and directed Sonja into the hallway.

"I'm sorry to interrupt, Chief, but I have some important information about the situation at the Midwest building and Dr. Diangelo," Sonja said.

"Sure. Let's hear it. What've you got?"

"There was a window washer from Windows on the World over on Jackson who saw some things when he was washing the Midwest windows early this morning," Sonja said.

"Really? He saw things at the medical building on Copeland?"

"Yeah."

"What did he see?" Tanya asked, leaning against the wall as Sonja talked. But she wondered how in the world this woman could possibly know some of the things she knew. Where was she getting her information? And from whom?

"He was in his bucket truck, and when he raised himself to the third floor, he saw Dr. Diangelo and another man wearing a nylon stocking over his head come into the room. Dr. Diangelo sat in this examination chair while the other guy watched him. Osmat, the window washer, observed all of this for a few seconds, but then he got nervous and lowered himself to the ground."

Pedretti pushed herself away from the wall and asked, "Was he able to identify this masked individual?"

"No. The nylon stocking smashed his features together, so he couldn't give a description of him."

Pedretti thought a moment. "I'm going to want to interview this window washer. You've got a name?" she asked Sonja.

"Yes, I do," Sonja said. She grabbed a scrap of paper from her purse, scribbled the name on it, then handed it to Pedretti.

She looked at it. "Osmat Bajwa?"

"Yeah, he's worked for Wally for about a year. He's Pakistani. Very reliable character. I've subcontracted him to clean some windows for some of my clients in the past. He does a beautiful job. Very hard worker."

"How in the world—" Pedretti started to say, but Sonja interrupted.

"I have my sources, ma'am. I'd like to keep them confidential."

"Only if you're telling me everything you know," Pedretti commented.

"Doesn't that kind of defeat the confidentiality issue?" Sonja asked.

"Yes, I guess it does, but I wouldn't want you to find yourself in a compromising situation in which a murderer gets off scot-free because of information you didn't share with me. Confidentiality goes out the window—no pun intended—when we're talking murder. Get my meaning?"

"Oh, I absolutely understand," Sonja said. "By the way, what's the scoop on Tina Diangelo? Was that foul play, too?"

"We're not sure. Too early to tell yet," Pedretti commented as she looked at the name scribbled on the scrap of paper. She looked back toward the classroom. "Hey, listen. I've got to announce this new piece of information to my crew." She grabbed Sonja's hand and squeezed it. "Thanks so much," she finished.

"Rest assured, Chief, I'm beatin' the bushes to figure this out, just like you," Sonja said sincerely.

"I'm glad you're in my corner," Tanya said. "Thanks for the info," and she turned and walked back into the classroom.

The meeting inside the classroom went on for some time. Pedretti shared the new information from Sonja about the masked intruder and the things the window washer had seen from his perch in his bucket truck. Questions were tossed around, and theories were presented. The note with political leanings found in Dr. Diangelo's suit pocket was discussed at length until Pedretti assigned Hatchet to put together a group of cops who could research the slogan written on the note and try to come up with some possibilities. Another group was assigned the tedious task of viewing the CCTV video. Maybe something would show up there.

Another topic of great interest was the death of Tina Diangelo which had not been mentioned in the report by Ed Phillips. Because her body was found high on a rocky trail under Grandad Bluff, the rescue squad had difficulty removing her body from the steep surroundings, but they finally arrived at the morgue with Tina's body shortly before noon. Ed had not had time to make an initial examination into what may have caused the death of the health guru, but several cops questioned the circumstances of her mysterious death.

At about three o'clock, the group finally broke up, some with specific assignments and others with a general mandate to keep their eyes and ears open and use their various contacts throughout the city to kick up leads that might explain the deaths of Tony and Tina Diangelo.

"How do you think it went?" Hatchet asked Pedretti as they walked down the hall to the chief's office.

"The information about the window washer gives us something to work with, but in the final analysis, unless we can find the masked man, it does us no good," she said wearily.

"Sounds like you're lookin' for the Lone Ranger," Hatchet said.

"Who knows? Maybe we are," Pedretti said. She walked

into her office, stepped behind her desk, and kicked off the low pumps she was wearing. She sat down at her desk and wiggled her toes in relief.

"There's one thing I need," she said frowning, leaning back in her comfortable swivel chair.

"Sure. What can I get you?" Hatchet asked.

"Some hot, fresh coffee," Pedretti grumped. Brousard nodded his head enthusiastically. *Always eager to please,* Tanya thought. *Nothing's changed.* "I doubt that you can find some in this building," she added. "That might be impossible."

"I'll get you some if I have to make it myself," Hatchet said, but he was smiling. "I'll be back."

After he left the office, Tanya sat at her desk, reveling in the silence. No phones. No eyes studying her every move and decision, nobody questioning her protocol, no Hatchet shadowing her around every corner. The peace wouldn't last long, but it was enough to revive her and get her through the rest of the day.

She thought back to her history with Hank Brousard. They'd been high school sweethearts at Logan with the same goal: becoming police officers in the city where they'd grown up in a place they loved with all their hearts. During their first year at technical college, several things threatened to upend their relationship. Hatchet's younger brother was killed in a motorcycle accident. To cope with his death and ease his pain, Hank began drinking heavily and was on the verge of flunking out of school when Tanya got hold of him and pulled him out of his depression. She'd spent hours every week tutoring him so he could stay in school and nights comforting him in his sorrow. It was an exhaustive journey, but when Hank walked across the stage and became a full-fledged cop, Tanya cried with joy at his success.

Some months later, Tanya discovered she was pregnant. Hank was appalled that she'd help save his career, but the pregnancy would jeopardize her own chances to become a cop. They agonized about what to do, but when Tanya was in her third month, she miscarried. It seemed the problem had solved itself on its own. But the loss of the baby was harder on Tanya than she expected. She began to push Hank away, avoiding intimate situations. Things came to a head one night, and despite their tears and anguish, they both decided to move on and date other people. Tanya met Roy several months later, and they were married within the year. Hank never seriously dated anyone else again.

That's the way things go, Tanya thought. *One day you think you're madly in love with someone, and six months later it's all over.* Tanya shifted in her chair, thinking about her marriage and family. Scott and Skipper, identical twins, were freshmen this year at UW–Madison: Scott majoring in biology with a goal of becoming a small-town physician and Skipper majoring in physics. *What do you do with a major in physics?* Tanya wondered. She wasn't sure, but their sons were bright, industrious, and hardworking. They'd be fine.

Leisel, their sixteen-year-old daughter, was a different story. Never one to hit the books, her life was a social whirlwind from the time she woke up in the morning until her head hit the pillow at night. Cheerleader, manager of the gymnastics team, member of the student council, the list of her activities seemed endless. Roy had tried to reassure Tanya that Leisel would be just as successful as her brothers;

after all, she had the gift of gab. "You'd be surprised where that can take you in life," Roy told her. *Yeah, right. Sometimes it takes you where you don't want to be,* Tanya thought.

A rustle at the door caught Tanya's attention. Hatchet walked in with a thermos of piping hot coffee.

"Where'd you find that?" Tanya asked.

"That new intern down in Admissions went in the back room, and ten minutes later she appeared with cups and a thermos. Some local brew. Hope it's okay." He poured the steaming liquid into a cup and handed it to Tanya.

She inhaled the aroma, closed her eyes, and took a sip. "I can feel the energy pulsing through my bloodstream," she said.

"Did you ever consider that maybe the reason for all your headaches is the stupid caffeine in the coffee?" Hatchet frowned.

"Don't even go there, and don't suggest I leave coffee out of my day. If I do, you'll pay the price, and believe me, it won't be pretty." She smiled, giggled, and took another swig of the steaming liquid, relishing the warmth as it slid down her throat.

Hatchet found a seat next to the wall, kicked his foot up on his knee, and studied his friend. Perceptive about human nature, Tanya had the uncanny ability to unite and lead her troops into the fray while still maintaining a personal connection with each person on the force. That was evident in the meeting today. When assignments were being handed out, she actively engaged in the process, delegating tasks to those officers she thought would be most effective.

Tanya noticed Hatchet's contemplative expression and

interrupted his quiet scrutiny. "Listen, Hatchet," she began, "don't overthink this investigation. We've got a lot of good people working on the evidence we've collected. Right now, it's a waiting game. The note, with its odd message, could develop into something that will lead us to a suspect. We might discover who did the deed if we can identify the masked intruder who was with Dr. Diangelo in his office this morning, but the question of why the dentist was eliminated is still out there—somewhere." She swept her hand toward the large window in her office that overlooked the athletic field of Logan High School. In the distance, the soaring sandstone bluffs rose in a rugged row to the east while eagles and hawks soared on the thermals in search of a meal.

Since moving to their new police headquarters, Tanya felt disconnected from the rest of the law enforcement community of La Crosse County, particularly from her colleague Lt. Jim Higgins and his team of investigators at the sheriff's department downtown. Tanya and Higgins had shared information and leads in several cases, and now, she felt like she was Huck Finn, floating on a raft down the Mississippi on her own. Of course, Higgins was only a phone call away, but the separation across town felt like a huge chasm, even though, logically, she knew that wasn't true. Higgins would always be available to lend his expertise and considerable experience.

As if reading her mind, Hatchet said, "Have you called Higgins yet?"

"Nope. We need to find out more before I give him a call. Besides, he's got his own set of problems to deal with," Tanya reminded him.

"Yeah. He's got Miss Elaine Turnmile, sheriff of La Crosse County." Hatchet shivered involuntarily. "She's a piece of work from what I hear."

"You've got that right. A sociopath with a caustic personality that only a seasoned veteran like Higgins is capable of handling," Tanya reminded him.

"And he's handling it?"

"By the skin of his teeth," Tanya said. "I feel for the guy. Maybe Turnmile will come around."

"When hell freezes over," Hatchet said bitterly.

CHAPTER 10 • SONJA
I Heard It Through the Grapevine

After I revealed my information to Chief Pedretti down at police headquarters, I got in my Subaru and headed back to the south side of La Crosse to Mrs. Ardell Vanderhorst's on Cass Street. Mrs. Vanderhorst has been a valued customer of the Dirty Business Cleaning Service since 1995, the year I began my services to the La Crosse community. Her home on Cass Street is one of several historic mansions throughout the Cass and King Streets neighborhood. These homes were built between 1880 and 1940 and represent the city's finest in Queen Anne, Romanesque, Prairie style, and Tudor Revival architectural styles. Reflecting the diversity of the professions of that day, the homes were built by men in the lumber, finance, construction, beer-making, manufacturing, and medical professions.

Mrs. Vanderhorst is a direct descendant of Ludwig Vanderhorst, the famous lumber baron who operated a mill and lumberyard in La Crosse during the early twentieth century. Her home is built in the classic Prairie style with a heavy emphasis on the Arts and Crafts movement (think Frank Lloyd Wright), which greatly influenced Ludwig and his wife, Gertrude, when they designed and built the home. I only know this because Ardell reminds me about the historic significance of this place every time I clean for her. When she starts telling another family history nugget, I nod pleasantly and paste a smile on my face, although truthfully, I could care less who built the house with all its special features. I'm just glad I have such a generous and faithful customer.

I let myself into the dark coolness of the back hallway with my house key, hung my jacket on the coat rack near the servant's bathroom, and walked into the modern, gleaming kitchen toward the back of the house. Despite the long, low roof line, a band of windows on the south side of the home let in abundant light. I looked out the kitchen window to see Ardell strolling through an expansive flower garden on the southern lawn in her broad straw hat. She clipped and pruned several lilac bushes, then cut a variety of flowers, laying them carefully in her gathering basket. She'll arrange them later into a beautiful bouquet to place on the kitchen counter. Ardell loves her flowers; she's always fussing over them as if they were her children. As I began my cleaning duties, I noticed a massive bouquet on a Victorian table near the front entrance of the home, as well as one that sat on the round parquet table in the library.

I moved efficiently and quietly through the lower level of the home, determined to tackle some of the cleaning jobs I'd been putting off. In the downstairs bathroom just off Ardell's bedroom, I poured a layer of salt over a half-cut grapefruit and watched the stubborn soap scum stains begin to lift as I rubbed the porcelain vigorously. With the sink sparkling clean, I poured two cups of white vinegar into the toilet bowl and let it sit. Before I left today, I'd scrub it clean. In the downstairs hallway, I squirted a glob of mayonnaise on a microfiber cloth and rubbed it into the wallpaper in the hallway where Ardell's great nephew had drawn a whimsical picture with crayons. After a few minutes, I rubbed the wallpaper gently with a clean cloth, and the crayon marks disappeared. These are the little extras I provide for my clients; they get the best of my cleaning knowledge and expertise with each visit.

After vacuuming the living and dining areas, I dust-mopped the wooden floors with a pleasant lemon oil cleaner. Things smelled bright and fresh as I walked back into the kitchen. Ardell was just coming in from the garden, so I invited her to sit at the small kitchen table. I poured a tall, cool glass of lemonade from the refrigerator and placed it in front of her while I put the cut flowers into a large bucket filled with water.

"Did you hear about the awful deaths of that dentist and his fanatical wife?" Ardell asked.

"Why do you say fanatical wife?" I asked as I placed several warm, wet sponges in the microwave to loosen the splattered food.

"Well, she's the one who owns that spa up in Onalaska. Everyone says she's an exercise nut. She's so skinny if she turns sideways, she disappears."

"Oh, really? I hadn't heard that."

"Now, Sonja, don't act innocent with me. There's no one I know in this town who knows more about people's comings and goings than you, so don't pull that little act," Ardell said tartly, looking at me over her glasses, which had slipped down on the end of her nose. Her hair was a frizzed-up mess from the humidity outside. She wiped the sweat from her forehead with a paper towel, waiting for me to enlighten her about the situation.

My shoulders slumped, and I sat down wearily across from her. The day was catching up with me. "Well, truthfully, I did hear about those deaths. What a strange coincidence that both would die on the same day," I commented.

"Yes, it is strange, but the workings of the Lord are sometimes mysterious and undecipherable," Ardell said stoically. "His ways are higher than our ways, and his thoughts are higher than our thoughts," she quoted seriously. She pushed her glasses up on the bridge of her nose, and we sat in silence for a few moments. "You know, sometimes those exercise nuts die a freakish death. Always huffing and puffing, lifting weights, jogging, jumping around. That's got to be hard on the old ticker, don't you think?"

She looked to me for wisdom. The trouble is, I had none.

Who knew what killed Tina Diangelo? I thought. *She died on the trail while exercising. You wouldn't think that would kill anyone as fit and slim as her. Still, strange quirks of nature do happen occasionally, I suppose. Or had her death been foul play, too?*

"I'm sure the coroner will have a reasonable explanation for her demise in the next few days," I said, getting up from the chair. I opened the microwave and began wiping it down.

"Is it true this Diangelo guy was found dead in his own

examination chair?" Ardell asked.

"That's the latest on Facebook," I said, spraying and wiping the kitchen countertop.

"Facebook, my eye," Ardell said sarcastically. "That internet stuff is a bunch of gobbledygook. You can't believe the garbage you see on those social media sites. Most of those people just shoot off their mouths. They don't know a squirrel hole from a donut hole."

Her lined, wrinkled face reminded me of her substantial age—ninety-two. Despite all that goes with advancing years, I loved Ardell for her blunt yet practical honesty. I'm going to miss her when she's gone.

Ardell continued her diatribe. "Didn't anyone see what happened to the dentist? You'd think the closed-circuit cameras would have shown someone or something suspicious or out of place, wouldn't you?"

"I suppose they're checking all that out, Ardell," I said while I thought about Osmat Bajwa perched in his window-washing bucket. I glanced at the time on the kitchen clock. "Hey, I've got to get going. I've got one more small job to do before I head for home." I leaned down and placed a brief kiss on her wrinkled cheek as she pressed a check for the week's services into my hand. "Take care. I'll see you next Monday," I reminded her.

"Thanks, love. You take care, too," Ardell said wistfully. I left her sitting at the kitchen table contemplating the mysterious deaths that had occurred in our beautiful city. "Be safe," she called out after me.

I hopped into my Subaru and was about to start the car when my cell buzzed. I checked the number but didn't recognize it.

"Sonja Hovland. How can I help you?"

"Well, you can't help me, but maybe I can help you," the caller said softly in a voice like velvet.

A chill raced up my arms. "Who is this, please?" I asked gruffly.

A little chuckle came over the line. "Relax, Sonja. It's Scottie Newcomb over at Suds and Duds."

I'm familiar with the laundry business and with Scottie, the owner. I've used their large washers and dryers a couple of times for some customers who needed curtains, drapes, and rugs cleaned.

"Hey, Scottie. What's up?" I asked, feeling relieved the caller was someone I knew well.

"One of my employees found something interesting in the laundry cart from Midwest Medical Services this morning. Some kind of old-fashioned nylon stocking."

"So why are you calling me?" I asked.

"Well, it's all over Facebook that some dude in Diangelo's office was wearing a stocking over his head to disguise his identity. And since you found Diangelo, I thought I'd pass the information on to you," Scottie explained.

I was shocked at the rapidity of the rumors flying around town about the incident at the Midwest Medical building.

"Where did you find the stocking? Was it the stretchy kind like pantyhose?" I asked.

"Yeah. We found it in a cart with some other towels and bibs from the dentist's office."

"How'd you know I found Diangelo?" I asked.

"Wally Leatherberry came in and told me that you found him in his dentist chair this morning. Boy, that must have been a shock, huh? He also told me about Osmat seeing a guy wearing a stocking over his face when he was cleaning the windows. What the hell is going on over there?"

"I don't know for sure yet; I'm still trying to figure it out myself. Do you have the stocking now?"

"Sure. Got it right here. Whaddya want me to do with it?" Scottie asked.

"Try not to handle it. Put on some gloves and place it in a baggie. I'll stop by and get it," I instructed him.

"Okay. I can do that, but you better get over here 'cause I close at five sharp."

"I'll be there in fifteen minutes," I said and hung up the phone.

I slammed my Subaru into reverse, backed down Ardell's driveway, and zipped across town to Suds and Duds on Lang Drive. When I opened the door of the business, a blast of air-conditioning hit me in the face. I thought it would be hot inside, but the washers and dryers were still. It was quiet and cool. A clothes rack near the front counter was loaded with clothes that had been dry-cleaned or laundered and would be picked up or delivered tomorrow.

A young man behind the counter held up a baggie with the nylon stocking inside. I grabbed it and yelled my thanks as I left the store. I made a beeline to the police headquarters several blocks away. Entering the shiny new building, I hurried up to the Admissions desk. A young female officer greeted me.

"Can I help you?" she asked, smiling pleasantly.

"I have to see Chief Pedretti," I said rather emphatically. I was out of breath and feeling frazzled by the day's unprecedented events. "It's really important. Urgent, in fact."

"I'll see if she's still here. Just a moment." The young officer dialed and talked while I drummed my fingers on the counter.

My feet were killing me, and I needed a shower. I hoped against hope that the chief was still in the building somewhere.

"I barely caught her," the officer said. "She was in the parking lot about to head for home. Here she comes now." She pointed behind me. I turned and saw Chief Pedretti enter the lobby. I went out to meet her.

"Hey. What's going on now?" Pedretti asked.

I held up the baggie with the nylon stocking. Pedretti's eyes widened. "Is this what I think it is?" she asked.

I nodded my head and proceeded to explain the story behind the discovery of the stocking.

"Unbelievable. What are you doing cleaning houses?" Tanya asked me. "You should be a detective. We could use more people like you."

"Oh, no, no, no," I argued, shaking my head back and forth. "I'm not interested in anything like that. I value my life too much to chase crooks and killers around town, trying to figure out their motives."

"Isn't that what you've been doing all day?" Tanya asked, cocking her head to one side.

The question stopped me in my tracks. I hadn't considered my activities to be secretive or subversive, but when I thought about what I'd been doing all day long, I realized the chief was pretty accurate in her assessment. I *had* been chasing down leads, talking to my contacts on the street, and gathering evidence that might lead to the identification of a possible killer.

"Well, I didn't plan any of this," I stammered. "It just sort of happened."

"Well, it's about the best unplanned investigation I've ever seen," Pedretti commented laconically. "So, are you headed for home?"

"Yeah. I'm beat," I told her, brushing a strand of hair away from my face.

"Are you up for a drink at the Bluffside Tavern up on Grandad?" she asked. "It's on my way home, and I need to wet my whistle."

I considered her offer carefully. I'm not in the habit of drinking before I go home from work, but considering how everything had played out today, I decided I deserved to relax a little bit. I dialed Trygve, telling him I'd be home by six-thirty. He promised to have supper ready and waiting. Then I headed to the Bluffside Tavern perched high on Grandad Bluff to meet Police Chief Tanya Pedretti for a drink.

The young man lowered the binoculars he'd bought at a secondhand store on the corner of Liberty and Logan Streets in La Crosse. *If you're going to do surveillance, you have to have the right equipment,* he thought. He watched Sonja Hovland and Chief Pedretti converse in the lobby of the police complex. Then he saw Sonja hand a bag to the chief. Inside the bag was something dark. He slammed his fist into the steering wheel, feeling his temper surge. The voices in his head reminded him of his incompetence. *How stupid can you be? You're just another loser who can't hang on to a job. Now you've botched this up. Can't you do anything right?*

He continued watching the exchange between the two women. They moved out of the building to their vehicles and drove out of the law enforcement parking lot. He carefully followed them, staying back several blocks, remaining unobtrusive. When they turned left on Main Street and continued to Bliss Road, which took them up the bluff, he wondered if they were headed for the Bluffside Tavern. It was a popular spot for a quick sandwich and a beer.

When both cars turned into the tavern parking lot, he drove by, winding his way up to Grandad Bluff Road, where he turned around and returned to the edge of the Bluffside parking lot in a shaded spot. He felt unsure of what he should do next. *Should I go in and sit by the ladies and listen to their conversation?* he wondered. That seemed awfully brazen—and stupid. He couldn't risk being seen now. He had to remain undercover until things settled down.

He reclined in the driver's seat of his car and sprawled his long, leggy frame out until he was almost below the window. Then he thought about his next move. He smiled wickedly. So many things had fallen into place in the last few days, except for that stupid sock. He kept believing in luck because he would need a lot of it with his next move.

In the seat next to him lay a book entitled *The Trouble with Capitalism*. The young man smiled, reached for the book, cracked it open, and began reading.

CHAPTER 11

How Do You Mend a Broken Heart?

The atmosphere inside the Bluffside Tavern was subdued, but after all, it was a Monday night. A few customers were seated at a couple of tables, the waitress scurrying around getting their drinks and sandwiches. Tanya and Sonja found a corner table away from the other patrons. The view of the lush, green trees surrounding the popular bar helped ease their frayed nerves. Tanya ordered a brandy old-fashioned sweet and Sonja a light pale ale.

When the drinks came, they made small talk for a few moments, each feeling rather awkward in this social setting. Tanya asked Sonja about her background and the details of her cleaning business, which seemed to break the ice. Sonja was proud of her success in the cleaning world and shared her business experience with Tanya.

"So, you started this business after you flunked out of college?" Tanya asked.

Nothing like a blunt approach, Sonja thought. *Must be all those years as a cop.* Although the police chief's assumption irritated her, she gave her the benefit of the doubt.

"Let me clarify that; I quit college," Sonja explained. "I never flunked out. The college scene was just one huge social experiment for me, and I might add, it delivered later, big time. Most of my customers are friends I made while I was in school, and I kept in contact with them. They became my first customers and have referred all kinds of people to me."

"And you're married?" Tanya asked, sipping her drink.

"Yes, to Trygve. He works for the Streets and Parks Department in La Crosse."

"Children?"

Sonja sighed heavily, and a familiar sadness welled up in her heart. "Three miscarriages—all about the third month. I couldn't do it again, so Tryg and I quit trying. We have two mules named Sonny and Cher, a bunch of chickens, and a very spoiled poodle named Coco, who basically runs the place. That's it."

"I'm so sorry," Tanya said sympathetically. "It must have been really hard to deal with the loss of your children." She thought of her miscarriage with Hank and the devastation she'd felt when it happened.

"Each time, we were absolutely shattered. But we adjusted and moved on. You really don't have much of a choice, do you?" Sonja said. "Besides, Tryg makes me very happy. He's my soulmate. What about you?" She sipped her beer and quietly watched Tanya's expression.

"Husband, Roy, twenty-three years together. Twin boys in college in Madison and a sixteen-year-old daughter whose social calendar would give the Kardashians a run for their money."

Sonja noticed the flat tone of her voice. *Oh boy,* she thought. *I hit a sore spot.*

"But you're happy, right?" Sonja asked quietly, sensing something amiss.

Tanya was surprised when her eyes filled with tears. She looked away quickly and struggled to regain her composure. *What's wrong with me?* she thought. She swallowed hard, cleared her throat, and said, "I'm kind of in a rough patch with my husband right now. I know we love each other, but I lost my mom recently, my boys left for college, and lately, things sort of crashed down around me. Sometimes I wonder if it's all worth it."

The sadness on Tanya's face filled Sonja with empathy. She leaned over and grabbed Tanya's hand.

"Hey, it's okay. I've been there," Sonja said gently. "There is happiness beyond your troubles."

"I'm not so sure about that. I can't decide if it's me fixating on the loss of my mom or if it's boredom on Roy's part," Tanya started. "If it's boredom, then that scares the hell out of me." Sonja let go of Tanya's hand and leaned back in her chair.

"When Tryg and I were going through our rough times," Sonja began, "I tried to come up with some routines that would give us both a breather from the day's stress and sadness. We started taking a short walk every night after supper, followed by a game of Scrabble or Kings Corner. It gave us a break from the sorrow and tension we were both feeling. And then we made a real effort to keep our love life from sputtering to a halt. Sex is a great outlet for letting yourself go and experiencing the joy of another person's presence."

The silence that followed seemed long and profound. Finally, Tanya spoke. "Thank you for sharing that. Roy just doesn't seem interested in me anymore." The tears began to flow, and Tanya cried quietly for several moments while Sonja waited. Finally, the police chief apologized. "I'm sorry. This isn't what I'd planned."

"Hey, what are friends for?" Sonja said, smiling bashfully. "Are you up for a little advice?" she asked.

"What have I got to lose?" Tanya said, shrugging her shoulders. She smiled weakly and wiped the tears from her cheeks.

"Tonight, when you get home after you've eaten something, lock yourself in the bathroom. Take a long bubbly soak, dress in your sexiest night stuff, spray on some perfume, and turn the sheets back."

"Are you serious?" Tanya said, leaning across the table.

"Dead serious. If that doesn't get you to first base, then you and I need to go down to Elaine's Lingerie on Third Street next to Doerflinger's and do some serious shopping," Sonja said. When Tanya continued to stare at her, she went on. "If boredom is your problem, honey, then you've got to spice things up. If you keep doing the same things, you're going to get the same results. Men are visual creatures, so give him something to look at."

"I'm not sure I'm really that…"

"Beautiful?" Sonja finished her thought. She noticed the threat of tears in Tanya's eyes again. "If your husband loves you, then you are beautiful to him. And you need to remind him why he fell in love with you in the first place." The quiet that followed made Sonja wonder if she'd overstepped some unspoken social boundary.

"Wow! Maybe you're right," Tanya said in a hushed voice. She thought a moment more and then said, "One more thing before you go: Can I put you on speed dial?"

"Absolutely. In fact, if you don't, I'll be offended," Sonja said, winking.

CHAPTER 12

What's New, Pussycat?

By the time Sonja arrived home, she was exhausted and hungry. Trygve met her at the door and appraised her condition.

"You look like you've been wrung through a knothole," he said grumpily. "And you're a half hour late."

Sonja bumped up against his broad chest and gave him a quick kiss. "Sorry, love, but I got into a very delicate conversation I wasn't expecting. I'm starving. Whatcha got to eat?"

"My famous goulash. Come on and sit down. I'll get you a plate," Trygve said gruffly.

They walked into the kitchen. Sonja washed her hands at the kitchen sink while Trygve placed a large scoop of goulash, two thick slices of toasted garlic bread, and a generous portion of coleslaw on a plate. Sonja sat down on a stool at the kitchen island and began ravenously wolfing down the food.

"You're gonna choke on it if you don't slow down," Trygve reminded her, setting a glass of wine next to her plate. "Are you even tasting it?"

Sonja pointed her fork at him. "Well, if you didn't make such an amazing tomato-hamburger goulash, I wouldn't have to eat so fast," she said, taking a sip of wine.

"It is pretty good, isn't it?" he said, finally giving her a wide smile.

"What's your secret, hon?"

"You'll never know unless you watch Lydia Bastianich," Trygve commented coolly.

"On PBS?"

"Yep. Now, quit avoiding the subject and tell me why you're late." He leaned against the countertop and crossed his arms over his chest.

"I ran into Sheriff Pedretti again, and we went out for a drink at the Bluffside," Sonja began. Before he could interrupt with more questions, she told Trygve about the discovery of the nylon stocking, which he found very hard to believe.

"What are the chances that would happen?" he asked when Sonja finished.

"Slim to none," Sonja said curtly. "Finding that sock was a stroke of luck we better not waste."

Sonja noticed her husband's wrinkled brows—a sure sign of some serious thinking on his part.

"What's this 'we' stuff?" he asked.

"Who was the one who told me I had to go talk to the sheriff and tell her everything I know?" Sonja tilted her head and waited for his answer. "That would be you, Tryg."

Trygve looked disgusted. "Well, yeah, I did say that, but I didn't think it meant you were going to be a participant in a full-blown police investigation."

"You better rethink that position, and I'll have you know I've found out more about this suspicious death in the last twelve hours than the whole police department has, and they've had the same amount of time as I have. Of course, my people are always there for me. So there," Sonja said brusquely, scooping up another forkful of goulash.

"Well, if the stocking was found in the Suds and Duds laundry cart, how did it get there?" he asked.

Sonja chewed a piece of garlic toast thoughtfully for a moment. "Might be someone who works at the laundry and decided it would be a good place to ditch it. But most likely, it's someone who threw it in the laundry bin at Midwest Medical when he escaped from the building this morning after he killed Dr. Diangelo," she said.

"Or … he might have hidden in the laundry bin and rode to Suds and Duds, where he escaped unnoticed," Trygve said, raising his eyebrows at this idea. "You said no one saw anyone leave the building this morning, right?"

He had a faraway look in his eye that Sonja had seen before. She was constantly surprised at the depth of the man.

He continued thinking out loud. "One more thing—how did the guy get into the building? That might be more important than how he got out of it. Was he employed there? He must have had access to the place somehow. Did he have some kind of ID or a key card or something?"

"I haven't gotten that far yet," Sonja said, "but I'll think about it." She finished her meal and put her dishes in the dishwasher along with a soap pellet. She closed the machine and pushed the start button.

"Up for a walk?" Trygve asked.

"Sounds good. Let's go." Sonja grabbed her sweatshirt off the hook in the hallway.

The evening air was cool and invigorating. Trygve and Sonja breathed deeply and walked hand in hand down their blacktop driveway onto Schilling Court, which bordered their land. Sonny and Cher, the two mules, walked along the fence, following them to the corner, where they began braying loudly.

"Should have brought them a couple of apples to shut 'em up," Trygve said.

"You spoil them rotten, Tryg."

"I know," he said quietly.

The evening sun was setting in the west, and the sky was ablaze with a profusion of pink and orange swirls, the wooded hills cutting a sharp silhouette against the blazing sky. They walked past the Stettlers' dairy farm, a beautiful turn-of-the-century operation with a red brick house and red outbuildings. Tom Stettler waved to them when he came out of the barn, done with the evening's milking. The odor of manure wafted into the air and mixed with the sharp scent of the towering pine trees along the road. After they'd walked for fifteen minutes, Sonja and Trygve turned around and headed home. A sliver of silver moon was rising in the east, and Sonja silently pointed to the yellow crescent hanging like a luminous bauble in the darkening sky. She thought of the times they'd both walked this road with tears in their eyes and heaviness in their hearts after the loss of their babies. Now the unity between them gave a deep, reassuring peace. They'd weathered several storms in their marriage and were still deeply in love. *Only by the grace of God,* thought Sonja.

They'd rounded the nearest corner and were heading back home when Trygve suddenly heard the terrible roar of a souped-up car engine. He looked behind and noticed a dark-colored vehicle moving fast and coming closer by the second. Trygve grabbed Sonja and shoved her into the ditch just as the car careened around the corner, heading straight for them. Trygve leaped to the side at the last possible second, almost landing on Sonja. The car's brakes screeched ominously, and the whole vehicle pitched wildly to one side, hitting the gravel shoulder, then fishtailed as the wheels grabbed the blacktop again. By the time Trygve was up and out of the ditch, all that was left of the threat was a black trail of exhaust and a dust cloud where the wheels had skidded onto the gravel shoulder.

"What the hell!" Trygve shouted, raising his fist at the disappearing car. He brought his fist down and slapped his jeans with disgust. Sonja picked herself up from the high grass in the ditch and joined him on the road. She was alarmed. Her husband seldom cursed or swore.

"Holy smokes, Tryg! Who was that?" she asked, panting. She winced as she rubbed her elbow.

"I don't know, but that's about the wildest driving I've ever seen on this stretch of road," he snarled angrily. "What's the matter with—" He stopped suddenly, still gazing in the direction of the car, a look of shock on his face.

Sonja laid a hand on his arm. "What are you thinking?" she asked.

"I think somebody just tried to kill you," he said softly.

Sonja studied her husband's face as he grabbed her hand and stomped down the road toward home.

When they got inside the house, Sonja headed for the

shower while Trygve located his cell phone and called police headquarters. When Sonja came out of the bathroom in her robe, Trygve was sitting in his La-Z-Boy, a look of dark anger on his face, the TV muted.

"Tryg? I can see you're mad. Furious, actually," she ventured timidly, standing next to his chair.

"That doesn't even begin to describe it, babe." He glowered at the TV.

"Did you call it in to the police?" Sonja asked.

"Of course I did. Talked to some guy named Hank Brousard." He looked over at Sonja. "You know him?"

"I met him this morning at the Midwest Medical building. He's Tanya's right-hand man. What'd he say?"

"He said he'd take it into consideration, whatever that means," Trygve spat. He stood up suddenly and pushed past Sonja into the kitchen. He spun around and pointed a finger at her. "Jeez, honey, how'd we get in this pickle anyway?"

"Now, take it easy, Tryg. It might have just been some drunk, crazy kid out for a joyride."

"No, it wasn't," Trygve argued loudly, his index finger poking the air between them. "That kid was out to run you over and kill you!" His shouting echoed through the house. Coco, the little black poodle, slunk down the hallway looking for a place to hide.

Sonja's eyes grew big with the realization that she had become a target in a murder investigation.

"Maybe what I found out today put me in the bullseye, ya think?" Sonja asked quietly. The question seemed to hang in the air.

"That's exactly what I think," Trygve said, looking defeated. "And if that's the case, then somehow this bozo found out about the window washer and the fact that you were the one who discovered the body. Not only that, but that means some of your friends could be in harm's way too." They stood in the kitchen for a few moments contemplating the situation.

Finally, Sonja sidled up to Trygve and put her arms around his waist, trying to comfort him. Trygve didn't scare easily, but she could see he was shaken by the incident.

"Come on, let's go to bed. Tomorrow's a new day," she said softly, giving her husband a tender kiss.

"Naw, I'm too keyed up. I'll be in later." He untangled himself from her hug and walked past her to the living room, where he collapsed into the recliner. Over his shoulder, he said, "You go to bed. You've had a big day."

A half hour later, Trygve slid into his side of the bed. Sonja rolled over and laid her head on his shoulder. "It'll be okay, Tryg. Don't worry."

He harrumphed with doubt. "You might have bitten off more than you can chew this time, darlin'," he said softly.

Sonja rolled on top of him and kissed him intensely. When she pulled away, she said, "And don't you dare tell me you're not in the mood, because I am." *Sometimes a woman just has to take charge,* she thought. She remembered the advice she had given Tanya at the Bluffside Tavern. *Give him something to look at.*

"I can get in the mood," he said, kissing her back. He kissed her neck, and she pulled her nightgown off over her head. "Oh, that helps. Why don't we just forget about today and start fresh tomorrow?"

"That is a very good idea, my man," Sonja said, returning his kiss.

CHAPTER 13
All in a Day's Work

When Chief Tanya Pedretti walked into her office on Tuesday morning, the phone was ringing off the hook. Her office manager wasn't in yet, so Tanya reached over and picked up the landline.

"Chief Pedretti. May I help you?"

"Hey, Tanya. Just wondering how last night went?" Sonja asked.

"Well, it wasn't a one-hit wonder, but it's a start. I'll tell you about it sometime."

"Do we need to take a trip downtown to Elaine's?" Sonja asked.

"Maybe. I'll think about it."

"One other thing," Sonja said.

Pedretti could hear a tentative quality in her voice. She was sure the other shoe was about to drop.

"Someone tried to kill me last night," Sonja said quietly.

"What? When? Where?"

"If you want the details, talk to Hank. My husband called him last night and described the incident to him. He wrote a report. It should be there somewhere," Sonja said, "maybe on your desk. You'll have to read it."

"I'll do that. You know what this means, don't you?" Tanya asked.

"I'm assuming someone is angry about my discovery of Diangelo's untimely death and is vowing to get even," Sonja summarized, "or permanently shut me up."

"Yep. You hit the nail on the head, and it also means someone is following you. Keep your eyes and ears open, and keep your powder dry," Tanya advised. "That shouldn't be too hard for you with all your contacts in the city."

Sonja didn't get the powder comment, but she deduced it meant she should be ready for action at any time. That didn't make her feel very secure. What did she know about killers and criminals? Somehow, since yesterday, she had entered a world she didn't recognize. Delving into little problems like infidelity, embezzling, and the dates and signatures on a birth certificate suddenly seemed rather trivial and petty. What she was involved in now was life and death stuff, and when she thought about it, her respect and admiration for Pedretti and her crew grew by leaps and bounds.

"Sonja? You still there?" Pedretti asked.

"Yep, but not for long," she replied. "I've got three big jobs today."

"Good luck. Call if you need something," Pedretti said, and the line went dead.

On Tuesday morning, Sonja entered the back door of a sprawling low-slung ranch home perched on a five-hundred-foot bluff above the Mississippi River off Malin Road on River View Lane near the tiny river town of Genoa south of La Crosse. The property owner, Timothy Mercer, was an executive at a convenience/gas store company in La Crosse, where he'd been employed since the age of eighteen. Now, at fifty-two, he had clawed his way to the top of the management heap and pulled down a comfortable three-quarters of a million dollars a year. His home reflected his style—casual and comfortable with the amenities you'd expect from someone of his status: a massive hot tub on the deck overlooking the river, a pool room with a fifteen-foot bar across one end, a movie theatre that seated twenty complete with surround sound and an eight-foot screen, six bedrooms, four bathrooms, a gleaming state-of-the-art kitchen and pantry, and a living room that jutted out over the bluff and seemed to defy gravity. The view of the Mississippi River was to die for, but all of it needed to be cleaned and maintained.

Mercer had been a valued Dirty Business Cleaning Service customer since 2010, when he'd built his blufftop mansion. Sonja had partied with him in college, and although he was an executive, she still had a beer and pizza with him once in a while when he happened to be home during the day. She knew his wife, Missy, casually, and Sonja made it her business to remember his children's names, marital status, and occupations. Four grandchildren often visited the Mercer estate, and Sonja's cleaning job grew exponentially when they did. There was no sign of Tim or his wife today, which was okay with Sonja. She had a lot to do and not much time to do it.

She began cleaning and polishing the kitchen. As she

mopped, vacuumed, and dusted her way through the huge home, her mind was occupied with the events of the last few days. It seemed like weeks ago that she'd stumbled on the dead body of Dr. Tony Diangelo, but in reality, it was only yesterday. A shudder ran through her when she thought about the handsome dentist, so still and lifeless in his chair. Sonja wondered when the coroner's report would be available. Of course, she'd probably have to rely on her friends at the sheriff's office to find out the real cause of the dentist's death. She thought of Ruth Miller, the part-time secretary at the city morgue housed at the law enforcement center on Vine Street. Ruth would have an inside track on the information Sonja needed.

During her first coffee break at ten o'clock, Sonja sat in a comfortable patio chair on the massive wooden deck in the sunshine and enjoyed a serene view of the great river below while she sipped a cup of coffee. Tows were moving up and down the waterway, and the current sparkled like a thousand diamonds. Overhead, she heard the screech of an eagle, looked up, and watched a mature male land in one of the massive pine trees on the edge of the bluff. *Such beauty,* she thought.

She plucked her cell phone out of her cleaning apron and dialed Ruth at the coroner's office. Explaining her situation, Sonja asked her to keep her ear to the ground and let her know of any preliminary results in the Diangelo autopsy. With that done, she resumed her cleaning routine.

Tanya Pedretti called her about noon when she was eating a salad at the kitchen island.

"Hey, I just wanted to let you know that Tony Diangelo died of a massive injection of fentanyl," Tanya began. "The dose was so big, he never had a chance. It killed him almost instantaneously—stopped his heart cold."

"Boy, that's upsetting. What about his wife, Tina?" Sonja asked.

"That's still up for grabs, but from what Ed told me, his ruling will be death from natural causes. It looks like she suffered a massive heart attack and died within a few minutes of the attack," Tanya explained.

"Don't you think it's kinda strange they both died on the same day? How often does something like that happen?" Sonja asked. "I can only think of one instance in my entire lifetime when a husband and a wife died on the same day, and that was in a car accident. Common sense tells you there must be a connection between the two events."

"Yeah, I know, that seems logical, but quirks of nature and circumstances sometimes do happen in real life," Tanya commented.

A considerable pause in the conversation made Sonja nervous, and she drummed a pen on the granite countertop waiting for Tanya to continue.

"Anyway, I just wanted you to know how Diangelo died. Oh, I also wanted to thank you for your advice. Although last night was nothing out of the ordinary, at least Roy and I seemed to reconnect on some level. Anyway, I was reassured. So, thank you again."

"Don't be shy. Keep on doing what you're doing. He'll notice your efforts eventually, and you'll both benefit from it. If not, remember to keep Elaine's shop in mind. I've had several people tell me her lingerie has played an important role in turning their love life around." The quiet that followed was awkward.

"That seems so ... conniving," Tanya said.

Sonja could almost visualize the disapproval on her face. It seemed laughable to her that someone like Tanya, who was familiar with the criminal world, could be so clueless about something as subtle as sexual relationships.

"Conniving, my eye," Sonja countered sarcastically. "The good Lord knew what he was doing when he made us. You've got your parts, and your husband has his, and the two were meant to work together for your enjoyment. Why do you think so many people get into trouble in the sexual area of life?" Sonja asked, not waiting for Tanya's response. "Because it's fun and pleasurable and exciting, that's why. I'm just trying to put a little zip back into your relationship, that's all."

"Well, I never thought about it that way, I guess," Tanya said. "Hey, I've got to go. Hank just walked into my office. Talk to you later."

"Yeah, later," Sonja said, and she hung up.

Sonja finished her cleaning duties at Mercers, locked the mansion, and started her journey back to La Crosse. As she drove, she thought about the vulnerability of people. Anyone who watched Tanya Pedretti carry out her duties as police chief of La Crosse as Sonja had would conclude she was successful because she was confident, intelligent, and bold—which was all true. But when you scratched the surface of people's lives, insecurities and pain often surged to the forefront, didn't they? No one goes through life unscathed by human problems and sorrow. How many times had she sat with her wealthy, upwardly mobile clients, listened to their tales of woe, and wiped away their tears? Too many to count. She'd concluded years ago that an outwardly successful life was no guarantee that happiness was an integral part of it.

After her revealing conversation with Pedretti last night, she was committed to keeping Tanya's marital concerns safe within the bonds of their newly formed friendship. There was really no other way to build trust between two people. In an age when people shared their intimate details on social media, privacy and discretion were at a premium. For Tanya and Roy's sake, she was rooting for them all the way, but nobody would hear it from her lips.

CHAPTER 14

There's a Hole in the Bucket, Dear Liza

Tanya Pedretti stood in the doorway of the crime scene lab at the new police headquarters on Ranger Road on Tuesday morning, gazing at the neutral walls, gleaming instruments, and a corkboard with various utensils hanging from small hooks. It reminded her of the challenges inherent in extracting DNA and fingerprints from everyday articles and surfaces. She watched the technician hover over a microscope. She quietly cleared her throat. The tech looked up.

"Sorry, Chief. Didn't hear you come in. You need something?" she asked, looking over at her, pushing her glasses up along her hairline.

"Just wondering if you've found anything significant from the Diangelo scene over on Copeland across town?" Tanya asked.

The tech leaned back in her chair and sighed. "At this point, the evidence is pretty slim, although we did get some significant DNA from the nylon stocking. Whether it matches anything in the DNA bank is still up for grabs. We're checking that. No fingerprints other than Diangelo's and some of his staff. Unfortunately, the cleaning lady wiped down most of the other surfaces in the office the morning of the crime. We did manage to empty the vacuum cleaner that was used, so we're going through that material. There might be something there. We're still working on the exam room where Diangelo was found."

Tanya leaned against the doorframe. The tech could see the disappointment on her face.

"Sorry, Chief. If I find anything exciting, I'll let you know."

Tanya turned to leave. "Thanks, Kay. Keep at it. We need to find the guy who wore the stocking." Tanya walked down the long hallway toward her office. Hatchet was up ahead having an intense conversation with another cop. He waved her down.

Mike Leland, the other cop, had been on the force for about ten years. He'd earned his detective license a couple of years ago. Since then, he'd had a few stints with Higgins over at the sheriff's department. Tanya remembered an investigation he'd been involved in a few years ago when Higgins's home had almost been burned to the ground by a relentless criminal. Mike was experienced, smart, and determined, and now he gave Tanya a sharp nod and met her curious glance.

"So, what's up, Mike?" Tanya asked. Hatchet glanced at Tanya, wondering whether any DNA evidence had been found at Diangelo's dentist's office.

"Mornin', Chief," Mike began. "We've been looking into fringe groups around the state, and we've come up with a few that seem to be operating within the greater La Crosse area. You got a minute to talk about it?"

"Absolutely, but I'm already familiar with a few of them."

Hatchet gestured to the door of the large room where the detectives shared a common space. "After you," he said curtly.

The three sat down around a laptop perched on Mike's desk. He navigated his way to a website that reviewed some of the political fringe groups currently active in Wisconsin.

"You said you're already familiar with some of these groups," Mike said, pointing to the screen. "So you know about the old standard John Birch Society, QAnon, and the Proud Boys listed here. But when we went through Diangelo's emails and Facebook posts, we found a few comments that referred to the Coulee Fifty for Democracy and Freedom. When we tried to find more information on them, we came up blank, but we found several lengthy diatribes on Facebook by Diangelo in which he raked the group over the coals. He referenced their conspiracy theories and their emphasis on guns as complete foolishness, taking apart their arguments one by one. He was very articulate in his criticisms. We also found a comment he made about the capitalist way of life, so we're thinking it's possible someone from the group took offense and decided to teach the doc a lesson. Diangelo's post used the *capitalist* term, and we thought that word might be important since it was repeated in the note you found in his suit."

Tanya listened carefully, then leaned back and studied the ceiling. She was quiet for a few moments and then sat up suddenly. "That's good work, Mike. It gives us a direction. Do we know any members of this group who are operating locally?" she asked, making eye contact with Mike.

"Not yet, but we've got every police officer in the city informed about the group, and they're keeping their eyes and ears open."

"Great." She turned to Hatchet. "I want you and Mike to head up the effort to find out more about this group and possibly locate some members. If you have to do something undercover, work together, communicate where you are and who you're with. Let's see what shakes out," she finished. She stood and left the room.

Hatchet looked at Mike and said, "Well, I guess we've got our orders."

"Yeah, we do. What's Pedretti gonna do with this new information?"

Hatchet shrugged. "She's got her sources she confides in, and it's not me these days," he said sarcastically.

"She's shuttin' you out, Hatchet?" Mike shook his head and continued. "Well, I guess you're going to have to earn your way back into her good graces," he said, insinuating Hatchet had been shown some kind of favoritism, although Mike always considered Pedretti to be above board and fair in her dealings with the cops under her leadership. However, the scuttlebutt and gossip about a possible long-standing romantic relationship between Tanya and Hatchet continued to swirl in the law enforcement gossip mill even though no one had ever seen them together outside of official functions or in their duties in the office and around the city.

"It must be that cleaning gal she met at the scene, the

one who found Diangelo," Hatchet said, his voice sharp with suspicion. "They seemed to hit it off."

"Yeah, I hear that gal's got an unbelievable network around town. Maybe we should plug into it," Mike said. "Whaddya think?"

Hatchet remained silent as if he'd never heard Mike's comment. He stared at Tanya while she strolled down the hall to her office. Mike noticed Hatchet's flint-like expression and wondered where this investigation was headed. *Looks like trouble is brewing on more than one front,* he thought.

CHAPTER 15 • SONJA

The Long and Winding Road

When I woke up Wednesday morning, my shoulder still ached from my fling into the ditch, and my black-and-blue elbow, where I'd landed hard on the turf, was throbbing with pain. I was reeling in disbelief that anyone would want to kill me. I limped into the bathroom and washed down two Tylenol with a glass of water. Then I hobbled back to bed for another half hour of sleep, but Coco jumped up on the bed and crawled between Trygve and me. The extra sleep I craved eluded me, so I got up, put on my robe, and went into the kitchen to make a pot of coffee.

Fifteen minutes later, Trygve joined me. I poured him a cup of coffee, and we silently sat at the dining room table, bleary-eyed, worried, and ornery. Outside the weather had turned a corner, and it was raining quietly but steadily. After a few moments of silence, I got up and stood by the patio doors looking out at the dismal conditions, cheered only by the row of purple lilacs blooming profusely next to the south side of the house. A few moments later, Trygve came up behind me and hugged me around my waist, kissing me tenderly on my neck.

"How ya feelin' about everything, sweetheart?" he asked quietly.

I'd heard that phrase before when we'd lost our babies and my parents had passed away. It was usually an invitation to vent and cry, but I honestly didn't know what to say this morning. Everything about the deaths of Dr. Diangelo and his wife, Tina, seemed to be on shaky ground. Where was the investigation headed? Was I still the main suspect? I hardly thought so. After all, I'd been instrumental in uncovering some important leads from Osmat, the window washer, and I'd located the nylon stocking at the Suds and Duds laundromat and given it to Chief Pedretti.

"Hon? Are you okay?" Trygve asked again, still holding me in his arms. I turned and kissed him tenderly.

"I will survive," I said with determined cheerfulness, although I felt anything but confident. To be honest, I wasn't enjoying the attention in the limelight, nor was Trygve. The morning edition of the *La Crosse Sentinel* lay on the kitchen counter, its headlines screaming the horror of the situation in big, bold letters: "HUSBAND AND WIFE DIE ON THE SAME DAY. CLEANING LADY DISCOVERS DENTIST'S BODY." I hadn't seen capital letters that big since the attempted assassination of Donald Trump in July of last year. Since the incident, we had completely ignored the calls coming in on our landline. Last night, in a fit of frustration, I threatened to cut the line, but Trygve convinced me restoring the disconnected line would be more costly than the satisfaction of ending the continuous calls.

"Don't worry about the phone calls or what the papers

say," Trygve said softly. His hazel eyes were soft with compassion.

"I'm not. But that nonstop ringing is getting to me. But the bigger question is: Do you want me to quit trying to find answers?" I asked him, looking into his kind eyes.

"That's like asking a bird not to fly," he responded with a sad smile. "But I think the discoveries you shared with Chief Pedretti should get you off the hook as a suspect."

I sighed loudly. "You'd think so, wouldn't you?"

Trygve pulled me into his chest and held me for a long moment. Then he stepped back, gave me a peck on the lips, and said, "I'm going to get dressed for work. You?"

"The same. I've got two jobs this morning, but my afternoon is free," I said.

Trygve groaned. "That spells trouble. I s'pose you'll be slinking around town trying to uncover more information about the mysterious pantyhose man."

"You never can tell, but hopefully some of my friends will come through with something that will move this case forward." I'm sure my determined expression at that moment sent daggers of worry through my husband, but he shrugged it off, knowing there was very little that could be done to dissuade me.

"Here's a loaded question for you: Are you making dinner tonight, or am I?" he asked me.

"I will. I promise to be home by five, and we'll have a nice romantic meal with candlelight, wine, and roses." I grinned mischievously. "And then we'll make mad, passionate love all night."

"Don't make promises you can't keep," he said gruffly, "or promises I might not be able to fulfill."

I saluted crisply. "Aye, aye, captain. Look for the whites of my eyes at five," I said, but from the look on his face, I knew he was still concerned about my safety.

Osmat Bajwa sat on the molded plastic chair in the interrogation room at the La Crosse Police Department on Ranger Street Wednesday morning. Outside the weather was stormy, but the intrepid window washer was cool, calm, and composed, a picture of serenity. Across from him, Police Chief Tanya Pedretti and Lt. Hank Brousard exchanged glances with the man who had witnessed the strange situation in the office of Dr. Tony Diangelo early Monday morning. There was tension in the stuffy interrogation room, along with a hopeful expectation that this humble blue-collar worker could tell the police something that would lead them in a new direction in the investigation. Whether he would come through with some enlightening tip was up for grabs. Chief Pedretti leaned over and started the video recording system.

She began. "Mr. Bajwa, thank you for coming in this morning. We are grateful to you, and we want to hear what you observed Monday morning, May 27, at the Midwest Medical Services building down on Copeland Avenue."

Osmat nodded his head briefly. "Before we begin, may I say something?" he asked politely.

"Of course. Feel free." Tanya smiled.

"In Pakistan, the police code begins like this: O you who have believed, be persistently standing firm in justice, witnesses for Allah, even if it be against yourselves, parents, and relatives. Whether one is rich or poor, Allah is more worthy of both. So, follow not personal inclination, lest you not be just. And if you distort your testimony or refuse to give it, then indeed Allah is ever, with what you do, acquainted." Tanya and Hatchet stared at Osmat in silence. "This is the code the police and its citizens are expected to follow in Pakistan," Osmat continued, "and I will do my best to tell you the truth so that justice may prevail. All praise to Allah. Thank you." He bowed his head slightly as if in prayer, closing his eyes briefly. For all Tanya knew, he might be praying. She looked at Hatchet out of the corner of her eye and noticed his expression of amazement.

"Thank you, Osmat. I can see you're taking this interrogation very seriously. We appreciate that. So, let's get started, shall we?" Tanya said.

Osmat opened his eyes and held the police chief's gaze for a long moment. He was a handsome man with smooth, velvety skin, dark eyes, jet-black hair, and a solemn expression that reassured Tanya he was committed to telling them what he'd witnessed as he looked through the third-floor window of the medical building early Monday morning.

"What did you see from your window-washing truck Monday morning?" Tanya asked.

"I was cleaning the windows on the east side of the building," Osmat began.

"Time?" Tanya interrupted.

"About five-thirty," Osmat said. Tanya nodded. He continued. "When I raised my bucket to the third floor, a light came on inside one of the rooms, and Dr. Diangelo walked into the room followed by another man who had a nylon stocking pulled over his head. The stocking made identification almost impossible. All his features were distorted, but I can tell you his hair was dark, maybe black or brown."

"Did you actually see him do anything suspicious toward Dr. Diangelo?" Hank asked.

"No, I didn't, but I didn't stick around because I was afraid he would notice me and come after me," Osmat said. "The situation seemed rather odd ... and rather threatening."

"Was there anything else you noticed about the man with the stocking over his head?" Tanya asked. "Can you give us some more details: perhaps his height and build, his race, any other features?"

"He was about six feet tall, slim build ... white, I think," Osmat's voice trailed off as he thought.

"Anything else?" Tanya asked.

The window washer remained thoughtful for a moment, his eyes closed as if he were visualizing the man again. Suddenly, his eyes popped open. "Oh," he said quietly.

"Yes, you remembered something?" Tanya asked, sitting forward.

"He was missing his little finger on his left hand. Actually, there was a little stub there, but most of it was gone," Osmat said.

"Really? That's an interesting detail we didn't have before," Tanya replied.

"Yes, I'd forgotten about that," Osmat said. "That's really all I saw."

"So, after you witnessed this strange scene, what did you do then?" Hank asked.

"I lowered my bucket and got in the truck. I left and went to my next job, but I couldn't get the strange situation out of my mind, so I called my boss, Wally, and talked to him," Osmat explained. "I knew something strange was going on, but I wasn't sure exactly what it was. It was obvious to me Dr. Diangelo was in trouble, but I didn't know how to help him. You understand?"

"Yes, I understand," Tanya said. "When you lowered yourself from the window, Dr. Diangelo was still alive, though. Is that right?"

"Yes, to my knowledge he was still alive, reclined in the dentist chair."

"And this was about five-thirty in the morning?" Tanya asked.

"Yes, between five-thirty and six o'clock, I'd say," Osmat answered.

Tanya nodded slowly, thinking about everything the window washer had told them. She was certain the nylon stocking man was an important link in the death of Dr. Diangelo, but whether he was the killer could not be definitively proven at this point. More evidence was needed. They reviewed the facts with Osmat again and then concluded the interview. Osmat was excused, and Tanya and Hank retreated to her office.

"This Osmat—can anyone confirm he was actually at the Midwest building Monday morning washing windows?" Hatchet asked.

Tanya was sitting behind her desk, ruminating on the facts of the interview, and she looked up, startled. "Well, no. I guess we're just taking his word for it. But I can give Windows on the World a call and talk to Wally to confirm it," she said, reaching for her phone.

"Might be a good idea," Hatchet commented.

While Tanya was on the phone, Hatchet answered his cell. Mike Leland informed him of the results of the CCTV video from the cameras positioned on the outside of the Midwest building on Copeland.

"There's someone on camera entering the building at the back entrance about 5:32," Mike began. "He had an ID badge of some sort, and he wore a hoodie pulled down around his face so his features couldn't be seen, but he was tall, over six feet, I'd say. So far, no one who works in the building has identified this guy. Dr. Diangelo arrived at 5:26 and used his ID card to get into the building," Mike said. "There's a problem here. This guy got into the building without Diangelo's help, so either he was an employee who had access via an ID badge or he got one from someone who works in the building. I can't see any other way he could bypass the system. We'll keep working on it."

"Good. It's important we establish a timeline of events on Monday. While you're at it, can you check to see if a Windows on the World truck was on the east side of the building about five-thirty?" Hatchet asked. "And also—if this guy entered the building, then he left somehow. Make sure to check the video for people leaving as well."

"Sure. I'll get back to you on that," Mike said, and he clicked off.

Tanya finished her phone call and looked over at Hatchet expectantly. He told her what Mike had learned from the videos at the Midwest building.

She summarized her call to Windows on the World. "Wally confirmed that Osmat was scheduled to begin his duties at the Midwest building on Monday morning at five-thirty," Tanya said, "although he says he can't prove it since he only goes to the work sites occasionally if there is a problem of some kind. But he said Osmat is extremely punctual, so if he tells him to be at a certain place at a certain time, he'll be there. The first Wally knew about the incident was when Osmat called him in a panic to tell him he thought he'd seen a murder."

"We should be able to confirm the truck was there with some of the outside video cam footage from the other buildings nearby. I've got Mike working on that." But Hatchet was still worried as he thought through the interview. "It just seems odd to me that Osmat would call the situation a murder when he actually hadn't seen anyone killed. All he saw was a strange circumstance he couldn't explain. So why call it a murder?"

"Yeah, I understand what you're saying," Tanya said. "That is odd, isn't it?"

Hatchet shrugged. "I just want to be sure we've covered all our bases, and we can confirm that Osmat was actually there when he says he was."

"Right. Makes sense. I agree," Tanya said, although she wasn't sure what Hatchet was after exactly. *He probably doesn't know what he's after, either. It's just a hunch,* she thought, *but hunches can lead to some interesting discoveries sometimes.* Tanya stood abruptly, then stretched her neck from side to side. "Let's get everyone together again this afternoon and go over what we know now."

"You want me to inform everyone?" Hatchet asked.

"Yeah. Get an email out to all available personnel. One-thirty in the incident room down the hall. Let's see what shakes out," Tanya said.

On Wednesday morning, Trygve Hovland made his way through the early morning traffic on Third Street until he came to Highway 61, which led to the big blue bridge that crossed over the Mississippi River to La Crescent, Minnesota. The river was shrouded in haze, but the rain seemed to be letting up. *Rain before seven, done by eleven,* he thought. He was on his way to Pettibone Park, specifically the octagonal pavilion located there, to repair some loose red stone along the base of the structure before the summer schedule became too busy. Pettibone Park was across the river from La Crosse's downtown riverfront district. The maintenance of the trails, docks, and buildings were the responsibility of the city Parks and Streets Department.

Trygve took a right on North Pettibone Drive and drove through the Barron Island lagoon until he came to the pavilion. At this time of the morning, the island was quiet. Trygve always enjoyed the solitude of this place, although he didn't get over this way very often. Early in the morning, the park usually teemed with a variety of birds and other small mammals, including deer, and as he walked to the back of his truck to get his tools and supplies for the repair, he heard the *skyowk* cry of a lone green heron who was perched nearby on a crooked branch of a gnarled oak along the shoreline. He stopped to observe the bird, then jerked the tailgate of his truck open and got out a couple of trowels, patching cement, a small hod, a few stiff-bristled brushes, and a hammer. He threw all the tools in a five-gallon bucket and began trudging to the pavilion, carrying the pail and a plastic jug of water.

He knelt to inspect the damage to the red stone and began mixing up a little cement. A few moments later, he noticed a young man pushing a bike toward him. The bike's back tire was flat, and from the expression on the kid's face, Trygve could see he was irritated. He stopped near the pavilion and stood there. Trygve looked up from his cement repairs. The young man was tall and lithe with dark brown hair in a shaggy style. He wore shorts and a T-shirt that said, "A penny saved is not worth it."

"Hi. You need something?" Trygve asked.

When Trygve spoke to him, the young man hesitated. "Well, my bike tire's flat, and I live on the north side of La Crosse. Could I hitch a ride with you into town?"

"Sure, as soon as I finish here," Trygve said, squinting up at the young man.

"How long will that be?" the young man asked impatiently.

"Oh, maybe another forty-five minutes or so," Trygve said. He continued cleaning brick and cementing them back into the foundation of the wall. For several moments the young man didn't speak; he simply watched Trygve working.

"You know the working man is very unappreciated in our culture," the kid finally said. "Nowadays, it seems if you don't have some kind of degree, you're just the shit under somebody's shoe," he commented sarcastically.

Trygve looked over at the kid and wondered why a strapping young man was riding a bike around a park on a workday. "Well, I might disagree with you there. I don't have a degree, but I've been working with my hands at this job for over twenty years, and I enjoy what I do—most of the time."

"See? You don't enjoy your job every day, I'll bet," he said in an argumentative tone. "My mom's always bitching about my attitude. She says I'm spoiled thinking that everything always has to be fun."

"Well, nobody probably enjoys their work every day," Trygve replied. "No matter what you do in life, every job has a downside. Keeping a balance between the enjoyable and the unpleasant aspects of a job are all part of the work experience." Trygve smeared cement on another red stone and glanced up at the kid. "It's not always doing what you like that counts. It's more about liking what you do. If you have that attitude, you'll be okay."

The young man frowned, his lips pulled downward in a sour gesture that reflected his low spirits.

"By the way, where do you work?" Trygve asked.

"Well … right now I'm unemployed, but I've got applications in different places all over town. I'm just waiting for one of them to call me for an interview."

Probably waiting for the perfect job to fall into your lap, Trygve thought, but he kept his ruminations to himself. "Well, good luck in your job search. Right now in this job market, if you have a good work ethic and a friendly attitude, you can pick just about any blue-collar job you want, and a lotta places will train you. Seems like I see 'Help Wanted' signs almost every place I go," Trygve said. The young man remained silent and sat in the grass, studying the river in the distance. Trygve continued working for another half hour, then gathered his tools and placed them back in the five-gallon bucket. "Bring your bike over to my truck. We'll throw it in the back."

Once they were on the road, the kid's attitude seemed to change. He was happier and even cracked a smile.

"Where do you want me to drop you off?" Trygve asked as they traveled back into the city over the big blue bridge.

"Somewhere over by the university. I called a friend of mine. He's in class until ten," the kid said. "He said he'd help me fix my tire."

"Sounds good," Trygve said as he maneuvered through the traffic. When he reached the corner of West Avenue and Main Street, the kid pointed. "Stop here. This is good."

Trygve eased over to the curb, parked the truck, and waited for the kid to lift his bike out of the back of the pickup. The young man waved, and Trygve returned the friendly gesture as he slammed the tailgate. Thoughts of tasks still ahead of him flooded his mind instead. He watched the kid push his bike down the sidewalk as he pulled back into traffic.

CHAPTER 16 • SONJA

You've Got Me Dangling on a String

On Wednesday morning I drove up to a large Victorian home in the historic Cass Street neighborhood near downtown La Crosse. Dale Devine has been a customer of mine for a long time. After his wife died in 2014, his large historic home would have fallen down around him had it not been for his children, who hired me to organize, dejunk, and maintain the inside of his mansion, keeping the place in somewhat respectable condition.

Cleaning Dale's house was a constant marathon of sorting and discarding. I'm sure he would have been buried alive years ago by his possessions if it had not been for my organization and constant removal of the stuff he wanted to hang on to. Newspapers and magazines were the worst, but knickknacks, junk mail, shoes, and old clothing were ongoing challenges. Who needs copies of the *La Crosse Sentinel* from forty years ago when you could view them online without the hassle of storing the paper? Try telling that to Dale and see how far you get.

This morning, I decided to tackle the front hallway closet.

My head was deep in the abysmal dark hole when my phone rang. Since the Diangelo case was front and center on my mind, I answered it immediately.

"Sonja Hovland," I said. A wool scarf fell from a closet shelf somewhere above me and flopped across the top of my head. I grabbed it and threw it in the discard pile.

"Sonja, it's Riley over at Pizza Hut. I found out something you might want to know about the Diangelo situation."

"Oh yeah? What's that?" I asked, trying to play innocent. *Does everyone in town know about my connection to this case?* I wondered.

"A couple of guys were in here late last night—about twelve-thirty—and I overheard a little of their conversation while I was cleaning tables and restocking the cheese and red pepper flakes. They were talking about some ID for the Midwest building. You know, the place where that dentist was found dead in his chair."

"Do you know these two guys?" I asked.

"The one guy I know from the university. He's a geography major. Real smart. The other guy I've never seen before, but they looked eerily alike."

"Were they twins?"

"Maybe. I guess I'm not sure," Riley responded. "They were probably brothers."

"Okay, so what's the geography guy's name?" I scrambled to find a pen in the pocket of my apron.

"His name is Sam Watson. That's all I know. He's a junior or senior at UW–L and probably lives off campus. Most upperclassmen do."

"And how do you know him?" I asked.

"We've been in a few classes together, and he heads up

a study group for those who are geographically challenged like me."

"So, they were discussing how to get into the Midwest Medical building with an ID?" I asked, not sure if I totally understood his point.

"Yeah, but that was all I heard. I have no idea what it means or even if it's important. I just know you were the one who found the dead dentist, and I heard the name of the building mentioned, so I thought I'd pass the information on to you," Riley told me.

"Does everybody in town know I found the body?" I asked.

"Well, anybody who's anybody in the cleaning and service business knows. News like that travels fast," Riley commented. "You're kinda famous now, Sonja. You put us on the map."

"Well, that was never my intention, but thanks for the great piece of information. I appreciate it, and I'll pass it on."

"No problem," he said, and then he hung up.

I sat on the floor and leaned against the door of the closet thinking about my next move. I knew whoever the nylon stocking man was, he had to have an ID to get into the Midwest building, or else he had somehow circumvented the system to gain access, or he'd hooked up with somebody who worked there and used their ID. Maybe he knew Diangelo and followed him into the building? That was another possibility. I'm sure Chief Pedretti and Lt. Brousard had already considered all those possibilities. I wondered if anyone had found any CCTV video. That was another way of determining how someone might have gotten into the building, but right now Mr. Devine's closet was calling my name.

I had no sooner shoved my way back into the black hole of the closet than I heard Dale creaking toward me with his walker. He stopped in front of a huge pile of boots, hats, coats, gloves, and other outdoor gear I had gleaned from the depths.

"Sonja? Are you in there?" he asked.

I unceremoniously backed out of the closet on all fours, turned, and sat on the floor, looking up at Dale. "I'm here, Dale. Just trying to sort out some of the things I don't think you need anymore. Why don't you have a look?" I suggested, pointing to the pile of outdated, musty clothes and old sporting gear.

Dale surveyed the pile, leaned down, and picked out a red and black-checked Stormy Kromer hat lying on the discard pile. He plopped it on his head and said, "I remember this hat. My dad bought it for me back in the sixties. Didn't wear it much. The kids at school called it my Sherlock Holmes hat."

"Is it something you want to keep?" I asked.

"Nope. Reminds me of all the bullying I endured when I wore it. Why would I want to remember that?" He threw the hat back on the pile. Although he had been thin and tall in his younger years, now he was stooped and hunched over with arthritis. He leaned forward on his walker, breathing heavily and looking exhausted. His daughter told me he'd recently been diagnosed with congestive heart failure. I got up from the floor, supported him around the waist, and gently turned his walker around so he could sit down.

"That's better," he said softly. "Thank you, Sonja."

"No problem. Maybe you can help me go through this discard pile. I don't think you'll use this stuff again, will you?"

Dale looked at the pile of tennis rackets, old deflated footballs and basketballs, a worn-out set of golf clubs in a brittle leather bag, several outdated stocking hats and wool mittens, a fedora with a sporty feather tucked in the rim, and a pile of mismatched leather gloves and wool mittens.

"Looks like the whole works can go to Goodwill," he said.

"I can take all of it over to the one on Mormon Coulee Road if you're sure you won't be needing it anymore," I said.

Dale leaned down and picked up the fedora, carefully placing it on his bald head. "I'll have you know I wore this hat on my first date with Dolly," he said cockily. "She didn't like the hat, but she liked the guy who was wearin' it." He smiled jauntily, and it did my heart good to see his moment of happiness remembering the years gone by. His face morphed into a more serious expression. "I still can't believe she's gone. My beautiful Dolly. Dolly the Devine I called her— and she was divine. This house is pretty damn lonely without her." A single tear trickled down his wrinkled cheek.

"I'm sorry, Dale. I'm sure you miss Dolly. Can I make you a cup of coffee?" I asked as I clasped his hand.

"Yeah. I'm going to watch *The Price is Right*. Can you bring my coffee into the living room?"

"Sure," I said, watching him sadly shuffle down the hallway.

After I got Dale settled in his recliner with a cup of coffee and a chocolate chip cookie, I finished organizing the closet and then tackled the rest of my cleaning duties. When I left, Dale was snoozing peacefully in his chair. I placed a kiss on the top of his bald head and loaded the closet discards into the back of my Subaru. I drove over to Goodwill on Mormon Coulee Road, where an attendant helped me fill a whole cart with Dale's castoffs. Then I drove over by the bluff to Pammel Creek Road. When I reached Apple Blossom Lane, I turned left and parked my car in the driveway of a sleek modern home that looked like a bunch of angles and corners to me, but considering who lived here, it made sense.

Art Ravenwald was a rather colorful local celebrity in the Driftless Area. He was a La Crosse native and came from a working-class family. His tastes were wide-ranging, and his interests were frequently off-the-wall and unorthodox. Instead of following his dad into the industrial job market as an electrician or carpenter, he used the skills he'd learned from his father in their garage on the north side of La Crosse to become a collage and metal artist. During the early years of his art career, when he sold very few of his quirky creations, he made a living by working at the La Crosse Rubber Mills. He'd finally come into his own the last ten years and was now steadily drawing attention and rave reviews from several art critics in the Midwest. The East and West Coast crowds had not caught on to his mobiles and other found-object art, but everyone around town decided the Midwest art vibe was more taught than caught, and since most coastal residents still had a flyover mentality when it came to the heartland, the residents of La Crosse claimed Art's genius for themselves.

I opened the side garage door, walked through the

darkened area where Art's Porsche and Ford Ranger pickup were parked, and entered the bright kitchen. I could feel a twinge of a headache starting behind my eyes, which frequently happened when everything screamed yellow, including the walls and their decorations: butterflies, sunflowers, daisies, you name it. Whatever hung on these walls had to be yellow. It made you wonder if you should wear your shades indoors. *Artists. Go figure.*

"Yoo-hoo," I yelled into the depths of the house.

"Sonja? That you?" Art called out from his studio on the east side of the house. I walked that way and stuck my head around the door frame of a large, airy room that served as an art studio. Art was sitting at his workbench on a stool, pliers in his hand, working on a mobile in the process of construction. Several completed mobiles were hanging from the ceiling waiting for delivery to an art gallery in Minneapolis. A roll of wire, a bunch of binder clips, rolls of masking tape, a soldering gun, and several small colorful, geometric shapes of metal were lying on the workbench. In front of him against the wall above his bench was an old card catalog discarded from the public library which held a variety of clips and fasteners he used in his artwork.

Watching Art create his mobiles was a fascinating experience; the physics of mobile construction was more complicated than anything I could imagine. The balance he had to achieve to make all the little shapes swing gently in the breeze was difficult. I admired him for his tenacity and determination. After all, it had taken him over thirty years to be recognized in his field. His casual clothes, full of stains and holes, were a testimony to his fierce work ethic. Yet his salt-and-pepper hair was carefully combed, his mustache trimmed and precise. It was good to see him so engaged in his craft. He looked up and gave me a warm smile.

Suddenly, a familiar greeting pierced the air from the other side of the room. "Sonja, Sonja," squawked Jocko. The large gray African parrot cocked his head, and his beady eyes zeroed in on me. He flicked his red tail in my direction. A small piece of pear that had turned brown and some discarded walnut shells lay in the bottom of his roomy cage, which sat in the corner of the studio near one of the large windows. Art had adopted Jocko when a friend of his threatened to put the beautiful bird to sleep. I understood the friend's reasoning since Jocko was always kicking up a fuss of some kind, injecting unwanted phrases into our conversations.

When the parrot focused his beady eyes on me, I always felt like an insect he was about to pluck and swallow with gusto. His large beak made me nervous, especially when he chewed on the wires of his cage or cracked nuts. The beautiful gray bird would often ruffle his feathers vigorously, and a cloud of dust would rise into the air. I was glad the studio cleaning was not in my job description. Due to Art's ongoing art projects and the messy habits of his large gray parrot, he cleaned this room himself. My cup overflowed with gratitude.

"How's my favorite ray of sunshine today?" Art asked me. "Find any more dead bodies?"

"Dead bodies, dead bodies," Jocko said, imitating his owner's inflection perfectly.

Although my friend's comment was meant as friendly fire, I was not in the mood to joke about something that had turned my world upside down. He noticed my sober expression, and a frown formed on his forehead.

"Sorry. Just another one of my offhand, asinine comments. You may completely ignore it or give me hell. Your choice," he said apologetically.

"Go to hell. Go to hell," Jocko mimicked belligerently.

I sighed, momentarily ignoring the parrot. "To be truthful, Art, finding Dr. Diangelo dead in his dentist chair at six in the morning was an awful experience, and it doesn't seem like anyone is making much headway in figuring out how he died or who did it."

"I'm sorry. I didn't mean to be crass," he said. "Are you involved in the investigation?" He carefully pushed a wire through a hole he'd punched in one of the metal shapes, then crimped the wire together with tiny pliers and looked up at me.

"Well, let's just say I'm watching from the sidelines, but … I have my hook in the water," I said. Truthfully, the investigation had completely overtaken my thought processes, interrupted my sleep, and made me tired and irritable. It hadn't done anything to improve my marriage, either. I waved a hand at him. A look of remorse crossed his face. "You're forgiven—" I started to say, but he interrupted me.

"You wouldn't be here if you hadn't forgiven me for a variety of transgressions a long time before this." He stopped his work and swiveled on his stool to face me. "Listen, let me tell you something. The scuttlebutt over at the university is that someone on the fringe was out to get Diangelo for his conservative views and his well-endowed bank account," he said, his expression turning serious.

"There's a radical socialist student organization on campus that's been recruiting new members, and the upshot of the whole deal is this group targets certain community leaders who are successful and wealthy. Then they hold them up as an example of the evil of capitalism in our society. In general, they do this stuff to attract students on the political fringe." He blew out a gust of air, clucked his tongue, and shook his head. "I don't see how their tactics are going to solve our divisive political attitudes. What about discussion and conversation as a way of understanding someone with an opposing view?"

"So do you know the name of this group?" I asked. I thought again of the note found in Diangelo's pocket: "Death to the Capitalists."

"Not really, but I have my hook in the water, too, so if I hear something, I'll give you a call."

"Hook in the water," Jocko said.

"Jocko, shut up!" Art said loudly.

"Shut up! Shut up!" the parrot screeched.

Art rolled his eyes toward the ceiling and mumbled, "He's on a roll today."

"Great, and since you're the one who has to deal with him," I said, turning back to the kitchen, "I'll leave you to it. I've got a house to clean and straighten."

"Carry on," Art said as he turned back to his workbench. "Your check will be on the kitchen counter when you finish."

As I walked back toward the kitchen, I heard the strains of Mozart's "Eine Kleine Nachtmusik" in the background. Music was the only way Art could calm Jocko's unrestrained, sometimes bawdy quips. Hopefully, the astute bird wouldn't add singing to his repertoire.

I scurried around the kitchen, cleaning the sink and wiping down the countertops. The yellow walls gave me a headache, but I ignored my distaste for the décor of the kitchen and scrubbed the black and white tiled floor. I moved to the large bathroom off the bedroom, where I scoured the shower, sink, and toilet. I put clean sheets on the bed and then vacuumed the bedroom carpet. I was going through the hallway to the eclectic living room area when my phone vibrated in my pocket.

I stopped in the hallway and leaned against the wall.

"Sonja Hovland. May I help you?" I asked politely, although I hated to think that more information about Diangelo's demise might be coming my way.

"Don't you ever answer your landline?" a cross voice said. "You know I hate calling you on your cell. The service is terrible—"

"Darlene. How are you, sis?" I interrupted before she could totally insult me with her rant.

"Damn ornery. What's the deal with you and this murder? I always told Mom you'd get yourself into some situation you couldn't handle someday. It's a good thing she's not around to see it. It would've killed her," she snarled, finishing her brutal analysis of my current situation.

"Well, since Mom died of cancer three years ago, I guess we don't have to worry about that, do we?" I snapped, my temper flaring. I promised myself several times in the past that Darlene's negative mental attitude would not affect my normally upbeat personality, but after only a minute on the phone with her, I felt myself plunging into a deep, dark pit of defensiveness and despair.

"So, what's with this guy you found in the dentist's

chair?" Darlene asked.

"How do you know about that? You live in Lake Elmo, Minnesota, for Pete's sake." I resisted the impulse to hang up on her.

"Like you, I have my sources," she said haughtily.

"Yeah, I bet you do." I tried to keep the sarcasm to a minimum. Darlene had worked as a dispatcher at the Lake Elmo Police Department for years until she was fired for disseminating choice pieces of information to the general public. Of course, she bragged incessantly about having her ear to the ground. I could just imagine her snooty expression, her nose lifted high in the air. Older sisters can be such a pain, even when they're two hundred miles away. "It just so happens I'm at a cleaning job," I continued, "and I don't have time to tell you about it right now. I'll call you later—"

"Wait!" Darlene ordered. "Don't hang up!"

"Sorry, sis. Time's a-wasting," I promptly hung up and breathed a sigh of relief even though I knew I'd pay a high price later for my impatience. I shut my phone off and finished vacuuming and dusting Art's living room, collected my check from the counter, and left.

As I drove across town, I thought about my sister, Darlene. Yes, I loved her, but she was a royal pain—what psychologists would call a very difficult person. Maybe that was the reason the bookshelf in my home office was littered with dog-eared copies of self-help books like *Navigating Life with Difficult People*, *Setting Boundaries with the Demanding People in Your Life*, and *The Survivor's Guide to Dealing with Unruly Siblings*. Darlene was divorced and unemployed due to "emotional instability," and I wondered if she would ever get her life back on track. I hoped she wasn't hopping in her car this very minute with her suitcase packed, heading for Barre Mills. The last time she tried that stunt, Trygve met her in the driveway, where shouting and choice words were exchanged for fifteen minutes. The result was six months of the deep freeze from Darlene. It was the nicest stretch of peace and quiet from my sister's legendary rude behavior that I had experienced in quite some time.

I pulled into the parking lot at the La Crosse Police Department on Ranger Street and walked into the new building. The smell of fresh paint and new flooring drifted in the air, along with the scent of Juicy Fruit gum. A young girl at the Admissions desk greeted me with a friendly smile, blew a bubble, and cracked her wad of gum with finesse. Had office etiquette changed that much since I was in high school? Since when did the help get to rudely chew and crack their gum when helping a client?

"Is Chief Pedretti in?" I asked with gritted teeth.

"I'll check. Just one minute. Who should I say is calling?" she asked, looking up at me, still rolling the gum around in her mouth. *Don't kids today have any manners?* I thought, my irritation piqued by the earlier exchange with Darlene. Rude behavior now seemed to be the norm, not the exception.

"Just tell her it's Sonja," I said, giving her a frosty smile. I leaned against the counter, waiting for permission to see the chief so I could relay my newest information about the Diangelo case.

After several moments, the young girl hung up and pointed to the elevator. "Get off on the second floor," she said, "and take a right down the hallway. The chief's office is at the end of the hall. She's waiting for you."

"Thank you so much," I said, my smile evaporating. When I arrived at the end of the second-floor hallway, I was surprised to see a spacious office with large windows that provided a gorgeous view of the bluffs and the river in the distance. I knocked quietly on the door, and Tanya waved me in.

"Hey, I was just about to call you," she began. "Hank and I interviewed Osmat this morning."

"Oh, yeah? How'd that go?" I asked.

"Not bad. He revealed an interesting detail about the nylon stocking man," Tanya continued. "He's missing most of his little finger on his left hand."

"Really? That *is* interesting," I agreed, although I wondered how many people in the city of La Crosse and the surrounding area were missing a little finger. Still, it was something. Tanya tipped her head and watched me closely. There was a certain intensity about her when she was on the prowl for information that might move a case forward. She leaned over her desk, planted her forearms on its surface, and clasped her hands. As always, she was immaculately groomed; her hair shone, her makeup was tasteful, and her clothing was businesslike yet with a flair of femininity.

"I'm assuming—although assumptions are dangerous territory for a cop—that you have something to share with me," she said, raising her eyebrows. "Some piece of information that you dug up from one of your informants in our fair city?" I detected a hint of sarcasm in her voice.

"Yes. Yes, I do," I said casually. "I've been told—"

"By your informants?" Tanya interrupted with a subtle grin.

"By my informants," I continued, "that there is a group over on campus who are targeting successful, conservative, wealthy residents of our city as examples of capitalism at its worst—capitalism gone amok, so to speak. Greed, materialism, and self-indulgence seem to be their beefs. According to my source, this group uses people like Dr. Diangelo to stir up dissension about our capitalistic system in an effort to recruit new members into their elite socialist club. What they're after exactly is still up for grabs at this point, but it's an interesting development. Apparently, they're serious about their intentions if Dr. Diangelo is any indication of their motives."

Tanya listened carefully and took a few notes on a yellow legal pad near her computer. "Hmm. Capitalism gone amok, huh? Well, in Dr. Diangelo's case, I think he lost his life because someone somewhere in our city has a burning hatred of those who are using our American capitalist system to better their lifestyle and boost their bank accounts and retirement plans. Remember that phrase: Death to the capitalists? Someone seems to be taking that motto seriously," she said, "although I have no idea who that might be." She was silent for a minute, shrugged her shoulders, and shook her head. "But, to be honest, I just don't get it. What's so offensive about our capitalistic system?"

I nodded my head in agreement. "I don't know. I don't get it either," I said, "but that doesn't negate the fact that we need to find the person who accompanied Dr. Diangelo to his office Monday morning and either killed him or watched while he killed himself." It was silent for a few moments, and during that time I wondered when something significant would blow the lid off this case and help Chief Pedretti figure out what in the world was happening to our peaceful river city.

"Anything else you want to tell me?" Tanya asked. I had drifted off in another direction of thought and was pondering our conversation about capitalists. "Sonja?"

I jerked my head. "Sorry. What did you say?"

"Was that what you wanted to tell me about or was there something else beyond the radical group on campus who might be targeting capitalists?" Tanya asked.

"No, that's just part of it." I noticed the chief's eyes widen at what might be coming next. I hurried to reassure her. "What I actually wanted to tell you is that someone called me this morning about a conversation he overheard at Pizza Hut late last night between two people he thought might be brothers or maybe twins. They were discussing an ID card for the Midwest Medical building." I dug in my pants pocket and retrieved the piece of paper I had written the name on. I walked over to Tanya's desk and handed it to her.

"Sam Watson?" Tanya asked, staring at the bit of paper. I nodded my head. The chief looked up at me. "You know him?" she asked.

"Never heard of him," I responded.

"Address?"

"Sorry, I don't know," I said. "I didn't have time to find out."

"Okay. We'll check into it." Tanya gave me a long, curious stare.

"What?"

"How are you getting these tips?" the chief asked.

"I told you before. My people come through for me when I'm in a jam," I said without fanfare.

"Yes, I can see that," Tanya said, but skepticism was written all over her face.

"I gotta go, Chief," I said, suddenly uncomfortable with her scrutinizing gaze. "Trygve is expecting me to fix dinner tonight, and I've got to pick up some groceries." I turned toward the door and waved over my shoulder. "Greet Roy from me. See you later," I said.

"Will do. Thanks for the tip," she yelled after me.

"No problem," I yelled back. But somehow, I just couldn't shake the sense of dread that had invaded the pit of my stomach. I felt like a thousand eyes were watching me from the shadows. *Don't overreact,* I thought. *You're getting paranoid.* But I wasn't comforted by my own counsel. I just couldn't shake the feeling that someone in the city was watching my every move, waiting to trip me up.

CHAPTER 17
Give Me Just a Little More Time

After Trygve Hovland dropped off the young biker at the corner of West Avenue and Main mid-morning on Wednesday, he drove to the municipal city maintenance headquarters, where he prepared for a day of filling potholes on several streets throughout the city. The smell of hot mix and car exhaust, along with the warm sunshine beating on his shoulders, made him sleepy. As he shoveled blacktop into potholes and moved the orange cones down the street, he wondered where Sonja was and what she was doing. The strange death at the Midwest building and the close call they'd had on their evening walk Monday made him angry and irritable. He could still remember the sound of the roaring engine as it came around the corner and the smell of screeching brakes and exhaust when they jumped into the ditch to avoid being hit. Although Trygve was still worried about her, he hadn't been married to Sonja all these years to begin distrusting her now. Her gutsy determination was at the very heart of her personality, and he knew her hard-headed practicality and common sense would rise to the top in every situation she found herself in. For just a moment during his lunch hour, as he leaned against a sprawling maple tree near Myrick Marsh, he could envision her cheerful smile and pretty face. He breathed deeply, said a silent prayer for her safety, finished his Pepsi, and walked back to his white service truck parked on the street.

While Trygve filled potholes, Beck Watson pushed his bike down the sidewalk, the tire making a *ka-thump* noise every time it made a revolution. If Beck were being totally honest, he would have to admit his brother, Sam, was much better at practical life skills, like fixing a flat bike tire. Sam not only had the know-how, but he also had all the tools to do the job. Beck shook his head when he thought about his brother.

Sam Watson, the college geek, lived and breathed university life. Who in their right mind expected to land a job with a degree in geography? Beck harrumphed to himself and smiled. *My brother, that's who,* he thought. When Beck compared himself to his brother, he almost laughed out loud. Despite his intellectual acumen, Beck had flunked out of college at the end of last year. By contrast, his brother had stuck to his college plan and would soon graduate and begin looking for a real job. But Beck's problem wasn't his intellect; instead, his problems boiled down to the everyday expectations of life: securing and hanging onto a job, cooking, cleaning and laundry, and fixing things like a flat tire on a bike. For those everyday things, he counted on Sam or his mom. That's why he was heading to his brother's apartment right now. He didn't have the faintest idea how to fix a flat tire.

When he arrived at Sam's apartment complex, he parked

his bike alongside the building, went inside, and rang the bell for apartment 223. Sam buzzed him through the secure door, and he took the steps two by two to the second floor. He knocked on the door and waited impatiently in the hallway. When Sam opened the door, Beck walked in like he owned the place. The apartment was clean and organized—another example of the stark differences between the two brothers.

"Boy, this is a far cry from my room at home," Beck commented. "I've got crap scattered everywhere, books piled up, clothes all over the place…"

Sam frowned at him, then raised his eyebrows, ignoring Beck's rant. "So, your bike is outside, I presume?" he asked.

"Yeah. I got stranded over at Pettibone Park, and some municipal worker gave me a ride across the bridge into town. You've got time to fix my tire, right?" Beck asked.

Sam sighed, still looking cross. His brother's expectation of help fired up his resentment. *Was the kid ever going to get his life together and start acting like an adult?* Instead of lecturing him, he said, "Yeah. I've got the time, I guess. I don't have to be at work until two o'clock. Let's head downstairs and get it done."

The two men walked down the hallway, descended the stairs, and went out to inspect the bike tire. "You got a patch for the tube?" Sam asked.

"There's one in this little saddle bag, I think," Beck said. He rifled through the bag's contents attached to the back of the seat and held up a patch. "You mean this thing?"

"Yeah, we'll need that. I'll run back up and get my Allen wrenches and tire pump," Sam said. "I'll be back in a minute."

When Sam returned, he removed the tire from the bike and began fixing it. Half an hour later, he was pumping up the tire. The conversation turned to the strange death at the Midwest Medical building on Copeland, something they had thoroughly hashed over the night before at Pizza Hut.

"So, do you know any more about that crazy death at the Midwest building?" Beck asked.

Sam shook his head and looked up at his brother. "I don't know. It's really a strange set of circumstances. I still can't figure out how someone got into that building without an ID. The place has a security system like Fort Knox. I oughta know. I work there. It's all but impossible to get in the place without the right identification badge," Sam explained. "If the police can figure that out, they'll be closer to solving who might have been involved."

A flutter of anxiety rippled through Beck, but he shrugged his shoulders. "Guess I wouldn't know anything about that."

"No, you probably wouldn't since you actually have to have a real job to understand those kinds of things," Sam said sarcastically. He tightened a bolt and gave the rear tire a spin.

"Hey! I'm working on it," Beck replied hotly, his temper flaring. His anger had been a major issue over the years, and now it flared like a hot coal with Sam's accusation.

Sam stood up, got on the bike, and took a spin down the sidewalk, returning to the apartment building, where he stopped and dismounted in front of his brother. "There you are," he said. "Fixed and ready to go."

Beck grabbed the handlebars. "Thanks," he said gruffly.

Before he could leave, Sam straddled the front wheel of

the bike, grabbed the handlebars, and held them firmly in his grip. Facing his brother, he said, "Listen, Beck, for Mom's sake, you need to take this job thing seriously. And you need to stop ranting about how unfair our system is. It gets old after a while, especially for Mom who works three jobs. It's not what she wants to hear from her unemployed son."

The brazen look of indifference in Beck's eyes alarmed Sam.

"Quit worryin' about me all the time," Beck snapped. "I'm gettin' it together. I'll get a job this week. You'll see." He jerked the bike from his brother's grip and pedaled rapidly down the street.

As Sam watched Beck pedal away, he felt like a lone man on an island out in the sea. Would his brother ever get his life together and quit weighing down his overworked, underpaid mom? He'd probably be homeless if it weren't for his mom's kindness. The kid couldn't even afford a car. But at least Beck had a bike now and didn't rely on him to get around the city. Maybe that could be considered progress, but as Sam turned and walked back upstairs to his apartment, he wondered what the future held for his troubled brother.

Officer Mike Leland and Lt. Hank Brousard sat in a black and white cruiser outside police headquarters in the spacious parking lot off Ranger Road. Chief Tanya Pedretti had given them orders: Find Sam Watson and question him about a conversation he had with another individual at Pizza Hut last night. She was due in court tomorrow to testify about another case and didn't have time to personally hunt the kid down. Mike and Hatchet were supposed to find out where this guy lived and question him about his knowledge of the security procedures at the medical building on Copeland Avenue. The two policemen made a couple of phone calls to the university.

"What's the address?" Mike asked, starting the cruiser.

"He lives at 1832 17th Street," Hatchet answered.

"That's over by the university, right?" Mike asked.

"Yep. It's an apartment complex where a lot of university students live. Let's get over there and see if we can find this guy," Hatchet said.

Mike drove south on West Avenue until he came to Main Street. He took a left, drove a couple of blocks, and then hung a right on 17th Street until he came to a large apartment building. The two cops parked by the curb, got out of the car, and followed a sign that said Manager's Office. As they walked down the hallway, they met a tall, young man coming out of the office.

"Hey, we're looking for a guy named Sam Watson," Hank said. "He lives in one of these apartments. Do you know the guy?"

The young man nervously flicked his eyes back and forth between the two policemen. "Well, yeah, I know him," he said quietly.

"Where can we find him?" Mike asked.

"You're lookin' at him."

Hank pointed at the young man's chest. "You're Sam?" he asked.

"Yup, that's me. Why're you guys lookin' for me?" he asked, nervously shifting on his feet. Hank noticed his deep-set hazel eyes and athletic build.

"Is there someplace we can talk?" Officer Mike asked.

"Sure, there's a patio with a picnic table under a shade tree around the corner. How's that sound?" Sam asked.

"Lead the way," Hank said.

The three men walked outside and sat down at the picnic table. After an awkward moment that was tense with anticipation, Hank began. "We've been told that you know something about the ID badges at Midwest Medical over on Copeland Avenue. Is that true?"

"How'd you find out about that?" Sam asked, bristling.

"We heard it through the grapevine," Mike said nonchalantly. Sam looked dubious. Mike continued. "Believe me when I say we have our sources."

Sam shrugged. "I guess that makes sense. I know about the entry badges because I work there part-time."

Underneath his seemingly cooperative attitude, Hatchet sensed a latent hostility.

"What kind of work do you do there?" he asked.

"I do custodial work Tuesdays and Thursdays on the second floor for the same-day surgery department," Sam said. "Why all the questions?"

Hatchet studied the young man. He seemed alert and sharp. Surely, he'd heard about the death of Dr. Diangelo on Monday morning. Everyone, especially the employees at Midwest Medical, must be talking about it. Police might have even interviewed him on Monday morning, although he did not allude to that.

"Are you aware of the suspicious death that took place early Monday morning at your place of employment?" Mike asked.

Sam leaned his arms on the picnic table and stared at the two cops across from him. His mind returned to the conversation he'd had with his brother last night—the conversation in which Beck seemed overly interested in the security system at his place of employment. Now a wave of panic coursed through his body. Was it possible that Beck was somehow involved in the bizarre set of events surrounding Dr. Diangelo? He'd had a few minor scrapes with the law that had conveniently been excused by his mom due to his depression. He'd had his fingers slapped by the judge and had been recommended for counseling to get in touch with his feelings. Sam's shoulders slumped.

"Yes, I know about that. You're referring to Dr. Diangelo, right?" he asked. Both cops nodded but remained silent. "You'd have to live under a rock not to know what happened on Monday. The whole city of La Crosse is talking about it," Sam said arrogantly.

"Yes, I would say that's true, and seeing as you don't live under a rock, why don't you tell us what you know about the security procedures for the building," Mike suggested, his voice gritty with determination. "I'm sure you're familiar with them."

"Yep, I am." Sam began explaining. "When you're hired there, you go through the typical security background check, and once you've passed that, you're issued an ID badge, which is swiped through the security reader at the back door. Everyone who works there enters through that door. I've had a badge now for about five months." Sam glanced sullenly at the two officers and waited for their response.

"Are you aware of the CCTV cameras throughout the

building?" Hank asked.

"Sort of," Sam said. "I don't pay much attention to that, but there's a couple on every floor, I guess, and at the main entrances."

"Tell us about your conversation at Pizza Hut last night with your friend," Mike said.

Sam's eyes widened at the cop's knowledge of his movements around the city. "How'd you know about that?" he asked. Officer Mike was about to speak, but Sam held up a hand. "Never mind. You're probably going to tell me you heard it through the grapevine." He shook his head with disgust. "By the way, that song is so seventies."

Hatchet shrugged his shoulders in a blasé gesture. "So ... your conversation at Pizza Hut?" he said. "Tell us about it."

"I got off work about eleven-thirty and met a friend at Pizza Hut. We talked about a lot of things."

"Like what?" Mike asked.

"Okay, okay, we talked about Diangelo's death," Sam huffed. "I don't think that's too unusual since everybody in La Crosse has been blabbering about it since it happened."

"Was there a discussion about ID badges for the Midwest building?" Hatchet asked.

"Yeah, my friend wanted to know how some guy could have gotten in the building without a badge," Sam reported. "I was wondering the same thing."

"By the way, who's your friend?" Mike noticed Sam's steely resolve.

There were several moments of silence. Sam continued giving both men an icy stare. "My brother, Beck, met me, and we had a pizza together."

"Your brother?" Hank said, his voice skeptical.

"Yeah. He has some mental health issues, and I try to check up on him every couple of days to see how he's doing," Sam explained.

"That's a good thing to do. Anything else we should know?" Hank asked.

"I don't really know why you need to know any of this stuff. I thought private conversations were still private, but I guess I was mistaken," Sam snarled.

"When a suspicious death occurs, and we're chasing down leads, we talk to anyone who might know something about the incident," Mike said. "Standard police procedure."

"Fine," Sam said huffily. "Are we done yet?"

"No. Does your brother Beck work at Midwest Medical, too?" Hank asked.

"He's unemployed at the moment. He has trouble holding down a job because of his mental health challenges."

"We'd actually like to talk to your brother. What's his address?" Hank asked, his thumbs posed above his phone screen.

"He lives with my mom up on the north side at 534 Prospect," Sam said, getting up from the picnic table. The two officers stood. "Please don't hassle my mom. She's overworked and underpaid, and the last thing she needs is another reason to worry about my brother."

"Thanks for the information. We appreciate it," Hank said solemnly.

"Sure. No problem."

As the two cops walked back to the cruiser parked next to the curb, Sam rushed back into the apartment building, climbed the stairs to his second-floor apartment, and let himself in. He fumbled in his pants for his cell phone. Beck answered on the third ring.

"Beck? The cops were just here asking about Dr. Diangelo's death," he demanded angrily. "Tell me what you know about that, and don't even think about lying to me."

CHAPTER 18 • SONJA
Silence is Golden

The aisles at the Woodstock grocery chain were crowded with shoppers. A lady in front of me suddenly veered off into another aisle, muttering something about baked beans. I headed for the fruit and vegetable section. Looking over the lettuce, I picked out a box of mixed greens and a head of Napa cabbage. The purple onions looked refreshing. I selected one and moved on to the tomatoes and cucumbers. Two women standing next to me were conversing while they eyed up each other's carts and the produce display in front of them.

"What do you think about the death of that dentist at the Midwest building over on Copeland?" the heavier woman asked as she poked a bunch of tomatoes with her finger.

"That's just crazy, isn't it? I thought our town was pretty safe, but I'm beginning to wonder. Where the heck are the police?" Miss Skinny said.

"Oh, they're investigating, don't worry."

"They are? Doesn't seem like they've gotten too far."

"Well, last night on the evening news they announced

Diangelo's death was suspicious. Something involving drugs. These things are complicated. They don't solve them overnight," the heavy woman huffed.

"Sounds like suicide to me," Miss Skinny replied with a haughty tone.

"Could be. Being rich has nothing over on suicide. I'm sure Diangelo was rolling in cash. Maybe he had marriage problems. Lots of people take their lives over divorce."

"You don't know that he had a bad marriage. Besides, he was a great dentist," Miss Skinny commented, seemingly offended that someone as successful as Dr. Diangelo might possibly be plagued with human problems like divorce or drug addiction.

"Money doesn't buy you happiness," the heavy woman said with pompous righteousness.

Miss Skinny rolled her eyes in dramatic fashion.

The other woman continued her analysis. "I've heard Diangelo charged outrageous prices for his implants. My question is: Who in their right mind would spend that kind of exorbitant cash on their teeth?"

Miss Skinny leaned toward the heavy woman and tapped her perfect front incisors. "See these ivories? Implants. Dr. Diangelo gave me my life back. He was a great dentist," she snapped. She whipped her cart around and began walking away. "And it was worth every penny," she spouted loudly over her shoulder as she marched off with her head held high.

I picked up a box of luscious-looking cherry tomatoes, nodded to the heavier woman still standing by the vegetables with her mouth gaping open, and walked on to the meat section. Trygve loved fish; I credited his taste to his

Norwegian genes. I selected two lovely salmon steaks from the meat cooler and moved on, picking up several other items for the tasty lemon sauce I planned to make to pour over the grilled salmon. In aisle fifteen, I met my neighbor, Mrs. Westley.

The Westleys were a foundational farm family in the Barre Mills area. Their farm had been in their family for over one hundred fifty years. Hardworking, industrious, and capable, their beautiful property of red buildings was immaculate, and their Jersey dairy herd was well-known throughout the agricultural community in Wisconsin and beyond. Just ask anyone in our neighborhood. Westleys' cattle dominated the Jersey awards every year at the World Dairy Expo in Madison, Wisconsin.

Although my neighbor wore jeans, a colorful scarf was draped over her shoulders, and a hot pink blouse reflected her rosy cheeks. She looked like a picture of health right in style with the latest fashion trends. Smiling at me, Stella stopped her cart next to mine. "Sonja, nice to see you. How are you, dear?" she asked.

"Well, I'm just fine, Stella. I trust you're not working too hard," I replied pleasantly.

Stella was my idol when it came to cooking and baking. She could whip up the most wonderful entrees, cakes, and pies with fresh ingredients, enthusiasm, her pots and pans, a good knife, a rolling pin, and a cutting board. To me, she seemed like Julia Child reincarnated. Her delectable food would make anyone swoon with delight. Trygve and I had dined at Stella's bountiful table many times. After her meals, I complained for days about the extra weight I probably had gained. Trygve would look at me and say,

"Sonja, just enjoy it. You're not going off the rails by eating at Stella's once every six months." This was true because I never really gained weight from feasting on her cuisine. I guess it was all in my head, not my hips, thank God.

Stella suddenly leaned toward me in a surreptitious gesture. Her face took on a grave expression, and she lowered her voice. "I've heard that you found that dentist dead in his office while you were cleaning. Is that true?" I noticed her eyebrows had crunched together like two woolly question marks.

I refrained from an exaggerated sigh that might offend my neighbor. I valued Stella as a friend, but no one understood how tiring it was to rehash my Monday morning discovery to everyone who asked. I spared Stella the gory details, although I was angry that the events at Dr. Diangelo's office had been inflated until they were downright lies. Blood-soaked carpets, a drug-infested orgy, and other blatantly false narratives about Dr. Diangelo's death had been rampant in the local gossip mills and on social media. Nobody had to tell me what had happened; I was there for Pete's sake. To me, it felt like the event was in every headline and on every radio talk show and newspaper in the area, to say nothing of social media, which I'd been avoiding like the plague since Monday morning. I didn't even want to know what wild rumors were circulating on Facebook and Instagram. For all I knew, people were calling me the new Sherlock Holmes of Barre Mills. *Ugh! How did I get in this predicament?* But instead of venting, I smiled anemically and considered how I might answer Stella's heartfelt question. I supposed the truth was the best option.

"Yes, I did find Dr. Diangelo," I began. "It was a very

unpleasant experience, but I've moved on, and the police are investigating. I have full confidence in their ability to find the perpetrator and bring him to justice," I said calmly.

"You mean ... he was murdered?" Stella asked, her eyes widening at my suggestion.

I squeezed my eyes shut for a moment. Another misstep. I tried to recover. "Well ... they're considering all possibilities but ... I don't think they've reached a conclusion yet about what actually happened."

"Oh," Stella said simply. She looked confused, so that made two of us. Finally, she spoke again. "I think it's about time we got together for dinner so we can catch up on all your activities. You do lead an interesting life, Sonja; I'll say that for you. I'll give you a call soon, and we'll get together after the dust has settled." She patted my hand and pushed her cart down aisle fifteen, disappearing around the corner. I continued to the checkout and then walked to the parking lot, praying I wouldn't see anyone else I knew. After the events of the last two days, I was ready to head to our one-room cabin near Towerville on the Kickapoo River for a few days of solitude and peace and some uninterrupted time to think.

On the way home, I stopped at Andy's Liquors and Fine Spirits near the Fox Hollow Golf Course and picked up a lovely light Moscato to go with the salmon and Trygve's favorite Spotted Cow beer. When I arrived home, Coco woofed and nibbled at my feet until I picked him up and cuddled him close for several minutes. Then I began my dinner plans. I made a small charcuterie board, including some wonderful pepper jack and sharp Cheddar cheese, red crispy grapes, whole wheat crackers, and thinly sliced salami, and slipped it into the refrigerator. Since it was only three o'clock, I walked down to the barn to check on Sonny and Cher and our flock of chickens. Sonny brayed loudly when he spotted me, came up to the fence, and bumped my hand with his wet nose. He expected a treat, and I didn't have the heart to disappoint him. I fed him a couple of apple wedges I'd tucked in my shirt pocket. Soon Cher arrived, batting her long eyelashes, wondering what all the commotion was about. More apple slices. I entered the chicken coop and picked the day's eggs, placing them carefully in my small wicker basket. Leave it to my animals to ease my tension and help me forget the problems of the last few days.

As I walked back to the house, I wondered how things were going for Chief Pedretti. I admired her grit. It couldn't be easy leading a group of strong-willed, well-trained officers of the law. No sooner had I dispelled thoughts of Pedretti and gotten down to my meal preparations when my cell phone buzzed on the kitchen counter.

"Sonja Hovland," I answered politely, but I could feel the tension building in my chest at the thought that more information about the Diangelo murder might be coming my way.

"Sonja, Tanya here."

"Hey! How's the Diangelo case going?" I asked with false cheerfulness.

"Well, we've made a little progress. Two of my officers had a conversation with Sam Watson, the guy who was at Pizza Hut last night."

"And?"

"He claims his brother, Beck, was with him. Apparently,

Beck has some mental health issues and is currently unemployed, but Sam didn't believe his brother would ever be involved in a serious crime like murder. But I looked him up, and he's had a few minor scrapes with the law. Nothing serious: breaking and entering, a fisticuff with another guy at a downtown bar, and trying to pass off a bad check. Still, minor incidents with the law can lead to more serious offenses."

"Well, I don't know anyone who'd want to believe their brother is a cold-blooded killer," I said. "Do you?"

"Well, I suppose that's a common reaction, but in my experience, people who commit serious crimes usually have major issues with credibility and truth-telling. We tried to find this Beck kid, but after checking at his mom's residence where he supposedly lives, my officers couldn't locate him. So, he must be floating around the city somewhere, or big brother warned him off, and he's on the run," Tanya explained.

"Sounds challenging," I responded. "Did you need some assistance?"

"No, you stick to your cleaning. We'll find him eventually," Tanya said with a gritty tone, "and bring him in for questioning."

"Do you think he might be involved in the Diangelo case somehow?" I asked.

"Don't know, but it's a line of inquiry we need to investigate."

Switching the subject, I asked, "How's life with Roy these days?"

It was quiet on the line for a few moments. "It's improving ... I think," Tanya said. "He seems less preoccupied, if you know what I mean, but there's always room for improvement."

"Glad to hear it."

"If you hear anything else about the Diangelo case, you'll let me know, right?"

"Absolutely, I will," I said. "Have a good night."

"Night," Tanya said softly, and she hung up.

I stood by the counter for several minutes wondering about Beck Watson, who seemed to have gone missing. *Missing?* I thought. *Missing my foot. That kid is on the run, or he's gone into hiding.*

CHAPTER 19
Dances with Wolves

Wednesday night turned cold and blustery with a staccato rain that pounded the hood of the black and white cruiser parked along the curb. The trees along Market Street danced in a sudden gust of wind, and a couple walking along the sidewalk pulled their hoods tighter around their faces, ran through the pouring rain, and climbed into a car a block away. Officer Mike Leland and Lt. Hank Brousard had taken it upon themselves to do an all-night surveillance in hopes of spotting Beck Watson riding his bike somewhere within the city limits. They'd cruised the city streets toward the north and south but came up empty. Since Sam Watson lived near the university, they parked in the neighborhood, hoping Beck might make a late-night visit to his brother's apartment.

"What did you think of Mrs. Watson's situation?" Mike asked, breaking the silence as they sat in the cruiser, wolfing down sandwiches from Subway.

"She seems totally exhausted by her kid's problems," Hatchet said, chewing thoughtfully as he gazed out the front windshield. "Can't blame her."

"Yeah, I agree. She did seem wrung out. Her son's unemployment is an ongoing issue," Mike added sourly, "but that's not surprising. The inability to hold down a job goes with the territory." Family problems involving mental health issues were nothing new to the two seasoned officers. Mental illness took a heavy toll on family life, erasing normality and leaving stress, fractured relationships, heartache, and often, poverty and homelessness in its wake. "Think we'll see him tonight?"

"Nope. If we do, it'll be a miracle," Hatchet commented.

"Miracles," Mike harrumphed. "Haven't seen too many of them lately."

"How's Lindsey?" Hatchet asked suddenly, changing the subject.

"She's busy workin' on her degree. She's got about eighteen credits left, most of it nursing practicum. Then she can get a full-time job and quit mooching off me," Mike said.

"But you're okay with her getting her education before you get married, right?"

Mike smiled. "Oh, sure. Once she gets a job and settles into it, then we'll tie the knot," he said. "Gonna be different being married."

"I bet. You've been together for quite a while, haven't you?" Hatchet asked.

"Four years this September."

"It's time," Hatchet said.

"That's what she said."

They sat inside the peaceful cocoon of the cruiser while the stormy weather outside buffeted the car. A half hour later, the rain lessened and became a steady, soft drumming that was hypnotic in its rhythm. Their full stomachs lulled them into a sleepiness that was hard to resist. Mike dozed off, and Hatchet watched the street while simultaneously scrolling through his messages on Instagram and Facebook.

About one o'clock in the morning, Mike jerked awake. He looked over at Hatchet and realized his partner had dropped off into a fitful snooze. Down the street at the corner, a lone figure on a bike stopped under the streetlight. The biker cast a lonely silhouette, looking like some kind of circus performer who suddenly found himself in the spotlight. He looked down the street at the cop car parked there. Mike sat up and shook Hatchet's arm.

"Hidey ho, neighbor. Look who showed up," Mike whispered.

"Huh?" Hatchet rubbed his face, squinting. He sat up. "What?"

"Down the street at the corner," Mike said, pointing that way. "Doesn't that look like that Watson kid?"

Hatchet looked at the kid sitting on his bike under the streetlight texting on his phone, and a dubious expression crossed his face. In his opinion it could have been any young college-age student. "Could be, but I doubt it. Want me to get out and talk to him?"

"Got your vest on?" Mike asked.

"Nah. It'll be fine. He looks pretty harmless," Hatchet said. He reached for the door handle and stepped out of the cruiser onto the sidewalk.

Mike watched his partner walk casually down the street lifting his arm in a salutation to the biker. The kid spit something in his hand, dropped it on the ground, then briefly reached into his jacket pocket. That simple action, a nimble sleight of hand, sent a flash of apprehension through Mike. What had the kid retrieved from his pocket? He had a sudden premonition of the potential danger his partner was facing, and then a wave of alarm coursed through his body. He noticed words being exchanged as Hatchet raised both hands in front of him. The biker suddenly looked very agitated. Mike blasted out of the driver's seat of the cruiser and began running toward the two men. That's when the kid pointed a pistol at Hatchet and shot a bullet into his chest. Hatchet collapsed and began writhing on the sidewalk.

"Stop! Police!" Mike shouted as he ran down the sidewalk. "Throw down the gun!"

The kid looked confused and halted momentarily, then dropped the gun on the sidewalk and took off down the street, pedaling madly until he turned into a dark alley behind a row of houses. Mike knelt beside Hatchet. He was bleeding profusely, and his eyes were glazed with pain.

"He had a gun! He had a gun!" Hatchet repeated hoarsely.

"Hang on, Hatchet. Help's coming!" Mike said desperately, but he could see his friend was losing too much blood. His face was white as paper, and he was shaking with shock. Mike ran back to the cruiser and called in the incident, then grabbed a blanket from the back seat and ran back to Hatchet. He covered his friend and continued talking to him in low, confident tones. Grabbing Hatchet's hand, Mike gripped it firmly. He was surprised at how comforting it was. "Help's coming, Hatchet," he said, trying to reassure the wounded man. "Hang on, buddy."

Although it seemed like an eternity to Mike, a cruiser

came screaming down the street in less than two minutes, followed by an ambulance. Seconds later the street filled with more police cars and emergency vehicles. Officers began flooding the crime scene, the surrounding streets, and the neighborhood. Some gathered around the wounded cop and Mike; others began running toward the dark alley looking for the shooter. Still, other officers walked across lawns and checked outbuildings where someone might hide. The ambulance personnel began working on Hatchet. Mike stood up to get out of the congestion, walked a few feet away, and watched the unfolding scene with a sense of disbelief and despair.

An officer came up to Mike. "Mike? I need you to come with me," he said. He steered Mike farther away from the chaos.

Mike stopped and stared at him. "I … I had a bad feeling about it. I should have made him put on his vest. I … I screwed up," he mumbled, "but it was just a kid on a bike. I didn't think he'd have a gun."

The other officer grabbed Mike's arm to get his attention, "Let me take you down to headquarters. You shouldn't drive," the officer said, "and you're going to need to make a statement about what happened."

"The chief? Anybody call the chief yet?" Mike asked.

"Don't know, but let's get you into a squad car," the officer said, directing Mike to a cruiser sitting in the middle of the street. Hatchet was loaded in the ambulance, and it drove away, the red lights reflecting on the house windows, the siren piercing the night air. The street teemed with officers who had spread out around the neighborhood looking for the shooter. Lights in the neighborhood began twinkling on.

A lady on Market Street near the scene opened her front door, looking confused. An officer shouted, "Stay in your home, ma'am. Shut the door and stay inside." The woman looked alarmed but shut the door and turned out her lights.

The officer led Mike to the police cruiser. He climbed in the back, then pulled his phone out of his pocket and called Tanya Pedretti's number.

"This is the Pedrettis," a deep voice said after several rings.

"Roy, Tanya there?" Mike asked.

There was a rustling sound and some mumbling. "This is Tanya."

"Chief, it's Mike Leland. I've got some bad news."

"Go ahead. What's happened?" Tanya asked.

"Hatchet was shot about a half hour ago. Chest wound. He's not good, Chief."

"What?"

"Hatchet—"

Tanya interrupted. "Where'd they take him?"

"Mayo, ma'am."

"Got it," and the line went dead.

CHAPTER 20
Ain't No Sunshine When You're Gone

The surgical waiting room at the Mayo Hospital was abuzz in the early hours of Thursday morning. Hatchet was in surgery, and Tanya was told if he survived, he would have a long, arduous recovery, and his physical abilities might be greatly diminished. His prognosis was grim.

Other police officers had heard about the shooting on Market Street and had come to sit and wait for the news of their friend and fellow officer. Several sat around on the padded chairs and sofas, their eyes red-rimmed, their faces lined with worry and anxiety.

Roy Pedretti met Tanya at the hospital after she'd visited the crime scene and given orders for an all-out city search. The gun the biker had used to shoot Hatchet had been recovered where he'd dropped it on the sidewalk. It was in the forensics lab being checked for fingerprints and DNA. Crime Scene had arrived, and they completed their tasks quickly. In three hours, Market Street returned to normal. The peaceful atmosphere of the street was restored; people shut off their lights and went back to bed, the stars came out after the rain, and the traffic was slow and quiet. It seemed incongruous that someone had just been shot and seriously wounded, and all that was left of the incident was a red stain on the sidewalk where Hatchet had lain and nearly bled to death.

Tanya walked up to the attendant's desk in the surgical waiting area after an hour had passed wondering if she could see Hatchet. The attendant held up a finger and said, "I'll check and see if he's out of surgery yet."

Tanya leaned on the counter and held her head in her hands. *How can this be happening?* she thought. *I just talked to him at five o'clock when I left for home. Now he's fighting for his life because some kid had a gun and, in a moment of panic, decided to use it.*

Roy walked up beside Tanya and wrapped his arm around her shoulders. "Let's sit down, honey. She'll come get us when it's time."

Tanya turned to Roy and leaned her head on his shoulder. She wanted to scream at the unfairness of all of this, but that would not be appropriate for the chief of police. She could imagine the headlines and chitchat on social media: "Chief of Police Loses her Grip on Reality When Her Right-Hand Man is Wounded."

"I can't believe this is happening," she said.

"Come on. Let's sit over here," Roy said gently. He guided her to a loveseat where they sat holding hands.

"What about Leisel? Will she be all right at your mom's?" Tanya asked.

"Absolutely. Mom will take good care of her," Roy assured his wife.

"The boys. I need to call the boys," Tanya said, digging

for her phone in her purse.

Roy gently held her hand. "I already did it, babe. They already know."

Tanya looked into her husband's eyes, and the tears began to flow. "This is so damn unfair. What if Hatchet dies?"

"Let's not think about that right now," he said, his eyes glistening with tears.

Tanya looked across the surgical waiting area and saw Lt. Jim Higgins and Sam Birkstein talking to several of the officers who'd gathered around them. Someone pointed at Tanya, and Jim caught her eye. He nodded his head and broke away from the group. Tanya stood and hugged Jim. Jim shook Roy's hand.

"I'm so sorry, Tanya," Jim said. "Do you know anything new? Hatchet still in surgery?"

"Still waiting. Don't know much, but it's not good," Tanya said, her voice cracking.

"What about the shooter? Any sign of him?" Jim asked.

"I've got every available man out on the street combing every neighborhood by the university. By now he probably dumped the bike and stole a car," Tanya said sourly, venting her frustrations.

"My staff is always ready to help," Jim said. "You've got good people to help Mike, right?"

"Yeah, we do. Thanks, Jim," Tanya said simply.

"If you need someone to be there for Mike, call me," Jim said. "I'd be glad to help. I've been through this."

"I know," Tanya said. "I appreciate it. You might get a call."

Jim wandered off and continued talking to other police personnel while Tanya and Roy anxiously waited for news from the surgical team. Someone found a deck of cards, and a game of poker started in one corner. Somebody else had gone to Kwik Trip and gotten a big box of donuts and rolls, and people dug into the sweets and sipped on coffee.

A half hour later, the assistant at the desk came over to Tanya and Roy.

"The doctor just got out of surgery and will meet you briefly and give you an update. Follow me." The young woman led them down a hallway and into a consulting room, where the doctor sat at a long table. He stood when Roy and Tanya came in, then fidgeted impatiently, waiting to deliver his report, ready to hurry to another crisis. Tanya glanced at his name tag: Dr. Sorenson. He was a middle-aged man, rather tall. His hair was graying at the temples, his face was drawn and serious, but his eyes were bright despite the late night and stressful situation. Tanya shook his hand. It felt strong, and for some unknown reason, she found great comfort in that. Her stomach felt like it was inside out, and suddenly, she realized how tired she was. She glanced at the clock on the wall above the doctor: 5:10 a.m.

"I'm going to give you a very guarded prognosis at this point," the doctor began. "Mr. Brousard had damage to the chest wall where the bullet entered. Apparently, the shooter was some distance away from him when he discharged the gun, which probably saved his life. The bullet exited his back on the right side between the fifth and sixth ribs. He has considerable damage to his right lung, which collapsed, and he lost a lot of blood, but fortunately, his heart was untouched by the bullet. That would have killed him instantly. He seems to be a fighter. His vitals are leveling out, but we have a long way to go. His recovery will be intensive, long, and painful."

Tanya laid a hand along her neck and clutched her blouse in her fist. "I can't believe this. I thought he was a goner for sure."

"The next few days will tell the story," Dr. Sorenson continued, "but this scenario is very tentative right now. Complications can crop up: infections, bleeding, and other problems. But, like I said, we are cautiously optimistic that Mr. Brousard can recover."

"Thank you. I'll report his condition to my team," Tanya said. She noticed the concerned look on the doctor's face.

"Don't exaggerate the hope," the doctor warned, holding up one hand. "We're not outta the woods yet. His condition is still very critical."

Tanya paused and nodded. "Don't worry, I've got it. I'm used to giving generic reports that don't panic the public. I realize he has a long way to go."

"That's right. Any other questions?" Dr. Sorenson asked.

"No, I have no other questions. You've given me a very realistic picture. Thanks," Tanya said. Tanya and Roy turned, left the room, and walked down the hallway back to the waiting area. After Tanya updated everyone about Hatchet's condition, she walked to the parking lot with Roy. The sky was changing; the dark night had crept away, and a pink blush of light was flooding the horizon with the promise of dawn. Tanya glanced at the sky and the changing colors. She stopped suddenly, laying her hand on

Roy's arm.

"Look, honey. Look at the sky. If we stand here long enough, we could watch the sun climb up over the bluffs. When was the last time you saw a sunrise over Grandad Bluff?" she asked Roy.

He looked at her and wondered about her state of mind. "Well, I haven't been up this early for quite a while, sweetheart, but if memory serves me right, it was back when we first started dating, and we spent the night in the back seat of my car."

"Oh, I'd forgotten that, but I think you're right. All I can really think about right now is that Hatchet might still get to see a sunrise again," Tanya said. She leaned back and looked upward in a gesture that looked like prayer. "God, Roy, our lives are so short—just a thin little thread keeps us here. We're so fragile, aren't we?" They stood there like that for a few moments, and then Tanya grabbed Roy's hand and began walking to the car in the parking lot. Climbing in the car, Roy started the vehicle. Tanya threw her purse between them on the seat. Roy was about to back out of the parking ramp when she touched his arm again. "Wait a minute," she said. "Before we go, I've got to tell you something."

"Okay." Tanya was not given to philosophical discussions, so her comments a few minutes ago about the sunrise had surprised him. "I think I know what you're going to say."

"No. No, you don't. What I'm going to say might come as a shock—" Tanya began.

"You're going to tell me that you and Hatchet grew up together and were—are—good friends to this day," Roy said, finishing her sentence. "I already know that. You're rooting for him—"

"Umm ... no ... it's not that simple," Tanya interrupted.

Roy turned his head slowly and looked at her. "Oh," he said.

Tanya blinked rapidly a few times. "Just listen and don't interrupt. I need you to hear me out on this. Hatchet and I grew up together, same neighborhood, same elementary school, same church, same high school. Before I met and married you, we were together like ... going together ... like probably-going-to-get-married together."

Roy shrugged his shoulders and made a wry face. "Yeah, so? Jeez, honey, I had other girlfriends before I met you, too," he said. He looked at her and held her gaze.

Even though he seemed calm, Tanya could tell this conversation made him uncomfortable. She hated disappointing him.

"I didn't live in a vacuum," Roy continued with an edge in his voice. "You had relationships, and I had relationships. So what?"

"I got pregnant with Hatchet's baby when I was at Tech," Tanya blurted.

"Oh."

"...and I miscarried. And after that, everything fell apart, and we couldn't sustain our relationship."

"Oh."

"And Hatchet still carries a torch, if you know what I mean."

"Oh."

Tanya let out a frustrated sigh. "Will you quit saying that and tell me what you think?"

"Well, what do you want me to say?" Roy snapped, his temper flaring. "I guess I don't understand why you're telling me this now after all these years."

"I'm telling you this now because lately, I've noticed you don't seem engaged. Our relationship feels like it fell off a cliff somewhere. I don't know what happened to us, but I told you about Hatchet because even though he's an important part of my life at work, you're the one I love. I'm worried about us, Roy. That's all." She turned away from him and stared through the front windshield. The silence dragged on for several moments. Tanya wondered if she should have left this territory unexplored. But she believed in honesty and truth and commitment. What they were doing wasn't working. They had to do something else— something different. This conversation was about doing something different.

Finally, Roy broke the silence. "I'm sorry. I know I've been preoccupied. Forgive me for being callous, but it has nothing to do with you. It was never my intention to hurt you, but working from home is harder than I thought it'd be, and honestly, I hate it. If I've been ignoring you, it's because I'm frustrated with this whole job situation."

"Really?" Tanya tipped her head as she stared at him. She grabbed his hand and held it.

Roy nodded his head. "Really," he said. He lifted her hand to his lips and kissed her fingers. "One other thing—I know you're close to Hatchet, but I never once suspected anything between you. Just so you know."

"Okay, that's good because nothing has happened since we broke up. In all fairness, I know I haven't been communicating much lately, either," Tanya confessed. "It's not all on you." She sighed loudly, and her throat felt tight. She could feel tears misting her eyes. "I miss Mom and the boys ... and now Hatchet is fighting for his life." As much as she didn't want it to happen, she began to cry.

Roy reached across the seat and pulled her to him, hugging her to his chest. "It's okay. It's okay," he said. "This is a tough thing, and the police chief has permission to cry on my shoulder anytime she feels like it." They sat in the parking ramp for a few minutes while Tanya cried.

"Can we go home now?" Tanya asked, pulling away from him, her voice still wobbly. "I need to take a shower and get ready for work."

Roy kissed her tenderly. "I'll make you breakfast."

"That'd be nice," Tanya said, and Roy backed out of the parking ramp and began the drive to their home above Grandad Bluff.

CHAPTER 21
Song Sung Blue

Thursday morning dawned with a pink and golden swirl of color that spread along the horizon. The craggy limestone bluffs surrounding the city of La Crosse reflected the soft yellow light that comes with the rising sun. South of the city off U.S. Highway 14 on a dead-end road called East Hill Road, Beck Watson huddled in a corner of an abandoned garage trying to keep the voices in his head at bay, but it was a losing battle. Lately the voices were more insistent and not easily quieted.

Last night, Beck had ditched his bike and stolen a small moped from a garage in a back alley near the Trane facility off Losey Boulevard. Through a series of evasive maneuvers, he'd frantically putted out of town, driving haphazardly with no real plan until he came to the end of a gravel road. He didn't know the name of the road, but he didn't care about where he was; he was just glad to get off the bike and into a building where he could rest and escape the citywide search being conducted by the police.

Now, in the early light of dawn, he lay sprawled in a corner of the garage, dirty and tired; he hadn't slept all night. The stress of the shooting kept coming back to him—the sights, the sounds, the smells. He squeezed his eyes shut and tried to think of a plan for the next few days, but nothing came to him. Forward-thinking was not one of his strengths.

His brain was on sensory overload brought on by the memory of the violent shooting of Lt. Hank Brousard. He wished he could erase it from his mind, but the scene kept looping back, over and over, like a needle skipping over a record repeating itself ad nauseam.

The vision of the police officer walking toward him in the darkness replayed itself in living color until his heart was pumping hard in his chest. He could feel the cold metal of the pistol in his hand and the kick of the gun when he'd pulled the trigger. He was convinced he could smell the gunpowder in his nostrils, even though the garage only contained a couple of broken-down lawnmowers and some old bushel baskets in one corner. The surprised look on the cop's face when he'd shot him popped into his mind again, twisting and tormenting his thoughts.

I *must be crazy,* he thought. *What the hell was I thinking?* He exhaled loudly and tipped his head back, resting it on the garage wall. *People already think I'm nuts, but now the cops are after me, and things will never be the same again.* He thought about his brother, Sam, and wondered if he'd heard about the shooting. His mother would be devastated when she found out. He reached into his pocket for his cell phone, but the screen remained dark; the battery was dead, and he didn't have a charger.

The moped he'd escaped on was propped along one wall in the decrepit, old garage. A small two-story farmhouse sat fifty feet away, its siding gray and brittle, the lopsided front door hanging crookedly from a couple of rusted hinges. The downstairs windows had shades that looked so ancient they'd probably crumble if you touched them. Beck wasn't sure if anyone lived in the house, so he spent the early morning hours inside the garage watching for signs of human activity, peering through a cracked board along the wall. The sun had been up for about an hour, and his stomach was rumbling with hunger when an old lady opened the rickety front door and let out a black cat. Then she shut the door again and disappeared inside the house.

Beck was surprised to see the old woman living in such a run-down house. He considered this turn of events, thinking about the situation he was in. He conjured up the possibilities this scenario presented; the woman and the old house on the dead-end road might be the solution to his quandary. Standing up, he moved out of the dark, dingy corner of the garage, dusted off his pants, and cautiously opened the side door. Walking toward the house, he was surprised when the front door suddenly sprang open, and the old woman appeared like a cuckoo from a clock. She was barely five feet tall, hunched with arthritis. Her arms were nothing but fragile twigs. Her hair was pure white and hung in long strands around her face despite an attempt to fashion it into a bun on top of her head. She wore a faded, dirty house dress and flip-flop rubber sandals on her feet. She stared defiantly at the tall man standing in her yard.

"Where have you been?" the old woman hollered with disgust. "You were supposed to be here three days ago." Her eyes flashed with irritation. Beck stared at the old woman, confused by the accusation.

"I don't understand how these businesses think they can get away with this," the old woman complained. "I called them four days ago, and you're just getting here. Where have you been?" she demanded again. "And where's your car?"

Beck shuffled on his feet and stammered, "I rode my moped here. It's parked on the other side of the garage. Your place was a little hard to find. I got lost." He wasn't very good at thinking on his feet, and the old woman's accusations further confused him.

"Lost?" the lady said, rolling her eyes upward. "Oh, my stars, what is the world coming to?" She shook a gnarled finger at him. "I left specific instructions about my location on the message machine. The incompetence of some people nowadays is unbelievable. Well, you're here now, so come on in." She waved her arm in a beckoning gesture. "I've got a list of jobs that need to be done. We might as well get started. Better late than never, I guess."

The old woman turned and entered the dark hallway beyond the front door. Beck climbed the rickety steps and tentatively followed her inside. The smell of cat urine assaulted him as soon as he entered the house. It was so strong it made his eyes water, but he kept his thoughts to himself. *Just shut up,* he thought. *Watch and make a plan.*

The kitchen was a chaotic, jumbled mess; newspapers were stacked in one corner, stinking garbage bags in another. An ancient stove was buried under pots and pans of all sizes and shapes, and the kitchen sink was filled with rancid, dirty water. A box of reeking cat litter sat next to the doorway. Everything stunk. Beyond the kitchen, Beck could see the living room, with an old threadbare couch and a shredded leather recliner the cat had used to sharpen its claws. In the corner a small television was flickering in the early morning light, the sound muted as the weatherman pointed to a map.

"Now, I left that list somewhere here in the kitchen," the old woman mumbled as she rummaged through a pile of mail and magazines on the worn oak table.

Beck stood mute, observing the woman's search, his mind racing with the possibilities of this place. *A hideout presented on a silver platter,* he thought. *If I play my cards right, this might work out.*

"Here it is," the old woman exclaimed, holding up a crinkled list in her arthritic fingers. "You can start with these jobs, and when you're done, we'll talk about your pay," she said firmly. "Don't try to pull any tricks, by the way. I'll be watching you. I don't tolerate shoddy work." Her blue eyes drilled a hole in Beck's forehead as she thrust the list at him.

He looked around the room again, grabbing the list from the old lady. "Shoddy work? That's rich," he said sarcastically, looking at the disaster in the house. "Have you looked around this place lately?"

"Now listen here, I'm not rich, but I'm glad to pay for quality work," she responded. The woman glanced at the clock. "It's time for *Wheel of Fortune,* and when that's done, I'll be checkin' up on you. I taught school for almost thirty years, so I can recognize a slacker when I see one."

Beck felt like giving the old woman a mock salute, but he knew that would go over like a lead balloon. Teachers didn't like smart-asses. Instead, he smiled at her, turned around, and went back outside. He scanned the list as he stood in the unkempt, weed-infested yard: straighten the trellis next to the back porch, haul the rocks from the overgrown flower bed along the house foundation, and fasten the loose step on the front entry stairs. He wondered if the old lady had any tools. He tramped back into the house and walked into the living room.

"You're not done already, are you?" she asked. "That's not possible."

"You got any tools?" Beck asked.

"Tools? What kind of tools?"

"A hammer? Maybe a screwdriver? A wheelbarrow??"

"Look in the garage. There might be some stuff on one of those shelves," the woman said. She got up from her chair and went into the kitchen, where she rifled through a drawer by the sink and found a screwdriver,, which she handed to Beck.

"By the way, what's your name? You never told me," Beck said.

The old lady scowled grumpily. "Mabel. Mabel Kimble. I left my name on the message at the agency. Didn't you listen to it?"

"No, I didn't."

Mabel shook her head in frustration. "I'm not surprised. So, your name, young man?"

"I'm known as Beck."

"Deck? What kind of name is that?" Mabel said in a huffy tone.

Beck shrugged his shoulders and smiled. "You asked for my name, and I told ya. Take it or leave it, lady."

Early Thursday morning, Trygve sat in his recliner in the living room, sipping a cup of coffee while he watched the local news. Suddenly he yelled to Sonja. "Honey, come in here. You've got to see this."

Entering the living room, Sonja stared at the face on the television screen.

"What's up?" she asked as the image on the television screen changed from the young man's face to the scene of a dark street flooded with the flashing lights of police cars and emergency vehicles.

"That kid—I met him over in Pettibone Park yesterday," Trygve said, pointing at the TV.

"What kid?" Sonja asked, confused.

"The one that was just on TV."

"You'll have to start at the beginning. I don't know what you're talking about," Sonja said, shaking her head.

For the next few minutes, Trygve told Sonja about the kid with the flat bike tire he'd met in Pettibone Park.

Sonja interrupted suddenly when Hatchet's face appeared on the TV screen. "Shh. Shh! Wait a minute! Listen." She pointed at the TV screen as Trygve turned back and watched.

With a growing sense of horror, they listened to the reporter talk about the shooting of Hank Brousard on Market Street in the early hours of Thursday morning. Then Chief Tanya Pedretti stepped to the microphone, her face serious and somber.

"God, she looks awful," Sonja whispered.

Police Chief Tanya Pedretti began to talk. "Early this

morning at about one o'clock, Lt. Hank Brousard was shot by someone who is still at large somewhere in the city. We have identified the perpetrator from Lt. Brousard's body camera as Beck Watson, who escaped from the scene on a bike and might be somewhere in the area. We are asking citizens in the surrounding La Crosse vicinity to be on the lookout for this man." She held up a current photo of Beck Watson. "Do not approach him. We believe Mr. Watson has some mental health issues, so we are asking the public to be cautious. Call 911 or Crime Stoppers or the La Crosse Police Department if you see Mr. Watson. Currently, Lt. Brousard is in critical but stable condition. We appreciate your prayers for his recovery."

The news report switched gears and went to other topics, but Sonja and Trygve sat frozen and mute, staring dumbfounded at the screen.

"This is going to rock Tanya's world," Sonja finally said softly. Trygve muted the TV.

"Promise me you won't get involved," he said, giving Sonja a stare that looked like a warning.

"Tryg, I told you before. My involvement in this whole thing was completely out of my control from the beginning. Weird things tend to happen when you find dead people in strange circumstances. I never went looking for any of this trouble. I happened to be in the wrong place at the right time ... or was I in the right place at the wrong time?" Her eyebrows crinkled together in a scowl, and she ran her fingers through her hair.

"Never mind," Trygve said impatiently. "The important thing is you were there in Diangelo's office and found him, which seems to have put a big target on your back."

He stood up and walked past Sonja to the kitchen. "Just promise me you'll be careful," he said over his shoulder.

Sonja followed him and set her coffee cup on the kitchen counter while Trygve made some toast. "You know I'm careful," Sonja reminded him. "As careful as one can be when dealing with people who've lost their moral compass."

"Or their everlovin' mind," Trygve said sarcastically. "Or a combination of both."

"My, my, aren't we ornery today?"

The toast popped up, and Trygve laid the slices on the counter, then slathered them with butter and some of Sonja's homemade raspberry jam. He took a big bite, chewed angrily, and said, "Look, babe. I would like to believe that everything will turn out all right, but when you're dealing with mentally disturbed people who've gone off the rails, that doesn't always happen."

"Now, Trygve, don't get all hot under the collar. I promise I'll stay out of it."

"Like you stayed out of it before?" he asked, his eyebrows raised in a look that could only be interpreted as a challenge.

"Okay. I can see we're not on the same page, and I don't want to fight, so let's just leave it at that." She walked over to him and kissed him on the lips. She then walked out to her Subaru parked in the garage while Trygve followed her, munching on his toast.

"Oh, wait a minute, I forgot to tell you," he said. "Some lady called our landline about a cleaning job. She said you never returned her call, so she called here. I talked to her and said I'd pass the message along. So, you better check your messages and return her call," he finished as Sonja got in the car and punched the garage door opener.

She slapped her forehead. "Oh my gosh. I've been so distracted I haven't checked my work phone for four days. I'll go through my messages this morning." She smiled at Trygve, who was resting his arms on her car's open front passenger window.

"By the way, thanks for the great dinner last night and all your extra effort later," Trygve said, smiling seductively. "It almost makes me want to forgive you for all this hullabaloo you're entangled in."

"Glad you enjoyed it. I'll see you tonight," Sonja said, backing out of the garage. She watched Trygve standing in the driveway as he waved to her. His face looked like granite, etched with worry and care. "How did my cheerful, optimistic husband change into a worrywart overnight?" she mumbled.

CHAPTER 22
I Can See Clearly Now

Sam Watson stood in his mother's dingy kitchen. Her 1950s two-bedroom bungalow was paid for, but the tiny, run-down home had diminished in value over the years due to neglect and economic hardship. Sam rushed over to her house on Friday morning to intercept the television report about Beck's involvement in the shooting of Lt. Hank Brousard. He had a growing sense of horror that his brother was involved somehow in the death of Dr. Diangelo, but he had no idea how that could have happened.

"Mom?" he yelled as he walked through the back door. "Mom? Are you here?"

His mother appeared in the hallway between the kitchen and the tiny living room. Sam could hear the drone of the television, and from the look on his mother's face as she walked toward him, he realized she knew about the manhunt being carried out in the city to locate Beck. Her haggard face and stringy hair were nothing new, but the absolute panic in his mother's eyes shocked him. She looked like she'd aged twenty years since he'd last seen her.

He thought of all the scrapes Beck had been involved in: writing bad checks, bar fights with other men over some misconstrued insult, dropping out of college, and his constant joblessness. And then there was his fixation on the U.S. government and his belief that the deep state was fronting a socialist-backed coup. It would happen any day now, and the damn capitalists would get their due. *Such malarkey,* sighed Sam. He was so tired of dealing with all the never-ending conspiracy theories.

Gwen Watson had been through hell and back dealing with her youngest son. She had scrimped and saved her money to send Beck to mental health professionals for counseling and advice about treatment for his bipolar and personality disorders. Beck's prescriptions alone just about broke the bank, yet she never complained. She worked herself to the bone day and night so that Beck could get everything he needed, and he still squandered the generosity she so freely gave. Sam boiled with anger when he thought about it.

"I heard all about it on the TV," Gwen said wearily. "Looks like Beck got himself in a real jam this time." She collapsed in a heap on the nearest dining room chair, put her elbows on the table, and rested her head in her hands.

"It's pretty clear from the video that it's Beck," Sam said, sitting down next to his mom.

"What am I goin' to do now?" Gwen mumbled into her hands. "He'll be in prison for the rest of his life."

"Let's not rush to judgment," Sam said calmly. "What we need to do right now is find Beck. According to the police reports, he escaped on his bike. I can't believe somebody hasn't spotted him yet."

"What about the gun?" Gwen asked. "Where'd he get that?"

"Well, the only thing I can think of is that old pistol Dad had, remember? We found it a couple of years ago when we cleaned out that back room and made it into a bedroom for Beck. He must have kept it," Sam explained, "and hid it in his stuff."

"Oh, I forgot about that," Gwen said, her eyes reflecting her confusion. "But why would he shoot a police officer? I don't understand. What would make him do such a thing?"

"Mom, you know that Beck's mood swings are huge when he doesn't take his meds. He gets difficult and feels threatened, and when he's like that, he does unpredictable things. He must have felt the cop was a threat, and he reacted." Sam sighed sadly. "What a mess."

"Poor Beck. He must be terrified with the cops chasing him and all," Gwen said softly.

Sam studied his mother silently in the dim light of the overhead bulb in the kitchen, pushing down the rage he felt at her sympathy for Beck. He would never truly understand the way his mother defended Beck at every turn in the road. How she constantly forgave his bad behavior and used his mental illness as an excuse for his poor decision-making and scrapes with the law. No wonder Beck couldn't think his way out of a paper bag. She'd never taught him accountability, and now look at the mess he was in. His mom had always provided excuses, but this time, the consequences were dire and life-changing.

"Mom, I need you to promise me one thing," Sam said. His mother looked up at him as if she were awakening from a bad dream. Unfortunately, the bad dream was just beginning. "Call me if you hear from Beck. Find out where he is. I might be able to convince him to turn himself in."

"I will," she said. Noticing the doubt reflected on Sam's face, she repeated, "I will. I'll call you if I hear anything," but Sam was unconvinced.

Maybe you'll call me, he thought, *but this is one jam you won't be able to rescue Beck from.*

Vivian Jensen sat across the coffee table from Officer Mike Leland at ten-thirty Friday morning. She'd made room in her hectic schedule to have her initial visit with Mike since the shooting of Hank Brousard last night. Vivian owned Jensen Family Counseling Services in Holmen, Wisconsin. Through her years as a liaison with the La Crosse Police Department and the La Crosse County Sheriff's Office, she counseled many police officers after incidents that involved physical harm and gun violence. She understood the performance factors that influenced police officers during high-stress events and deadly force confrontations. In fact, it was all too familiar to her, and sometimes she wished it could be different, but it seemed to be getting worse. She'd come to accept that shootings, murder, and the violent mayhem police officers often confronted left scars and deep wounds on their psyche. Helping the officer understand and cope with the anguish and torment following a violent confrontation was an area of expertise she knew quite well, and she was more than willing to help.

"So, Mike, how are you feeling this morning?" she asked gently. Mike sat erect and stiff, his senses on high alert—something Vivian had seen before in law enforcement officers who'd come to her for help. "Relax, Mike. It's just you and me. Everything you say here stays here."

Mike let out a deep breath and relaxed his shoulders, making a visible effort to ease the tension he felt. He kicked his feet out in front of him and leaned back into the comfortable chair, but his face reflected a lack of sleep and the disorientation that comes from events that are out of your control.

"I knew I'd eventually end up here someday," he said, looking at the floor.

"Boy, I hope it's not as bad as all that." Vivian smiled. "My office is not a prison."

He looked up at her. Then he grinned shyly. "Well, I know it's a required part of the job after an incident," he said, his hazel eyes taking in Vivian across the coffee table. He said "incident" like it was a dirty word.

"Yes, it is required, but I hope you'll find what we do to be very practical and helpful. That's why I'm here, Mike. To give you some pointers and strategies that will help you return to normal life as soon as possible."

"Great. So, let's get at it," he said.

"Okay." Vivian picked up her clipboard and pen. "I'm just going to take a few notes to remind me of your initial feelings and reactions to the shooting. It will help me tailor specific strategies for you and your particular situation. Are you okay with that?" she asked.

"Sure, I guess," Mike said, but Vivian could tell he was less than thrilled about it.

"Why don't you tell me what happened Thursday morning," Vivian said. "Use as much detail as you can, and then we'll make a plan."

"Where should I start?" Mike asked.

"Let's start with the beginning of your shift," Vivian suggested.

For the next half hour Mike Leland told the story leading up to and including the shooting incident involving Hank Brousard. His voice cracked a couple of times, and Vivian watched him as he carefully struggled to control his emotions. He was calm and rational until he talked about Hank lying on the sidewalk, bleeding profusely. "I felt so helpless," he croaked, tears streaming down his cheeks. "I thought for sure he was dead." When he finished, he seemed utterly exhausted. Vivian handed him a couple of tissues and waited for him to calm down.

"What you experienced, Mike, was a traumatic incident," Vivian began in a soothing voice. "Your brain is built to respond to danger in a specific way. The shooting you experienced imprinted itself on your brain; the sights, sounds, smells, and your reactions to it are now a part of your emotional circuitry. It's what's commonly known as PTSD. My job is to help you learn to manage your emotional responses to the shooting so that you can return to the job and resume a normal life again."

"Will I be able to forget this?" Mike asked.

"No, but the symptoms of PTSD can change over time. It's a matter of reeducating your emotional circuitry. I won't sugarcoat it; it will take hard work and a good support system, but you can recover. That's what I'm here to help you with. You've already started by telling me the details of the shooting incident, which is the first step on your way to recovery."

"I ... I just feel so responsible for what happened, and

I'm so jumpy and nervous, like someone is waiting for me around every corner," Mike said.

"That's pretty normal in these situations. Hypervigilance, jumpiness, and nightmares are all symptoms of PTSD that you will likely experience in the next few months and then less frequently as time goes on. But remember, by retraining your brain, you can rebuild your life," Vivian said. "And I'm here to help you do that."

"Okay. Can I call you if I need something?" Mike asked.

Vivian took a business card from her pocket and handed it to Mike. "Absolutely. Call anytime, day or night. Let's schedule your next appointment, too."

Mike stood and headed for the door to the lobby. He turned at the last minute and said, "Thanks, Dr. Jensen."

Vivian's eyes misted and she nodded. "No problem, Mike. If you have any questions, just call my number, and don't forget to make your next appointment before you leave."

"I will," he said.

After Mike left the office, Vivian returned to her desk, picked up her phone, and dialed.

"Jim? I need a favor."

"Sure. Mike Leland, right?" Jim Higgins asked.

"Yep. Can you check in on him and be there for him?"

"You got it. I'll do it today."

"Thanks. That's a great help. He doesn't know it yet, but he can't do this alone. He seems a little reluctant to ask for support, but you and I both know he's going to need it," Vivian said.

"Yeah, we're all changed after an incident like this. I'll look in on him. Count on it, Viv," Jim said. "Any news on Hank?"

"Nothing much. He's hanging in there."

"Watching a partner go down is a cop's worst nightmare," Jim said.

"I believe you. Thanks again. I have patients waiting," Vivian said. "Keep me in the loop," and she hung up.

CHAPTER 23 • SONJA
The House of the Rising Sun

I looked in the rearview mirror Friday morning as I drove out the driveway on my way to work and watched Trygve staring after me. I was overcome with guilt. Our lives had changed so much in the last four days, and I couldn't blame him for feeling confused and angry. The simple life we'd led before Monday's grisly discovery on Copeland Avenue seemed like eons ago, but despite the recent turmoil we'd experienced with the death of Dr. Diangelo and the shooting of Lt. Brousard, I was confident that our life would return to some kind of normality when everything blew over. We could go back to a more predictable, peaceful lifestyle. There was no doubt in my mind that we had experienced a groundbreaking shift in our view of reality. It's one thing to watch murder mysteries unfold on TV or in a movie; it's another thing to actually be involved in one, to witness events firsthand. Somehow, the week's turmoil had drastically curtailed my enthusiasm for *Masterpiece Mystery*.

I drove from our home through the beautiful farm country of Barre Mills to the south side of Onalaska. As I traveled through the countryside, I took pleasure in the vistas before me—the pristine farmsteads built by German immigrants in the late nineteenth century, cows grazing hungrily in lush fenced-in fields, budding apple trees and lilacs filling the air with their perfume, their crisp leaves juxtaposed against the robin's egg blue of the sky overhead. My worries seemed to retreat. I headed into town to the stoplights on the corner of Losey Boulevard and La Crosse Street. Waiting for the light to turn, I savored the beautiful spring season. Puffy, cotton ball clouds drifted across the sky, the marsh was alive with birds, and the surrounding bluffs reflected the sunrise against the sandstone escarpments that jutted above the highway. When the light changed, I turned right and then right again on 24th Avenue, rolling up to a quaint little bungalow where Ms. Collette Tierny resided. She'd been a faithful customer of mine for over ten years. She was employed at the La Crosse Public Library as a desk clerk and research assistant. Her amazing mind encapsulated levels of knowledge I didn't even know existed. It was my personal belief she had read every book in the public library, but I knew that was impossible. However, pick any topic, and this lady could recite several books you should read about the subject. To me, she seemed like a living, breathing, walking encyclopedia.

I parked on the street, opened my hatchback, and gathered my cleaning tote, then walked to the side entrance of the house and let myself in. I paused for a moment at the kitchen window, which overlooked Myrick Marsh. Several groups of waterfowl were gathered there, and they splashed and chattered with animated spirit. The spring morning beckoned from the window. Warm rays of sunlight bathed my face, and suddenly, I had the urge to be somewhere else, to forget all the tragedy that had struck our small college town. *It'd be a great morning to take a bike ride on the River Valley trail and forget all this drama and death and chaos*, I thought.

"Good morning, Sonja," a voice behind me said.

I jumped at the unexpected greeting and turned around. There stood Collette dressed in a boho purple tiered skirt, a long-sleeved lacy white blouse, dangling silver earrings, and knee-high brown leather boots. Her hair was styled in a slightly messy but still very attractive updo. She looked stunning as usual. No one in their right mind would believe she was a librarian, and that's exactly how she wanted it. Her inquisitive eyes took in my presence, and suddenly, I felt uncomfortable. Did she know about the incident at the Midwest Medical building and my role in finding Dr. Diangelo dead in his examination chair? I'm sure she did; everyone in town was talking about it. I could imagine the questions and remarks Collette might have about the murder. Knowing her formidable research skills and intelligent mind, I was sure she'd ask questions about the facts of the case. Maybe she'd even propose some kind of motive for the murder. I stopped my ruminations. *Since when was I paranoid about being in the presence of a friend?*

"Oh, Collette, good morning," I stammered. "You startled me. I wasn't expecting you to be here. I thought you'd already left for work."

"Well, I told the head librarian I would be in later than usual today. I wanted to see how you were doing after your terrible ordeal," Collette said. "I'm so sorry this happened to you, Sonja. What can I do to help?"

Maybe it was the way she said it, or the sympathetic look in her eyes, or the way she'd always treated me with such respect and love, but at that very moment, the week came crashing down around me, and I found myself leaning against the kitchen countertop crying like a baby. Collette rushed to my side as I blubbered on about the terrible events on Monday and the way my life had changed forever.

"I'm so sorry this happened to you. Come over here now," Collette whispered, placing her arm around my waist. "Let's sit down, and I'll make you a fresh cup of coffee." She guided me to the small dinette table in her cozy kitchen and busied herself preparing a pot of coffee. While the coffee was brewing and I was trying to get a grip on my crying jag, she dug in her breadbox and found two cinnamon rolls, which she heated in the microwave. Setting a mug of coffee and the cinnamon roll in front of me, she sat down and reached for my hand.

"Now, listen to me, Sonja," she said. Her hand firmly grasped mine, which I found comforting. Her luminous brown eyes shone with empathy. "You may be feeling guilty, or you may be feeling like things have gotten out of control, but you're a smart woman, and you have a very successful business that you built from scratch. You're going to recover from this terrible shock and go on to do great things," Collette counseled me.

"I am?" I said through my tears. Collette reached for a box of tissues and pulled one out.

"Yes, you are," she said firmly, handing me the tissue.

Somehow that seemed unbelievable to me, considering the crazy things that had transpired during the week. I blew my nose noisily, wondering what had gotten into Collette.

This pep talk was totally out of character.

She continued. "I've watched you over the years. You do a marvelous job cleaning my house. You're respectful, you're conscientious, and you're efficient. You have a wonderful reputation among your clients. This murder has rocked your boat, but you're still in the boat, and now you have to pilot yourself into the harbor." Collette's eyes gleamed with purpose.

I was glad someone thought I was capable of great things because, lately, the facts of the Diangelo case had overwhelmed my common sense and reasoning ability. I felt like an utter failure, completely out of my depth.

I stared at her and said, "I don't think you know what you're talking about."

"Oh yes, I do," she countered. "I know you, and you're going to be just fine." She pushed a cinnamon roll toward me. I lifted the gooey bun to my lips, took a generous bite, and felt the sugar and starch begin to do their magic. I began to feel better immediately.

"You heard about the policeman who was shot last night, right?" I asked, wiping a tear from my cheek. I licked some frosting from my lips.

"Yes, our prayer chain at St. Joseph's was notified early this morning. I know Hank personally. He comes to our parish when he can get away from his police duties. He's a very nice man," Collette said, taking a sip of coffee, "and this shooting is a terrible thing."

"You know Hank Brousard?" I asked, my cinnamon roll poised in midair.

"Of course. I've lived in this town my whole life. I know Tanya and Roy Pedretti, too. Wonderful family. They live up above Grandad Bluff, you know. I've been to a few of their patio parties. Great hosts."

Once again, I was brought up short by my own ignorance. I stared at Collette as if I were seeing her for the first time.

"I had no idea," I mumbled stupidly.

"You know a lot, Sonja, but you can't know everything." Collette patted my hand.

"So, you know that Hank is Tanya's right-hand man," I said.

"Depends on what you mean by that," Collette said. Her green eyes sparkled about some kind of confidential matter I had not been privy to. I sipped my coffee, hesitating to bite the bait she had put before me.

"Well, I meant Hank is second-in-command at the city police department," I muttered, "but you probably already know that."

"Yes, I'm aware of his position." Collette suddenly went quiet. After a few moments, she said softly, "You do know that Hank and Tanya have a history, don't you? They grew up together."

I looked at her blankly.

"I'm sure this shooting is very upsetting for Tanya. She's a great cop, and most people wouldn't believe it, but she has a very sensitive heart. It must be awful for her to watch her childhood friend suffer."

"Yes," I said. "I'm sure it is, and she is a wonderful person." Now it was Collette's turn to be surprised.

"How do you know that?"

"Tanya and I have gotten acquainted and become friends since this whole Diangelo murder business started," I explained. "I met her Monday morning when she showed up at the Midwest Medical building, and we kind of hit it off."

Collette's eyes grew wide with amazement. "I didn't know you knew about—"

"My lips are sealed. You know, friend-to-friend secrets and all that," I said confidently, even though I didn't know a single thing about Tanya and Hank's relationship. Nor did I want to.

"Oh. Oh, I see," Collette whispered. "Of course, that makes sense."

There was an awkward silence. To tell the truth, I wasn't sure where this whole conversation was going or what Collette knew about Hank and Tanya, but I was ready to move on. My hard-headed Swedish nature did not pander to hush-hush secrets and innuendos. "Hey, thanks for your concern, Collette, but I've got to get going, or my whole day is going to be thrown off course. Thanks for being so understanding. The coffee and cinnamon roll were just what I needed."

Collette stood suddenly, put her dishes in the sink, and gave me a peck on the cheek. "I've delayed you. I apologize."

"No, you haven't. Not at all. You just helped me haul in the anchor," I said.

"I did what?" she said. I gave her a knowing smile and nodded enthusiastically.

"You helped me realize this investigation isn't done yet, and I need to see it through to the end," I said cockily. If I'd been a rooster, I'm sure I would have been strutting and cock-a-doodle-dooing in the kitchen. Little did I know how foolish that remark would seem later when I recalled my conversation with Collette.

"Just remember this," Collette said, her eyes taking on a peculiar intensity, "Our greatest weakness lies in giving up. The most certain way to succeed is always to try just one more time."

"Is that from your own lips, or did somebody else say that?" I asked, frowning.

"Thomas Edison. Good luck with the case, Sonja. I'll see you later." She picked up a bag of books and her briefcase and headed to the garage. "Remember—you're destined for great things. Your check is on the coffee table in the living room, as always."

I waved and thanked her, then watched her walk briskly to the garage. I began my cleaning routine, mulling over what my librarian friend had told me. I was vacuuming the living room carpet when I remembered the phone messages I had neglected the last four days. After cleaning and collecting my check, I walked to the Subaru, opened my phone, and retrieved my messages. Only five. That wasn't so bad. I scrolled through them, listened to each one, and sent a response. I was down to the last one. I frowned as I listened to the message: "This is Mabel Kimble out on East Hill Road. I need some assistance with my house. Somehow, it's gotten ahead of me, and I have a number of things that need attention. You were recommended to me by Carl Stigen. He said you've helped him out occasionally." I noticed she'd called on Monday. She ended her message by rattling off her phone number. I called, but Mabel did not answer. I decided to take a chance and drive to Mabel's since it was on the way home anyway.

I sat in my car for a few moments while I called Trygve and left him a message, telling him I'd be home later, around six o'clock, because I was going to meet with a new client named Mabel Kimble. I hung up, feeling good that I'd gotten my business life back on track. I started the car and drove to my next job feeling optimistic that everything was going to turn out alright after all. Little did I know that my day was about to turn into a nightmare. Like *Alice in Wonderland*, I was about to fall down the rabbit hole.

Hank Brousard briefly regained consciousness late Friday morning. He noticed the clatter of a hospital cart in the hallway, the rustle of a nurse's uniform as she checked his IV, the murmur of voices in his room. He opened his eyes just a slit, and the sunlight burst through and struck him like a lightning bolt, so he squeezed his eyes shut again.

I must be in the hospital, he thought. *But why? How did I get here?*

The voices in the room continued in low tones. Hank recognized the deep familiar bass voice of his dad. Someone else was whispering, but he couldn't understand the words. Everything seemed garbled, and he felt like he was in a fog.

"Waking up?" a nurse asked, hovering over his bed.

Hank's eyes opened a crack. "Sort of," he mumbled.

"Do you remember what happened to you?" the nurse asked.

"Not really," he croaked. He closed his eyes again.

"You were shot last night while you were on duty," someone said. Hank recognized his dad's voice. He felt a big, warm hand clasp his, and suddenly, the terrible events of the past evening spilled into his brain like a waterfall roaring over a precipice. He groaned, remembering the kid on the bike under the streetlight, the blast of the shot, and the burning pain in his chest.

"Yeah, it's coming back to me a little bit," Hank whispered.

"Don't worry," his dad said softly. "The people here are gonna take care of you. You're in good hands, son. Father Jackson was here and said some prayers for you."

Hank drifted off again when the nurse gave him another dose of morphine. She looked over at Bob Brousard. "He's coming around. That's a good sign, but he's gonna be hurtin' for a while."

Bob nodded. "He's tough. The Italian genes go way back to Sicily. He'll be okay."

The nurse smiled wanly. *You have no idea what he's in for,* she thought. *It's gonna be a very long road.*

CHAPTER 24

Raindrops Keep Fallin' on My Head

At one o'clock on Friday afternoon, Tanya Pedretti closed her office door and sat down at her desk. She was exhausted from the long night at the hospital and the continuing search for Beck Watson, but she knew her day was not finished yet. She'd spent the morning talking to the officers patrolling the streets, getting hourly updates about the search for the elusive Market Street shooter. About eleven o'clock, an officer called in saying he'd found an abandoned bike leaning against a garage on the city's south side. A moped had been stolen from the garage at the same residence. Later, Pedretti got the official coroner's report on the death of Dr. Tony Diangelo—death by a massive injection of fentanyl. Tanya struggled to balance the coroner's report with the interviews of his employees, who spoke highly of his kindness and concern for his staff and patients. She was convinced that Tony Diangelo's death was no accident; someone had viciously injected him with a massive amount of fentanyl.

She went downstairs just before lunch and listened to the

interrogation of Sam Watson. He seemed to be the typical big brother who babysat his disabled, irresponsible sibling. There was nothing especially revealing or shocking about the information Sam shared with the two interrogators, although Tanya learned some things about Gwen Watson, the overprotective mother who refused to teach her son accountability despite his issues with mental illness. A house search was being conducted at the Watson residence on the north side this morning. Officers were especially focused on Beck Watson's bedroom. *We're doing all the right things; we're just not getting anywhere,* thought Tanya.

When Tanya arrived at the office early on Friday, she'd immediately chosen a new lieutenant, advancing Officer Chad Hepple to the position temporarily vacated by Hatchet. The choice had been easy; Hepple had proven his mettle in a number of cases and situations in which his grit, determination, and knowledge of the community had proven invaluable. In addition, he'd been working on his detective license, demonstrating his desire of service to the community. Tanya had seen him in action. He was a team player and frequently went out of his way to encourage the new recruits who had graduated from the technical school across town.

Just before lunch, Tanya retreated to her office. She felt defeated, tossed about like a lone leaf blown helter-skelter in a stiff wind. How could a mentally ill young man breeze through town on a bike, steal a moped, and nobody had seen him? Maybe he had the power to become invisible, like something out of Harry Potter. Tanya harrumphed to herself. *Not likely,* she thought, *but the kid is obviously resourceful and calculating. Or he's just lucky.*

The absence of Hatchet left her feeling overwhelmed, like a fish out of water. She leaned back in her chair, trying to come to terms with the shooting of her childhood friend and former lover. She was gaining a new perspective about how she'd relied on him over the years. What previously had irritated her—his hovering presence, nit-picky perfectionism, concern for her, and lingering attraction for her—now left Tanya with a sadness that throbbed like a dull ache in her chest.

The police chief turned in her chair and looked out of the large office windows that faced south. The brilliant sunshine and the powder blue sky billowed with wispy, cirrus clouds. As Tanya watched them form and reform into intriguing shapes, a couple of bald eagles soared on the updrafts caused by the heating of the air currents around the bluffs.

Tanya was seldom in a philosophical mood; her job required her to use logic and reasoning. The police chief's skill set—her hard-headed knowledge gained from years patrolling the streets and environs of La Crosse and her common sense—didn't leave much room for sentimentality or emotional angst. Today, though, she felt as if she should write a poem or sing a song or paint a picture, something to pay tribute to one of her own who'd been needlessly shot and lay critically wounded, close to death. Her mind wandered. *Ode to a Policeman? A poem? What a joke!* She scoffed at the idea that her brain could produce anything worthy of the sacrifice made last night by her partner and friend. She hadn't written a poem since she'd had fifth-grade language arts, for Pete's sake. She blew out a breath, threw her pen on the desk in frustration, and ran her hand through her thick hair. *Enough of this*, she thought disgustedly. *I've got a murder to solve and an injured officer who's teetering on death's door. I don't have the luxury or the time to mourn over things that can't be changed.*

She reached for her cell and dialed.

"Hepple? I need you in my office right away," she said curtly.

"I'll be right there."

Sure enough. In less than two minutes, Officer Hepple knocked on her door and came in without waiting for permission to enter. Tanya eyed her new second-in-command: crisp dark blue uniform, fresh face, neutral expression, and spit-shined shoes. If Hepple was feeling any emotion about last night's grisly event, it didn't show.

"What can I do for you, ma'am?" Hepple asked, standing at attention.

"We need to compose an agenda for the meeting at two. Do you have some suggestions?" Tanya asked.

"Absolutely. I took the liberty of writing one up," Hepple said. He handed a paper to Tanya and waited for her feedback.

Tanya spent several moments perusing the document. When she finished, she looked up at Hepple. "This is well done," she said. "Good work, Chad. Has everyone been notified?"

"Yes, Chief. I told everyone to report to the classroom down the hall at two o'clock as you directed. I estimate the meeting will take a couple of hours at the most."

"Great. Thank you. I appreciate all you've done for me. I realize this is a tense situation, and you've been thrown into the deep end, so to speak," Tanya explained.

"Not a problem, Chief. I'm ready to serve in any capacity wherever I'm needed."

"Hmm, if that's the case, then how about a fresh cup of coffee before we walk down to the meeting? Can you do that for me?" she asked, raising her eyebrows.

"Absolutely. I'll be right back." He turned and exited the room, closing the door quietly behind him. Tanya leaned back in her chair and stared at the ceiling. *Well, Hepple is efficient. I'll say that for him,* she thought. *But it's just not the same without Hatchet.*

A little after one o'clock on Friday afternoon, Sonja drove through La Crosse to Industrial Commodities on the city's south side. She entered a big blocky warehouse in an area of large industrial complexes behind Gundersen Lutheran Hospital and walked up to the service counter. Darcy, a familiar face at the cleaning supply business, greeted her with a cheerful smile.

"Hey, Darcy," Sonja said. "I need a few things." She slid a handwritten list toward the girl at the counter. "Can you get this stuff ready right now? I've got a job over here on the south side, and I don't want to have to double back again to pick this stuff up before I go home to Barre Mills."

"For you, Sonja, it's no problem," Darcy took the list and disappeared through a swinging door to the back, a massive open area filled with shelves of industrial supplies. She was gone for several moments. During that time, Sonja reviewed the facts of the Diangelo case in her head.

Dr. Diangelo's death was caused by a massive injection of fentanyl. Motive: possibly politically based on the note left in his coat pocket, although drug addiction was not out of the question. Sonja had not ruled out suicide, either. Witnesses: a window washer who noticed the strange situation in the doctor's office early Monday morning but didn't actually see a murder take place. The evidence of the crime was slim. Sonja hadn't been informed about any CCTV video, but she knew the police were working hard reviewing footage. The discarded stocking the intruder had worn over his head during his confrontation with Dr. Diangelo had been found, but no one had identified the intruder who had worn it, so right now, it was a moot point.

Through her contacts around the city, she found out about Sam Watson, a university student, and his brother, Beck, who were overheard at Pizza Hut discussing the procedure for gaining entrance into the Midwest Medical building. When questioned, Sam was cooperative and shared his brother's delicate mental condition and details of his own work history at the Midwest building, but he seemed to have underestimated his brother's mental condition when it came to the shooting of police officer Hank Brousard. Was Sam innocent of any involvement in the crime, or was he in cahoots with his brother in a plot to kill Dr. Diangelo? Something to consider. Furthermore, what had led Beck to shoot a policeman? Was he feeling threatened because he'd committed murder and feared being caught? Sonja remembered his scrapes with the law and wondered if someone as unstable as Beck could carry out a complicated crime. Now he'd disappeared and, for all practical purposes, had eluded the police. That might have been a stroke of luck, or maybe Beck had gone into hiding with the help of his brother. Sonja sighed, feeling frustrated at the slow progress. Unless Beck Watson could be found, things were at an exasperating standstill.

While she waited for her order to be filled, her cell rang.

"Sonja Hovland."

"Sonja. It's Art Ravenwald."

"Hey, Art. What's up?"

"I gleaned some information from some of my contacts at the U about a couple of political groups operating on campus."

"Great. Just a minute while I get my notebook out," Sonja said, rifling through her purse to find pen and paper. "Okay, let fly. I'm ready."

"Before I get into the specifics, let me say when we're talking about political organizations today, there are a couple of things to remember—most people no longer get their information from a newspaper. Instead, they get it from the internet, television news, or other media sources. Groups on the fringe, like the John Birch Society, used to focus on diabolical conspiracies to overthrow the government in order to attract new followers. While those tactics seem old hat, some of today's political activists have forged a new way of communicating their culture and ideology, frequently mixing conspiracy theories with partial truths. The outsiders are out, the Birchers have been birched, and in their wake are these new savvy groups who have updated their rhetoric to fit the contemporary political scene," Art explained. "They use ad agencies to craft their internet image, hire top-notch spokespersons to get their message across, and have tremendous street smarts, which come in handy when they want to take the political temperature of the average American citizen—that includes college kids.

In other words, they're chameleons who can change their color at the drop of a hat to suit the situation they find themselves in. And they're all over the internet, complete with websites and social media pages that are usually very glossy and professional-looking."

"Okay, so how does that tie in with Diangelo?" Sonja asked, getting to the point.

"Good question," Art said. "I don't know for sure, but the note found in Diangelo's suit coat is important. I'm convinced of that. It seems to suggest some kind of conspiracy against our economic system."

"Well, we do know from some of Diangelo's Facebook posts that he was vehemently opposed to the slick solutions some of these groups proposed," Sonja said. "He was especially opposed to the use of guns, violence, and subversive tactics. He frequently ridiculed doomsday preppers and conspiracy theorists as preposterous fringe groups not to be taken seriously."

"There is one group that has been active on campus recently—the Coulee Fifty for Democracy and Freedom," Art explained. "They seem to be loosely organized, still in the developmental stages. Supposedly they have fifty beliefs in their party platform, but no one has actually seen them. They have a website that looks legit and is peppered with a few tantalizing mantras, but if you read between the patriotic drivel, there's an underlying tone of resistance and violence. The killer could be tied to a group like that, a local organization where he was groomed into committing a radical act in the name of the group. Something that would elevate their status in political circles."

"You mean they might set someone up as a stool pigeon?" asked Sonja.

"Yeah, someone from the group might have been chosen to commit Diangelo's murder to promote their political agenda," Art said. "Maybe someone who is easily persuaded and even more easily controlled."

Sonja felt a chill race up her spine. *Could Beck Watson have been set up by some local political group seeking the spotlight so they could influence a bigger segment of the population?* she thought. *This sounds like something out of a spy novel.*

"Do the police have any leads yet on who the perpetrator might be?" asked Art after a few moments of silence.

"They're zeroing in on a couple of potential suspects," Sonja said, her mind still racing with the possibilities Art had presented.

"Well, my best to them in their hunt. I hope they find whoever did this. Always good to talk with you, Sonja."

"Take care, Art, and thanks for the tip." Sonja was still standing by the counter, deep in thought, when Darcy returned with the supplies she needed.

"Sonja?" Darcy said, waving her hand in front of her face.

Sonja jumped.

"Oh, I'm sorry. I was just thinking, I guess," she said apologetically.

"Nothing wrong with that." Darcy smiled. "How's the case going?"

"Case? You mean the case of Clean as a Whistle?" Sonja replied. "I haven't used any of it yet, but I've heard that stuff can take off any stain you can imagine, from dog poop to blood, but I've found nothing beats Borax, baking soda, vinegar, and a little elbow grease."

"No, no, no. I meant the Diangelo case. I hear you've been helping the police," Darcy said, leaning forward across the counter, waiting for a juicy tidbit to come her way. She lifted her eyebrows in a "tell-all" gesture.

"I don't know where people get these ideas," Sonja responded angrily. Her exasperation knew no bounds. If she'd been a teapot, her whistle would have been screeching. She resisted the urge to level Darcy with the facts. "Listen, Darcy. I told the police what I saw and heard on the morning of Diangelo's death. The other stuff you've been told is someone's overactive imagination spiked with a lot of crazy drama."

Darcy held up her hand palm out. She shook her head several times. "I knew it. I just knew it. That doggone busybody Marion is spreading a bunch of ugly rumors. And they wonder why women are called gossip machines!" Darcy's eyes danced with frustration, and her cheeks were flushed with embarrassment.

Sonja reached over and patted Darcy's hand. "I'm relying on you to straighten her out, Darcy. I know I can count on you."

Darcy brought her hand down on the counter with a bang. "You're doggone right, Sonja. I'll straighten out those tongue waggers. Just wait 'til I get a hold of Marion. She might have a hissy fit, but she's gonna get an earful."

"Atta girl," Sonja said. She turned and waved as she left the building. Driving south into the heart of La Crosse, she wondered about the information Art had shared. Who would be crazy enough to even believe some of the political rumors and half-truths she'd heard recently? They seemed outlandish—everything from the death of Hillary Clinton in Guantanamo Bay to the Democrats who controlled the weather to an AI replica who was a stand-in for Joe Biden. Really? That sounded absolutely freakish, like something out of a sci-fi movie. Then she thought of Beck Watson. Anyone willing to shoot a police officer over a verbal exchange might believe some of those rumors. She shivered, but it had nothing to do with the temperature in her car.

CHAPTER 25
Tossin' and Turnin'

Tanya Pedretti stood at the back of the classroom on the second floor of the La Crosse Police Department, where several police officers and detectives had assembled for the two o'clock update concerning the Diangelo murder and the shooting of Lt. Hank Brousard. Her officers had been out on the street, to the Watson home, and to the shooting location on Market Street, collecting evidence and talking to people. In front of the classroom, Officer Chad Hepple was calmly studying the agenda for the meeting. The room was buzzing with conversation, and Tanya had cracked open a few windows to let in some fresh air. In the front and to the left of Officer Hepple, a rolling whiteboard held photos, notes, and possible motives in the death of Diangelo. To a casual observer, the board looked like the scribblings of a young child let loose with a set of new markers, but Tanya knew better. Several officers assigned to the case had spent hours hypothesizing, synthesizing, creating mind maps of the crimes in their current state. These maps were crucial in visualizing possible motives and organizing events into a workable timeline and theory of the two crimes. She was pleased with her team's work.

"You want me to run the meeting?" Chad had asked in the hallway before they went into the classroom.

"Yes, I'm feeling a little disoriented. Frankly, this shooting has hit me hard. I don't know if I can hold it together when the conversation turns to the details of Hatchet's injuries, but I have every confidence you can manage. Your agenda is well organized; you've covered the main concerns in both cases." Tanya explained. "We'll assess the new information we get from the street and develop a plan of action. Besides, I'll be right here, and if you miss anything, I'll jump in."

Hepple continued to stare at her in disbelief.

Tanya noticed a light sheen of sweat on his forehead.

"You're going to be fine, Hepple. Just fine." She patted his shoulder. "I have every confidence in you."

Hepple stared at the floor and shook his head several times. He gazed at his boss, unsure of his abilities to run the meeting. "Okay, ma'am. I don't know what I did to deserve this, but I'll do my best," Hepple finally said.

Tanya nodded her head confidently. "I knew you'd say that. Come on. Let's get this show on the road."

Now Chad Hepple looked out at the group that had gathered in the classroom. *These are my people, my brothers and sisters in blue,* he thought. *Just act normally, and everything will be okay.*

"All right, listen up, everyone," Hepple said in a loud voice. "Let's get started." The room turned quiet, and during the silence, Chad felt a ripple of anxiety. He squared his shoulders and began to review the facts surrounding the strange death of Dr. Tony Diangelo. Occasionally, he glanced to the back of the room, where Tanya gave him a thumbs-up. When he finished, he asked, "So where are we at with the CCTV video at the Midwest building? Anybody have anything on that?" Hepple asked.

"Yes, sir," a female officer spoke up. Jenny Lasinsky was a seasoned cop and usually dealt with school and college incidents. "We were able to retrieve some video from the appliance store across the street from Midwest Medical. We can confirm from the video that Osmat Bajwa, the window washer from Windows on the World, was on the premises of the Midwest Medical building at 5:30 on Monday morning. He was there washing windows until approximately 6:08 when he lowered himself to the ground in the bucket of his truck and left the grounds."

"Good. So, we can establish his presence and testimony about what he saw on the third floor that morning as accurate, correct?" Hepple asked. "He was actually there?"

"Right. He was there, so his claims about what he saw have been recorded and verified," Jenny said. "Chief Pedretti and Hatchet conducted the interview with Osmat."

"Yes, that information has been passed along," Hepple repeated. "Now, what do we know about the arrival of Dr. Diangelo and the suspect at the building the morning of the twenty-fifth? Any CCTV video on that?"

Jenny Lasinsky continued with her report. "We have been able to verify that Dr. Diangelo entered the building at 5:26, and the suspect, who kept his head down and wore a hooded sweatshirt to cover his hair, arrived about 5:32. The suspect used an ID that the system recognized. We've questioned every worker in the building. Using the height, weight, and build of the man in question, the only employees who come close to matching that description are Sam Watson and another kid who works on the first floor, Dominic Rodriquez. Both have alibis that cannot really be verified because they say they were at home, alone, at the time of the incident. But let's remember, Beck Watson could be the man on the CCTV video since physically he is of similar height and weight. Of course, it's possible someone else borrowed or stole an employee's ID to get into the building. Since Sam Watson is an employee at Midwest Medical, his brother Beck would have had access to his brother's ID, so he is a strong suspect. However, there is no video of the suspect leaving the building. What that means is the suspect may have hidden in some container within the building. We wondered about the stocking found in the Suds and Duds laundry cart. Could someone have hidden in the cart and ridden to the laundry facility where he escaped unnoticed?"

A buzz of discussion started at Jenny's suggestion. Chad motioned to the group to quiet down again.

"Yes, that is a possibility we'll keep on the table," Chad said. "Thanks, Jenny. We'll do some more investigating along those lines, but for now, let's move on. Who interviewed the manager of Fitness Forever?"

"I did," another officer said. Gordy Smith was a large man with a receding hairline and a florid face, which was constantly flushed as if he had a sunburn. Hepple turned to him.

"Go ahead, Gordy. What did you discover?"

"The manager of Fitness Forever, someone named Mckenzie Lane, was in shock at the death of her boss. Couldn't believe she'd died of a heart attack. Said Tina and

Tony's marriage seemed stable and happy, that her boss was demanding, but that was understandable considering all the pressure she was under. Lane didn't believe anyone had it out for Tina. In fact, she said everyone adored her. She concluded that Tina must have died of natural causes, because nobody she knew would want to kill her. Several of the other employees said the same thing. Tina was well-loved and respected as an employer and businesswoman."

"The coroner told us about the heart attack, so I believe at this time we can disregard the theory that the deaths of Tony and Tina Diangelo are related. It looks like a very unusual coincidence of a husband and wife dying on the same day. Doesn't happen very often, but it does happen," Hepple said. At the back of the room, Tanya nodded in agreement and gave another thumbs-up to Hepple. He took a big breath and continued.

"Let's talk about the Watson brothers and the shooting of Hatchet," Hepple said. At the mention of the violent incident involving one of their own, the room began to buzz again with an angry tension. Hepple tensed, fearing he was losing control of the meeting. He looked back at Tanya, who gave him a gesture, her pointer finger going in a circle. He read her lips from a distance: "Move on."

Hepple raised his arms up and down, trying to tamp down the anger in the room. The officers quieted briefly, but Hepple felt like he was holding a lid on a barrel that was about to explode.

"I know this subject, especially the shooting of Hank, is a sensitive one and is on everyone's mind. I understand how you feel, but we have to think clearly and put our emotions to one side right now," Hepple said calmly. He reviewed what they knew about the Watson brothers: Beck's continuous struggle with mental illness, his chronic unemployment, and high intellectual ability. Sam Watson seemed to be the stabilizing force in his brother's life, was a good student and hard worker who had held the family together after their father had deserted them.

"We haven't completely finished going through the kid's room yet, but what have we found from the search of the Watson home so far?" Hepple asked.

Several hands went up.

"Johnson, let's start with you," Hepple said, pointing to a man dressed in jeans and a Wisconsin Badgers T-shirt.

"We found some interesting reading material in Beck's bedroom," Johnson said, glancing down at some notes in front of him on the table. In a voice devoid of emotion, he read the titles. "*Karl Marx and Capitalism, Gangsters of Capitalism, Capitalism's Toxic Assumption,* and *Capitalism Must Die.*" His eyebrows went up. "Interesting bedtime reading, huh?"

Hepple tipped his head to one side, thinking. "Those books could certainly skew your thinking against our economic system. Anyone else?"

Officer Tim Cassidy spoke up. "I spent a lot of time talking to Mrs. Watson. She's had a tough go of it with her younger son, Beck. She's very protective, allows him to come and go as he pleases, says she doesn't know what her son does all day long, but he's rarely at home except later in the evening, even though he doesn't have a job right now. His employment record is very chaotic. He gets a job but, after two or three weeks, finds some excuse to quit. This has gone on for years, apparently. She, on the other hand, works three jobs to make ends meet."

"What about the interview with Sam Watson?" Hepple asked. Tanya spoke up from the back of the room.

"Hatchet and Mike Leland conducted that interview, and I listened in," she said. She walked forward until she was standing by Hepple's side. He moved over as Tanya took her place at the podium. "Sam has frequently covered for his brother and bailed him out of jail when he got into some minor scrapes with police over the last few years. I'm not ready at this point to relegate Sam to the sidelines. I believe he may know more about Beck's involvement in the Diangelo murder than he's letting on. For one thing, Sam had access to the building via his ID badge. His brother could have used it to gain access to the building, as Jenny suggested, or Sam could have been involved and framed his brother for the incident. But considering Beck Watson is responsible for the shooting on Market Street, it's also very possible he could be the one who killed Tony Diangelo. That's still uncertain, but we'll continue to investigate. Does anyone else have any information pertaining to the Diangelo case?"

Another officer raised his hand and stood. "I managed to track down a couple of guys from the Coulee Fifty group. They told me the meetings were loose, informal, and infrequent. When I showed them photos of Sam and Beck Watson, they recognized both as having attended a couple of their meetings. Both the guys I talked to claimed that violence was not part of the group's political stance, but…" The officer shrugged. "Who knows? Someone who's unstable could interpret their goals in a different light. You can justify almost anything if you're feeling threatened, and what's threatening to one person could be totally benign to another."

Tanya listened carefully. She was encouraged that everyone was working so hard trying to uncover the motivations behind the Diangelo murder. Although what had been discovered wasn't earth-shattering information, with other evidence and eyewitness testimony, it could lead to some significant progress and possible apprehension.

"Now, when it comes to the shooting of Hatchet ..." Tanya stopped briefly, struggling to maintain her composure. Her eyes misted with tears, but she took a deep breath and continued. "We have the Market Street incident on Hatchet's body cam, so there's no question that Beck Watson was responsible."

Several hands popped into the air. Tanya patiently answered questions about Hatchet's current condition and his possible release from the hospital. More discussion followed about Beck Watson's disappearance. "Officer White, could you tell us what you found at the residence on the south side this morning?" Tanya asked.

Officer Jeremy White stood. "We received a call about a missing moped on Hagen Road. When we arrived at the residence, we found an abandoned bike leaning against the back of the garage. So sometime last evening, the bike, which we identified from Hatchet's body cam as belonging to Beck Watson, was dropped off, and the moped was taken."

"I want every cop in this city to be on the lookout for Beck Watson," Tanya responded, her voice hardening with resolve. "I've issued a BOLO for him in neighboring counties, and hopefully someone will spot him. Consider him armed and dangerous. Wear your vests. I think he's proven that he can't be trusted. Be careful and keep headquarters informed of your movements and discoveries. If you spot him, call for backup. You know the drill." Tanya stopped briefly and scanned the audience. Her face took on a hard, flint-like expression, and her eyes flashed with anger. "We're going to find this Watson guy and bring him in for questioning in the Diangelo murder case, and he'll be prosecuted for the shooting of Lt. Brousard. Mark my words. It's just a matter of time and coordination. We. Will. Get. Him."

The officers returned Tanya's stare with solemn reservation.

"That's all for now. Be careful and stay safe," Tanya finished. Everyone stood, and a loud buzz filled the room. Tanya leaned over and said to Hepple, "You did great. Thanks for helping me out."

Hepple nodded his head. "No problem, ma'am."

Sam Watson lay on his bed in his apartment on 17th Street, his arm slung over his forehead as he stared at the ceiling, trying to make a new plan. Since Beck had shot the police officer, Sam wondered what was next on his brother's agenda. His mind was spinning with the possibilities. *Where was he, and what was he doing?* Sam groaned. Beck wasn't the best at planning or thinking on the fly, especially without Sam or his mom to temper his wild ideas.

Sam brought his fist down on the mattress, sending a flurry of dust into the air. He watched the dust particles dance in the beam of sunlight coming through the bedroom window as he thought about the years gone by: his mother's constant worried expression, the inordinate amount of time she spent fussing and fuming over Beck. Then there was Beck's defiance of any kind of house rules and the continual job hunt that always ended with him either being fired or walking off the job. Sam simmered with unresolved resentment and anger. Why did his father abandon them, leaving Sam in charge at such a young age? When was it all going to end? He was so exhausted from the years of conflict and turmoil.

At the same time, he wondered what the police had learned about the Diangelo murder. A growing sense of panic filled his chest as he thought about the possible outcome of this whole situation. What would happen when they finally figured it all out? Maybe Beck was smarter than all of them. He'd had enough sense to run and hide. Somehow, that seemed like the only solution to the problem.

Tanya Pedretti stopped at the hospital to see Hatchet after work on Friday evening. He was still heavily sedated, but he opened his eyes briefly and squeezed Tanya's hand. She returned home feeling hope swell in her heart. The Pedrettis had finished their evening meal and were relaxing in the living room, the TV murmuring in the background, the Brewers and Twins slugging it out in the eighth inning.

"I quit my job."

"You did what?"

"I quit my job," Roy repeated. He slowly lowered the *La Crosse Sentinel* far enough to look into his wife's eyes.

Tanya stared at him, her mouth gaping. "Why would you do something like that?" she asked. She grabbed the remote and shut off the TV.

"I realized I'd been neglecting you, and I wanted to make amends. Start over, so to speak," Roy began to explain.

"Well, that's something, but I'm not really sure quitting your job is the means to the end," Tanya sputtered, trying to understand.

Roy laid the newspaper in his lap, folded his arms across his chest, and began his defense. "I hated working from home. And besides, I think I need a change of scenery. Maybe do something totally out of my element. What do you think?"

Tanya blinked rapidly a few times, trying to maintain her sense of fair play. *Is this what they call male menopause?* she wondered. She shook her head. "Well, you could have knocked me over with a feather. You've been a successful CPA for years, Roy. You could start your own agency if you wanted to, I guess. Is that what you're thinking?"

"Nope. Getting out of the numbers game. I'm looking at horticulture," he said confidently.

"You mean plants and landscaping? That kind of stuff?" Tanya tipped her head to one side. She looked at her husband with something bordering on bewilderment. If this was Roy's answer to their marriage difficulties, then she wished she'd kept her mouth shut.

"La Crosse Landscape Design over by Grandad Bluff needs a facilities manager," Roy explained. "The pay isn't great, but I suggested doing their books as well, which would increase my bottom line. I'd be managing the installation team and setting their schedule. When the weather's bad, I'll have time to work on the books and make sure the vehicles and equipment are in good working order—stuff like that. It's a much more hands-on job than what I've been doing. I won't be chained to a desk, and I'd be around people again. They're thinking over my offer. Five days a week, one Saturday a month, two weeks paid vacation the first five years, and a 401k retirement plan.

"So, you'd be managing people's schedules and workload and doing the business books?" Tanya asked.

"Yep. Total change of scenery. Whaddya think?"

"Well, it looks like you already made your decision, so I'm not sure what you want me to say," Tanya replied brusquely, the anger just below the surface.

"Now, honey, don't be like that," Roy admonished. "Ryan Howard from Landscape Design knows me and contacted me when they decided to reorganize the business. He thought I'd be a good fit. This wasn't just some harebrained idea that came to me out of the blue. You told me yesterday that we were in trouble. I took it seriously and respected you for telling me. I thought it over and took action. I thought you'd be happy about it."

"I'm trying to be. It's just kind of a shock. A little bit unexpected," Tanya said, softening her tone.

Roy got up from the recliner, walked over to the couch, and sat down by Tanya. He pulled her close and kissed her cheek. "Baby, what I'm trying to say is that I love you, and if you're unhappy, then I'm willing to make some changes so our relationship can stay strong. I thought that was what you wanted me to do."

Roy turned her face toward him and kissed her tenderly on the lips. Tanya continued staring. *Boy, I must really be out of touch,* she thought, *if this is his answer to our marriage issues.*

"Okay," Tanya said softly. "But could I have a few days to absorb all of this? It's just such a surprise."

"Sure, no problem." He kissed her again, briskly this time, got up, and walked to the kitchen. He called over his shoulder. "Want something to drink?"

"Yeah, a stiff brandy—a very stiff brandy," Tanya yelled. She leaned back, reviewing their conversation in her mind. *Never saw that coming,* she thought. *Have a little faith. Roy's not stupid. He's making sacrifices for the sake of our relationship. It'll be alright.*

At that moment, Leisel walked into the room and plopped down beside Tanya. "Mom, there's this boy named Craig, and I was wondering if he asks me out will you and Dad let me go on a date alone with him?"

Tanya looked at her daughter—her beautiful brown eyes, her hopeful expression, so much like her father.

"You always told me to come to you, and you'd help me understand men and what they wanted. Remember when you told me that?" Leisel said.

"I do remember." Tanya smiled at the incongruity of the moment—like she understood men—then cuddled her daughter, drawing her close. "I'm still learning, but tell me about this Craig guy," she said.

CHAPTER 26 • SONJA
I Wanna Hold Your Hand

By the time I packed my supplies from Industrial Commodities into my Subaru, it was already two o'clock. I hurried to another cleaning job on Market Street. Although, I hated driving along the street that had just been the sight of an attempted murder of a police officer. It turned my stomach that Beck Watson had so callously shot Hank Brousard in the chest without any forethought or hesitation. *Why do people do these things?* I wondered. *Desperation? Panic? Stupidity?*

I rolled to a stop by the curb in front of Mrs. Cadwallader's English Tudor bungalow. She has been my customer for about a year, and her position at Viterbo, the Catholic university in town, explained her penchant for crucifixes and religious artwork. I let myself into the side door by the garage. The home was quiet, and Mr. Bojangles, her black and white tuxedo cat, greeted me with a husky meow and a generous leg rub. I reached down and petted the feline, who purred with utter contentment, then followed me into the kitchen, meowing loudly, looking for a treat.

I began my cleaning duties and finished the home in a little over an hour. I moved on and drove south beyond the roundabout past the turnoff for U.S. Highway 14 to Old Town Hall Road, which led to the home of my next clients, the proprietors of Mt. La Crosse, the recreational ski area on the outskirts of town.

The Halstads' home was designed to resemble a Swiss chalet. It overlooked a wide valley below the ski hills peppered with homes built in the late nineties. Just beyond the ski area stood the Shrine of Our Lady of Guadalupe nestled against the steep hills. Trygve and I had spent time walking the grounds there searching for peace after the death of our children. Usually the Halstads were not at home, but occasionally they were here. Today was one of those days. As soon as I entered the home carrying my bucket of supplies, I heard cross voices engaged in some kind of argument in the living room. I walked that way and found Julie and Ralph Halstad hotly discussing the finances of the ski business in preparation for the upcoming summer slump.

They looked over at me when I walked into the room.

"Sonja! Find any more dead bodies?" Ralph teased. I resisted the urge to turn around and walk back out of the room. Instead, I smiled widely and shook my head.

"No such luck, Ralph. And how is your life these days?"

"Well, we had a good winter season with all the abundant snow," Julie said, beating Ralph to the punch, "so I guess we'll be in business for another year. We've got a lot of maintenance to do this summer to get ready for next year's season. Snowboarding is definitely the most popular winter sport, so we're busy designing a new hill with jumps and other challenges."

"That sounds interesting, but I've got to get busy. I'm seeing a new client on East Hill Road after I do your house. Her name's Mabel Kimble," I said.

"Mabel? You're going to Mabel's?" Ralph asked. His pointed finger left me feeling exposed and vulnerable.

"Yes, I am. She called earlier in the week, but somehow, I didn't get her message until this morning." I silently berated myself for being so preoccupied that I neglected to return inquiries about my cleaning services. Then I noticed the suspicious look on Ralph's face and the pointed finger still aimed in my direction. "Something wrong?" I asked innocently.

"Are you sure you want to do that?" Ralph asked.

Julie gave her husband an annoyed look. "Ralph, that's unkind."

"Well, just so you know, Mabel's considered the eccentric in the neighborhood," Ralph said haughtily. "She lives in a damn shack even though I'm sure she has a decent retirement and could afford something better than that old dilapidated farmhouse she lives in. And the road to her place is a dead end. Not exactly the most hospitable situation for a woman all alone. Make sure your cell phone is charged up," he warned.

"Oh, most of that is just neighborhood gossip," Julie said, waving her hand at Ralph. "Mabel was a teacher for years. How dangerous can she be?"

"Don't worry," I blustered confidently. "I think I can handle a retired teacher."

"Okay, but don't say I didn't warn you," Ralph said.

Julie shook her head in disgust.

Seeing an argument brewing, I quickly got to work cleaning and sprucing up the Halstad home. Two hours later, I was on the road again.

Trygve Hovland cleaned out his city truck after a day of patrolling the streets of La Crosse. He'd replaced several signs around town, smoothed an approach with gravel in a parking lot near the university, and repaired a catch basin over on Pearl Street. He hung up his shovels and rakes, cleaned the day's food refuse and garbage from the truck cab, and then walked wearily across the parking lot to his vehicle. Sonny Lewison walked quickly toward him.

"Hey, Tryg! Wait up," he said. Trygve stopped and turned around.

"How's Sonja these days?" Sonny asked as he approached Trygve.

Trygve frowned. *Why does he want to know that?* he wondered.

"She's fine. Why do you want to know?"

"Well, she's famous. After she found that dead dentist, I bet people are callin' her and lookin' her up. Askin' for her advice and stuff. Her name's all over the internet on Facebook and Snapchat. Maybe she'll get interviewed by Joe Rogan."

Trygve looked directly at his co-worker, and his hazel eyes smoldered with resentment. He took in Sonny's frizzy hair, yellow teeth, shit-eatin' grin, and torn T-shirt.

Sonny finally backed away when he noticed Trygve's stoney-faced expression and tight-lipped silence. *What was it about Trygve?* he thought. There was something vaguely threatening about Trygve sometimes. Generally, most of the guys at the street department steered clear of him, avoiding any serious arguments. Was it his muscular physique coupled with his quiet, serious demeanor that kept everyone at arm's length? Of course, there was always someone who dared to get closer to the fire than he should—like Sonny. He lacked the prudence to avoid a confrontation with the big Norwegian. As Sonny stood there, the lyrics of a song popped into his mind. The song was "Big Bad John" by Jimmy Dean. The words ran through his head ... *And everybody knew you didn't give no lip to Big John.*

"Look, if it's all the same to you, I'd rather not discuss my wife's activities with you," Trygve said, his face flushed with aggravation. "It's none of your business."

Sonny's eyes widened at the hostility in Trygve's voice, and he held up one hand. "Okay, Tryg. I got the message."

"Good, I'm glad you did, and if you missed anything, you can just check on Sonjahovlandinvestigations.com. I update her website every hour," he said sarcastically. Trygve turned abruptly and trudged to his truck, then leaned out the window. "I'll see you Monday," he said. As he drove out of the parking lot, he glanced in his rearview mirror. Sonny had a puzzled expression on his face while his thumbs madly texted something on his phone. *More BS being posted on social media,* Trygve thought sourly. He shook his head and traveled toward home through the countryside of Barre Mills.

On the drive, Trygve considered the gossip swirling around town about Sonja's involvement in Dr. Diangelo's murder investigation. He wished for once she would just do her cleaning jobs and come home without all the innuendos and gossip trailing behind her like a dark shadow. He had to admit, though, that the investigation was a change of pace from the other problems they'd faced in their marriage—the death of their three babies and the passing of Sonja's parents.

Despite his warnings to the contrary, Sonja seemed to be energized by the Diangelo investigation. She'd taken on the challenge of seeing this thing through to the end, although he wasn't really surprised. Sonja had always been headstrong, and honestly, that was one of the things he'd found attractive about her. She was willing to tackle anything from the first moment he met her. She'd proven her mettle early in their marriage when they bought their tiny run-down farm in Barre Mills, fixing and remodeling every building until it was just right. She knew how to operate woodworking tools and was not intimidated by hard work, dirt, and sweat.

He remembered the day that stupid drunk had driven his car through the living room wall of a home on French Island where Sonja had been cleaning. When he'd gone into the house to check on the occupants, there she stood, impertinent and bold as brass. In charge. And he'd fallen in love with her right then and there. He smiled now when he thought about that moment. He knew as long as he was married to Sonja, life would never be boring. But in the last few days since this whole ruckus had started, he also knew life would never be the same again. *Is that a good thing?* he wondered. *We can't say our life is boring, but am I willing to exchange what we had for this?* Somehow, the thought gave Trygve little consolation, and his mood remained dark and sullen.

CHAPTER 27 • SONJA

Like a Bridge Over Troubled Water

After I finished my cleaning job at Halstads, I stopped at a small drive-up coffee kiosk on Highway 35 and ordered an Americano with hazelnut syrup and a generous portion of whipped cream. I was going to need some quick energy to finish my last stop of the day at Mabel Kimble's. I headed to the southern outskirts of La Crosse looking for East Hill Road. After a series of wrong turns and backtracking, the road sign came into view. Next to it was another sign that said DEAD END. I recalled Ralph Halstad's warning about Mabel Kimble and felt a twinge of uneasiness, but I headed down the road toward her house anyway, trying to shake off my misgivings.

The blacktop highway narrowed to a gravel lane bordered on one side by a thick hedge of small pine trees. As I negotiated the lane that led to Mabel's residence, I thought back to the words I'd spoken earlier in the day to my librarian friend, Collette: "I need to see this investigation through to the end." The trouble with rash statements of bravado spoken without any real forethought is it sets you up for disappointment. Nothing about the Diangelo murder was any clearer to me now than when I'd first gotten tangled up in it on Monday morning. A whole week had gone by, and to my untrained eye, it seemed the solution to the murder was at a standstill. I sighed loudly and parked the Subaru at the end of the driveway. All I wanted to do right now was meet this Kimble lady and then go home to Trygve and my peaceful little farm.

I sat in my car for a long time taking in the decrepit appearance of the residence. I've seen some very chaotic, dirty homes in my career as a professional housecleaner, but nothing prepared me for Mabel Kimble's disastrous abode. If this was what the *outside* of the home looked like, I couldn't imagine what was inside. I grabbed my phone and looked up the address again wondering if I'd made a wrong turn. Was this the property mentioned in the message Mabel had left me. Did I miss the house on the way in? Was this where I was supposed to be? *There must be a mistake*, I thought, but after checking the address again against the house numbers near the front entrance I realized that this was Mabel's place.

I swept my eyes over the property through the windshield, studying the layout carefully. A tumbled-down barn lay rotting in a heap toward the back of the property. At one point in its history, I'm sure it was a beautiful structure that housed cattle and hay. Now it had collapsed into a jumble of boards, bricks, and rotten shingles. The house was still standing, but it looked like something out of *The Addams Family* TV series. Gray weathered siding, a sagging front door, and rickety front steps made me reconsider this endeavor. The house was dark and seemed to be unoccupied. A garden plot of tumbled weeds and dead plants lay near the back side of the house, and a burn barrel next to a barbed wire fence was smoldering with gray smoke, filling the air with an acrid smell. Everything about this situation was disturbing. The house appeared to be disintegrating before my very eyes. When I went inside, would I fall through the floor to the basement? If conditions inside were like the ones on the outside, then I wondered if the more expedient solution might be to burn the place down. All I needed was a gallon of gasoline and a match. I shook my head and reminded myself I was not an aspiring arsonist.

Finally, after several moments of trepidation, the better angels of my nature won out. It really was a lovely spring evening; the sun was sinking in the west, and the steep hills surrounding the farm were burgeoning with spring greenery. I stepped from my Subaru and tramped through the tall grass to the front door. The steps creaked ominously beneath my feet. I knocked and was surprised when a petite elderly woman opened the door after a few moments. She stood there with an expression of genuine surprise. Apparently, she did not get very many visitors. Raising her eyebrows, she examined me with skepticism.

"Hello," I said in a friendly tone. "I'm here to talk to Mabel about some cleaning."

"Cleaning? You must have the wrong address," the woman snapped, tipping her head to one side. Her floral housedress had a yellow stain on the front that looked like egg yolk, and her fluffy blue slippers were dirty and ragged. Her snow-white hair was disheveled, her face a map of wrinkled skin.

"Are you Mabel Kimble?" I asked.

"Yes, I am. Who are you?" she demanded rudely.

I hurriedly tried to explain. "I'm Sonja Hovland from Dirty Business Cleaning. You called my agency at the beginning of the week, but I've been busy. I apologize. Your message got lost in the shuffle somehow."

Mabel waved her hand in front of me. "No, no, you're mistaken. Someone from your agency has already been here and did some of the work I requested, which brings me to my next question. Is this the way you normally operate your business?"

I could see by the cantankerous attitude of the old woman I would get nowhere with flimsy excuses. "I apologize," I started again, but Mabel rushed on.

"Well, I certainly deserve an apology, thank you very much. Without Deck, your helper, my jobs would still be undone." Mabel's eyes flashed with impatience. "I assume this is not your normal response to inquiries. If it is, your business will crash and burn. It'll never get off the ground." She clamped her mouth shut and planted her feet obstinately in the doorway, blocking my view of the interior of the house.

"I can assure you I answer my business calls in a timely manner," I began to explain. By now I was getting a little hot under the collar, and I could feel my cheeks flushing with embarrassment. "I'm confused about something you said. I don't have any employees. I run Dirty Business Cleaning Services by myself, so who is this Deck person you're talking about?"

It took a few moments for Mabel to internalize my question. She squinted and asked me to repeat the question. I did, and during that time her expression changed from one of confrontation to utter confusion. The information I gave bewildered her. She stood silently in front of me and stared at me for a very long time. Finally, she said, "Well, if you don't have any employees, then who is Deck?"

I shrugged my shoulders. "I don't know any guy named Deck. I apologize for the mix-up, but I'm here now, so why don't we go inside and discuss your cleaning needs?"

"Well, I suppose it wouldn't hurt," Mabel said, turning into the dark hallway behind her.

She beckoned me with a gesture. I followed her wondering what I was getting into. The smell was the first thing that assaulted my senses. The strong odor of cat feces and urine and the dark, despondent atmosphere made my nerves tingle. My skin prickled as I imagined hordes of fleas and ticks crawling from the woodwork to bite my skin. I followed Mabel into the living room, where a small lamp provided some much-needed light. A young man who'd been sitting on the couch suddenly sprang to his feet and stood in front of me. I looked at him, and he looked at me.

"This is Deck," Mabel said confidently, pointing to the young man. "He's not a figment of my imagination, as you can see." She crossed her arms over her scrawny chest and waited for my reaction.

I tentatively held out my hand. The young man gave me a weak handshake while he studied my face. I met his gaze, but my heart thumped wildly, and my mouth went dry. Standing in front of me was Beck Watson, the man who'd shot Lt. Hank Brousard.

"Hello. It's nice to meet you," I said carefully, concealing my shock behind a friendly smile. "Thank you for helping Mabel."

Officer Mike Leland stared at the boxes the crime scene investigators had dropped off on his desk Friday afternoon. The La Crosse police force, under the leadership of Tanya Pedretti and Chad Hepple, were steadily gathering evidence about the shooting of Lt. Hank Brousard and the ongoing mysterious death of Tony Diangelo. Now the evidence was piled on Mike's desk.

Officer Leland was feeling jumpy and agitated since he'd returned to police headquarters after the shooting incident. Despite his long conversation on the phone with Lt. Jim Higgins in which he bared his true feelings about Hatchet's incident, he was still disoriented, and he had an intensely painful headache. The last person who'd entered Mike's workspace had backed away, apologizing profusely for startling him while he was concentrating on his task. At home his girlfriend, Lindsey, had been hovering over him, watching every move, constantly asking him how he was feeling. He was sick of it, but with each passing day, he realized his PTSD response to the shooting on Market Street would take longer to recover from than he'd anticipated.

Since Mike had been taken off active duty, it was his job to sift through the boxes of materials taken from Beck Watson's bedroom on Thursday afternoon and record the contents. Mike took two Tylenol, tamped down his frustrations, and continued taking items out of the first box. Besides the books they'd found in the bedroom on the evils of capitalism in a free society, a couple of officers were convinced other important clues were hidden somewhere in the boxes of jumbled materials—evidence that would solidify Beck Watson's attempted murder of a La Crosse police officer but also materials that would prove he'd been involved in Tony Diangelo's death as well.

Mike eyed the cardboard boxes and sighed. *Might as well get started,* he thought. He leafed through a bunch of receipts from Walmart. After studying them, he continued sorting through other random items in the box, which included a comb, a book of matches from a tavern on Gillette Street, several paperclips, pencils, and binder clips, a couple of college notebooks, three paperback novels, an American Legion button, and a condom. Mike listed the items on the correct form, then looked in the box again. A piece of yellow legal notebook paper lay crumpled at the bottom of the box. Mike reached in and grabbed it, then unfolded it. It appeared to be a list of proprietors and their businesses. He read the names on the list with growing alarm. Tony Diangelo—Midwest Dental Services, Timothy Mercer—Allied Gasoline Company, Kevin Gottleib—Strobe Brewing, Steve Deerfield—Midwest Aggregate. The list went on and included about ten names of prominent businesses, some Mike recognized and some unfamiliar to him. He noticed Tony's name at the top of the list. Most of the cops Mike had talked to believed Diangelo had probably been murdered. Mike recalled the odd note found in Tony's suit pocket: "Death to the Capitalists." Here was a list of capitalists doing business within the city of La Crosse, but why did Beck Watson have such a list? Was this further proof that he'd been involved somehow in Tony Diangelo's strange demise? Then another chilling thought came to him. Was this some hit list Beck had composed?

Mike stood up beside his desk to stretch his legs. He was

deep in thought about the list dangling from his hand when he heard his name from across the room.

"Mike? Are you okay?" Chad Hepple asked.

He'd been watching him and now Hepple walked over to the desk. "What's up? What did you find?" he asked.

Mike remained silent but laid the crumpled yellow piece of notepaper on his desk and flattened it with one hand. "Take a look at this and tell me what you think."

Chad leaned over the desk and silently studied the list. He turned to Mike and said, "What do I think?"

"Yeah. Do you think this list is important?"

"It could be, but just remember that Beck Watson has some mental health challenges. We know that from the way he reacted to Hatchet and from what his family told us. This list could be the ramblings of a seriously ill person whose mind went on some kind of weird tangent, or—"

"It could be an actual hit list that Beck is planning to carry out," Mike said.

"And how do we know which one it is—"

"Or is it just a dumb list that has nothing to do with the Hatchet's shooting or Diangelo's murder?" Mike said.

Chad paused a moment. "You do realize we're completing each other's sentences, don't you?" he said.

"Great minds connect on a higher level," Mike said, smiling. "Seems like a good sign to me."

"Right," Chad said, grinning. "But, seriously, the chief needs to see this." His grin disappeared.

"Agreed. Let's go," Mike said.

Mike and Chad walked down the hall to Tanya Pedretti's office. She was sitting at her desk, the phone pressed to her ear. Despite the lateness of the day, she looked fresh and alert. When the two men walked in, she acknowledged their presence and held up her hand in a "wait" gesture. She continued her conversation, and when she hung up five minutes later, she looked at the two cops and asked, "What's up? Find something?"

"Yeah, Mike found this list in the bottom of one of the boxes from Beck Watson's bedroom," Chad explained as he laid the note on her desk. Tanya studied it briefly.

"I don't like the looks of this. You think this list has something to do with Diangelo's death?" Tanya asked.

The two men nodded.

"Explain," she said tersely.

"A couple of things come to mind," Mike began. "We know Beck Watson had several books on the negative effects of capitalism which ties in and supports the troubling note found in Diangelo's suit pocket. This note," he said, pointing to the piece of paper lying on the desk, "seems to suggest he formulated a list of capitalists within the city of La Crosse. What he intends to do about it is still up for grabs. Maybe Watson is planning more havoc within the city, possibly with these individuals in mind."

Tanya looked doubtful. She cocked her head and studied the ceiling tiles for a moment while she thought about the list. When she looked back at Mike, he noticed the skepticism written on her face.

"You mean you think this is a hit list? These might be people he's decided to get rid of because of their capitalist success?" Tanya asked.

"Exactly," Mike continued. "If I was on this list, I'd be worried, but it's just a theory at this point, ma'am. It could also be the ramblings of a seriously unhinged person who might be harmless, but that's a calculated risk in itself. It's interesting that Diangelo is dead, and his name appears at the top of the list. I doubt it's coincidental."

Tanya listened carefully as Mike theorized.

"We've got to start somewhere," he finished, shrugging his shoulders.

The police chief sat at her desk thinking for a few moments. "Well, the first thing we've got to do is find Watson. We're working on that, but it doesn't seem to be going anywhere. For argument's sake, let's run with your theory since we haven't got anything else to go on right now. If this is a hit list, we would be remiss if we didn't inform the people on the list they may be in danger. And the public and media fallout if we ignore the list—and another person is eliminated—would be catastrophic. So, it seems to me, the least we should do is contact each of the people listed so they're aware of the situation." She looked at Chad. "You take care of that, Chad. Keep it serious but lowkey. Emphasize the confidentiality aspect and tell them to stay safe and take extra precautions. They should call immediately if anything at their home or business environment seems out of the ordinary."

"Yes, ma'am. I will," Chad said. "I'll get on it right now." He picked up the note, and the two men exited the office.

"Well, we told her," Mike said sullenly. "She didn't seem too impressed."

"Don't worry about it. I think it was a good call. I'll make the phone calls to the people on the list," Chad said. "You keep looking through those boxes. There might be something else in there that could help us locate Beck Watson. He seems to have disappeared from the face of the earth on a damn bike. How is that possible?"

"I don't know," Mike said, "but I'm hoping something will happen that will break this case open."

CHAPTER 28
Stayin' Alive

The sun sank slowly toward the horizon on East Hill Road Friday evening. Mabel Kimble's run-down farmhouse remained dark and silent. Beck Watson was gone, and as Sonja reviewed the last hour, a sense of regret and frustration flooded over her.

When Sonja had arrived at Mabel's, and the introductions were made, things went downhill rapidly. Beck Watson made threats and demands which Sonja valiantly tried to rebuff, all to no avail. After several intense moments of negotiation over the fate of the two women, Beck decided to take them to the dank basement of the farmhouse. When he ordered them to turn around so he could tie them up, Sonja tried to grab the rope from Beck, but in the tussle that followed, he proved to be too strong and quick for her. He tackled her onto the basement floor, and she hit her head hard on the cement. He slapped her several times across the face, then roughly turned her over and tied her securely. Mabel was no problem; she proved to be too old and weak to resist. He finished tying them up with a long cord of plastic clothesline, pushed them against the cold stone wall of the basement, and shut off the lights as he ascended the stairs.

"You won't get away with this!" Sonja yelled angrily as Beck retreated.

"Watch me!" Beck shouted back at her as he slammed the basement door. Sonja's hope of reprieve melted away when she heard Beck start her car and leave the farm. Her phone was in the vehicle; now they had no way of calling for help. Then another thought occurred to her—a handgun was in the glove box of her car. The two women were hidden away at a place that, for all practical purposes, looked abandoned, imprisoned in the basement without options, while Beck Watson roamed the countryside empowered by a car, a cell phone, and a gun.

"Well, I guess there's a first time for everything," Mabel commented quietly in the dark, breaking the silence that followed Beck's departure.

Sonja leaned toward her until their shoulders touched. "I'm sorry," Sonja began. "I should have fought harder." Tears of disappointment rolled down her cheeks. Moments later she asked Mabel, "Are you cold?"

"Not too bad, but the longer we sit here, the chillier it will get." Mabel was silent for several moments, then she spoke again. "Sonja, I want you to listen to me. I was a teacher for over thirty years, and in my career, I've dealt with some pretty tough kids. There's something wrong with this Beck kid. He has some problems, especially with people in authority. He's going to be punished, don't you worry. He can't run around doing stuff like this and get away with it. You wait and see; he'll be caught. I know I'm right. I can feel it in my bones."

Sonja appreciated Mabel's confidence about the scales of justice, but at the same time she wondered how many criminals were wandering around free after they'd committed serious crimes. She knew not everyone was apprehended. Hunting down perpetrators took time, effort, money, and manpower.

Sonja took stock of the situation they were in. It wasn't that she'd been seriously hurt, but her pride had taken a blow. Her bravado and spunk had disappeared. When she thought about how easily Beck had overwhelmed her, she was embarrassed and vowed to improve her skills in self-defense when this was all over. Maybe take a few classes in self-defense or karate at the Y. She felt a surge of anger at the casual violence Beck had used on her. Her cheeks burned where he had slapped her several times, and more tears came. Thinking about Lt. Brousard languishing in the hospital with life-threatening injuries from the shooting, her temper bristled. *Someone is going to catch you, Beck Watson, and you'll get a well-deserved dose of justice,* she thought. However, Sonja knew vengeance was a slow-cooked meal best served by someone wiser and smarter than her.

"You can't beat yourself up over this," Mabel said as if reading Sonja's mind. "Just let it go."

Sonja remained quiet for several moments.

"Well, when I don't show up at home tonight," Sonja said, leaning against Mabel, "my husband Trygve will be all over this, I can tell you that," she said. Her voice had regained some of its strength, and her tenacity and confidence were returning slowly. She took a deep breath. "Believe me, when Trygve finds us, he'll be hoppin' flyin' mad. And a mad

Norwegian is not something to take lightly. Beck is going to get his comeuppance; I can tell you that."

"Your husband's Norwegian, huh?" Mabel retorted. "My husband, Lars, had some Norwegian blood, too, and I remember how mad he got when I told him about some of the shenanigans my students tried to pull on me. He called the offenders little *drittsekks*."

"Which means what?"

"Shitass in English," Mabel said. She chuckled softly.

Sonja smiled in the dark, amused by the language lesson. Trygve did not swear in Norwegian, although she was sure he knew some choice words since his parents were both fluent in the language. She could see his rugged profile in her mind and imagined him hunched over his phone dialing her repeatedly. *When I don't answer, he'll figure it out,* she thought, *and he'll call Tanya. That'll get things moving.*

Sonja's stomach growled with hunger. "I wish we had something to eat," she said.

"A good cup of coffee and a sandwich would go a long way to help us feel better, wouldn't it?" Mabel asked.

"True," Sonja replied, "but the chances of that happening are pretty slim."

They fell into silence. Sonja tried to work the rope loose that was digging into her wrists and ankles, but it seemed impossible to disentangle them. Finally, exhausted from the ordeal, both women leaned against each other in the cool darkness of the basement and fell asleep.

Beck Watson breathed deeply as he sped down the Great River Road to his destination. On his right, the Mississippi

River reflected a riot of pink and red hues as the setting sun slipped behind the bluffs. A flock of geese rose gracefully into the air, flying south, their silhouettes framed in the glow of the sky. Driving Sonja's car filled Beck with a sense of freedom and power. Nobody could touch him now. He had a car, a phone, and a plan. *Just watch me,* he thought. *I know what I'm doing, and it's for the good of everyone, even if they don't know it yet. I'm going to be a hero.*

Beck leaned back in his seat, enjoying the hum of the engine and the fresh, clean scent of the spring air. After being cooped up in Mabel's house yesterday, he was glad to leave the ramshackle joint behind. Mabel had been good to him, but her house was a dump. The only solution to that mess was a match. He grinned to himself. When he finished at Mercer's, maybe he'd go back to the farm and take care of those two nosy women. A little gas, a match, and whoosh! It would all disappear.

He remembered the spark of anger in Sonja's eyes when they'd argued and the satisfaction he'd felt when he overpowered her and tied her up. *That'll show her. Her spunk got her nowhere. She needed an attitude adjustment, and I'm the one who gave it to her.* Towering over the two women in a raw show of force had satisfied him in a way he couldn't explain. The brute force he'd used when he shoved Sonja to the floor was intoxicating. The way she had gone limp in submission when she realized he was stronger than her gave Beck confidence. As he drove through the darkness to his destination, he mulled over his actions with the two women and then decided he wasn't going to waste any time rehashing his feelings like Dr. Connie had suggested he do during their last counseling session. *Who cares about two stupid women?* he thought bitterly. *They deserved what they got. Forget 'em and move on.*

As he hurtled down the road, he glanced at the speedometer—ninety miles an hour! *Whoa! I better slow down. Don't want to get in a row with a cop now. That would ruin everything.* He briefly took his foot off the gas, then cruised down the road at a comfortable—and legal—speed. Finally, just outside Genoa, he saw Malin Road. He put on his signal and turned. Traveling a few miles farther, he came to River View Lane. He smiled again. *I've got a plan,* he told himself. *Nobody can stop me now.*

Trygve Hovland banged the feed pail against the fence in the descending dusk. In another hour it would be dark. He wondered where Sonja was. After the latest flurry of detective work had come to a dead end, Trygve got nervous thinking about what his wife might be doing. Just four days ago someone had tried to run them over on their evening walk. Now she was late—again. *Why hasn't she called?* he wondered. *Was she in another mess of trouble?*

He absentmindedly stroked Sonny's long, shaggy ears as the donkey munched on his feed. A few minutes later, Cher joined him at the fence. Trygve dug an apple from his pocket, cut it in half, and offered it to the mules. Then he walked to the chicken coop and sprinkled feed and lettuce scraps in the trough and filled the hens' water container. When he finished, he walked slowly to the house, stepped up on the deck, and entered the kitchen through the sliding glass door. He picked up his cell from the counter and checked his messages. Nothing. He grumbled under his breath in frustration as he sent another text to Sonja, hoping she would respond. He couldn't understand where she was. It was after seven o'clock.

Trygve walked to the oven and turned it off. He removed the chicken and vegetables and set the pan on the island counter. Then he walked to the spare bedroom, sat down at the computer, and looked up Mabel Kimble's address. He knew his search for Sonja would offend her sense of independence and autonomy, but, from his perspective, he had no other options. His wife was missing, and he was going to find her somehow. A chill of apprehension prickled his arms. He sat at the computer thinking about all the things that had taken place during the week— the murder of Tony Diangelo, the close call with the driver who tried to run them over Monday evening, the shooting of Lt. Hank Brousard, and the flight of Beck Watson who was still on the loose somewhere. All of it was very disturbing.

He decided to call Police Chief Tanya Pedretti at home. Maybe she had talked to Sonja in the last few hours.

"This is the Pedrettis," a deep male voice said.

"Hello. Trygve Hovland here. I was wondering if I could speak to Chief Pedretti for a moment?"

"Sure. Just wait a minute. I'll get her," Roy said.

"This is Chief Pedretti. How can I help you?"

"Trygve Hovland, here. I'm looking for Sonja. Have you talked to her or seen her in the last few hours?"

"No, I haven't talked to her. She's not home yet?" Tanya asked, feeling a prickle of apprehension.

"Nope. She was going to stop at a new client's house on the way home, but she's still not here. I expected her by five," Trygve explained, glancing at the clock. "It's 7:45 now. Something must be wrong."

"How can I help?" Tanya asked.

Trygve ran his hand through his hair and sighed deeply. "I'm not sure yet, but I'm heading out to 534 East Hill Road, where this client lives, to see if she stopped there. If she's not there, I'll call you back," Trygve said.

"Sounds good. Keep me in the loop." Tanya hung up, but she was worried. Sonja had a lot of contacts around town. Was she snooping around trying to get information about the Diangelo murder, and she'd run into trouble? Where was Beck Watson? Although it seemed inconceivable at the moment, Tanya wondered if Sonja had hunted down the fugitive and caught up with him. Thinking about the possible consequences of a confrontation with a mentally deranged man who had a hit list of successful entrepreneurs in the La Crosse area did not reassure her. After all, Sonja was an amateur; she lacked experience with hard-core criminals. Tanya stood in the living room, a frown creasing her forehead, the phone clutched in her hand.

"Everything okay?" Roy asked from across the room.

"I'm not sure yet. There might be trouble brewing."

"What kind of trouble?" Roy asked.

"Sonja Hovland trouble."

"From what you've told me about her, she could be in over her head."

"Yeah, somebody's in over their head. I'm just not sure who," Tanya said softly.

CHAPTER 29
Give Me Just a Little More Time

Trygve Hovland pressed his foot on the gas pedal and accelerated down the curving country road on his way to East Hill Road. His GPS in the pickup droned on until, in disgust, he disabled it. He didn't need some discombobulated voice telling him how to find Mabel Kimble's farm. He knew most of the roads around La Crosse like the back of his hand. He could find the Kimble place without the help of MapQuest.

The sun had set, but the horizon was still luminous with reflected light. Overhead, the sky had turned a deep shade of purple, and stars were beginning to twinkle in the night sky. The trees on the rolling hillsides along the road had turned to dark smudges, and a rising moon hung low in the sky. On any other night, he and Sonja would be out for their evening walk, enjoying the moonlight and the company of each other. *Not tonight*, he thought sullenly. *Instead, I'm on some wild goose chase.* Trygve noticed a fire number along the road and wondered if he'd missed the turnoff. He grabbed the address he'd scribbled on a Post-it note, looked at it, then slammed on the brakes. He'd driven past the driveway. He rammed the truck in reverse, backed up a hundred feet, and turned onto East Hill Road until it narrowed to a one-lane driveway. A barn owl suddenly swooped low in the path of his headlights. Trygve braked and swerved to miss it, cursing loudly at the disruption of his mission.

"I hope this is the place," he muttered. He drove to the end of the road and came to an open area where a collapsed barn and a weathered, ramshackle house sat in the gathering darkness. Trygve groaned in frustration. "Looks like Spooksville," he grumbled. Grabbing the piece of paper again, he glanced at the address. *This is the place,* he thought, *but there couldn't be anybody living in a house in such a run-down condition.*

Trygve sat in the truck, dejected yet determined to find Sonja. He leaned his arms on the steering wheel and thought hard, wondering what had happened to prevent his wife from calling home. *Where was she?* Obviously, she wasn't here at Mabel's farm. There was no sign of her vehicle. Trygve reached for the key in the ignition but stopped when he noticed a wadded tissue lying in the driveway just beyond the truck's headlights. He felt a chill race up his arms. *What was that doing here?*

He opened the door of the pickup and stepped out onto the gravel driveway. The truck's headlights lit a path leading to the rickety house. Standing in the glow of the headlights near the wadded tissue, he could see someone had recently trampled down the grass. Then he noticed the fresh tire tracks in the gravel where he'd parked the truck. *Someone* had been here recently—probably this evening.

He returned to the truck and took a flashlight out of the glove compartment, then flicked on the switch and began making his way toward the house. Somewhere close by an owl hooted. Shivers raced up and down his arms. When a cat meowed close to his feet, he jumped sideways, then continued toward the house.

Stumbling through the high grass that surrounded the dwelling, he arrived at the front door and climbed the wobbly steps, then hesitated, feeling foolish knocking on the door of a home that was obviously unoccupied. *There's no one here,* he thought, but he decided knocking would be the polite thing to do even if no one was home. He timidly tapped on the door and waited. When no one answered, he got angry and pounded his fist hard against the door several times, venting his frustration. Finally, he stopped and listened. It was quiet for a moment but then he thought he heard voices. *My imagination has run amok.* He tried the door handle, which turned easily. He went inside and groped along the wall of the entryway. The cat smell threatened to overwhelm him. He covered his nose with his hand and searched the wall until he found a light switch. He was not surprised by the chaotic disaster that appeared when he flicked on the light.

"Sonja? Are you here?" he yelled loudly. He listened carefully, and this time he heard a distinct response. Someone was yelling inside the house although the sound was muffled.

"Sonja? Where are you?" he yelled again. He walked into the living room, then stopped and listened again. The voices were coming from beneath him. The old house must have a basement. He went back into the kitchen then noticed a door in the far corner opposite the entrance door. He flung the door open and hollered again.

"Sonja?"

"We're down here, Tryg," Sonja yelled back.

Trygve turned on the light, maneuvered down a steep set of wooden stairs, and found Sonja and Mabel sitting against the stone wall, looking tired and bedraggled, their hands and feet bound tightly with clothesline rope. He rushed over to the women and knelt in front of them. Sonja's face was red and swollen, but the older lady next to her looked fine.

"How long have you been down here?" Trygve asked.

"Too damn long, that's for sure," Mabel snarled.

"I stopped here about four o'clock," Sonja began explaining, but Mabel interrupted.

"You need to untie us, and then we'll explain," Mabel ordered. "There's a wire snips up in the kitchen in a drawer next to the sink. That should cut through this clothesline."

Trygve nodded. "Right. I'll get it." He climbed the stairs, found the snippers, and returned to the basement, cutting the restraints from the women's hands and feet. Then he helped Sonja and Mabel back up the stairs and outside while the women chattered about the events that had overtaken them late in the afternoon.

Sonja bent backward, looked at the night sky, and breathed deeply of the cool air. After a few moments, she walked over to Trygve and hugged him around the waist. "I tried to loosen the rope, but I couldn't do it. When did you figure out where I was?" she asked.

"Since your message said you were going to Mabel's before you headed home at six, I took a wild guess that you might be here," Trygve said, wrapping his arms around

Sonja. His eyes, normally kind, were blazing with some kind of resentment. "Did the jerk hurt you?" he asked, running his thumb along Sonja's red cheek.

"Not really. I'm fine, Tryg," Sonja responded.

"Hey, you two love birds, what about Sonja's car?" Mabel asked as she sat on the front steps, frowning.

"Yeah, Tryg, what about my car? And my cell phone? And my gun?" Sonja asked.

"Just a minute. Before we do anything else, I want to make sure I have this whole affair straight," Trygve said.

Sonja nodded.

"So, according to your story, this Beck character came here after he shot Lt. Brousard and hid out in the garage until he met Mabel." Trygve pivoted toward Mabel sitting on the stairs leading to the front door. Pointing to her, he said, "You thought he was someone from Sonja's cleaning service, and you invited him in to do some jobs for you. Is that right?"

"That's right," Mabel said, nodding her head energetically, "but obviously I was wrong about his intentions."

Trygve switched his gaze to Sonja. "Then today, after you finished your cleaning jobs, you stopped in unannounced to talk to Mabel, but Beck was still here hiding out, so to speak," Trygve said.

"Right—hiding in plain sight," Sonja answered. "As soon as we were introduced, Beck started asking questions."

"Like what?" Trygve asked, trying to understand the whole convoluted affair.

"Had I heard about the policeman who was shot in La Crosse? Who do the cops think did it? What was I doing here? He wanted to know what my plans were," Sonja explained.

"And you said?" Trygve had crossed his arms over his chest and listened carefully. He could tell by the look on Sonja's expression that she was about to give him the lowdown.

"Well, Tryg, you know me and my big mouth," Sonja started.

Trygve let out a groan and swiped his big hand across his face, wondering what his wife would say, although he had a pretty good idea already.

"I told him I knew who he was, that I believed he had shot Hank Brousard for no justifiable reason, and that he should turn himself in because he was also the primary suspect in the death of Dr. Tony Diangelo. Furthermore, I told him the police would eventually catch up to him, and he'd pay for what he did." Trygve groaned loudly. "You know me, Tryg. I told him the no-bullshit truth as I understood it," Sonja finished resolutely. Sonja crossed her arms over her chest, cocked her hip, and watched Trygve's reaction.

"And the guy went apeshit?" Trygve asked, raising his bushy eyebrows.

"Not really, but I could sense a change in his demeanor," Sonja said diplomatically.

"I can believe that," Trygve muttered under his breath.

Mabel joined the conversation. "In reality, he got pretty ticked off. That's when everything went up in smoke."

"And that's when he took you to the basement and tied you up?" Trygve asked.

"Yep, but I want you to know I fought him, Tryg." Tears flooded her eyes. "He pushed me down on the floor, but I fought back. He slapped me a couple of times, but then he overpowered me." Sonja's voice wobbled as she retold the incident, but inside, she was furious at the way she'd been manhandled.

Trygve put his arm around her and pulled her close. "It sounds like you're lucky he didn't do more."

"Okay, okay, so the guy is a little unhinged. What's new?" Mabel said impatiently. "There's whackadoodles running around all over the place nowadays. We need to get this show on the road. What are we gonna do about all this?" When Sonja and Trygve continued to stare at her and remained silent, Mabel continued. "I've been hog-tied and insulted, and the guy who did it just disappeared down the road." Mabel pointed a gnarly finger in the direction of the main highway. "He's not going to get away with this if I have anything to say about it!"

"Ladies, before we jump from the kettle into the fire, I think we need to call in the reinforcements," Trygve said as he pulled his cell out of his pocket.

"The reinforcements?" Sonja asked.

"Yeah, as in your friend, Police Chief Tanya Pedretti," he replied, "and the La Crosse Police Department."

"Sounds like a plan," Mabel said, smiling for the first time that evening.

CHAPTER 30
Knock Three Times

Tanya Pedretti, Jenny Lasinsky, and Lt. Chad Hepple sat in a squad car at the bottom of River View Lane. Tanya leaned over the steering wheel and looked up at the bluff above. At the top of the craggy precipice, lights from Tim Mercer's mansion glowed steadily in the dark. Tanya wondered whether Beck Watson had gotten into the executive's residence yet.

After a harried conversation with Trygve and Sonja Hovland in which she learned of Beck Watson's presence at Mabel Kimble's, she'd made an educated guess and driven down the Great River Road with a couple of squad cars to Tim Mercer's residence. Beck was obviously desperate, and his thought processes were muddled and confused. That was a bad combination in anyone's book. Coupled with the fact that he had shot a policeman at point-blank range, Tanya could not afford to take any chances the young man might escape again. Of course, there was always the possibility that Beck had never come this way and was now driving frantically out of state in a stolen car. Tanya sighed loudly, her frustration evident to her cohorts in the back seat.

"Whadda ya think, Chief?" Officer Jenny Lasinsky asked quietly from the back seat.

"I think we're going to be engaged in a hostage situation or something very similar. This Beck guy will probably not be willing to negotiate, so it could get ugly."

"What about Mercer's family? His wife and kids? Do we know whether they're at home?" Chad asked.

"Right now, we don't know, but I would assume they're in the home somewhere. After all, it's well into the evening. I doubt they would be anywhere but here, which adds to the complexity of the situation," Tanya said. Earlier, she'd sent three officers up the driveway on a covert mission to the sprawling mansion to see if Beck Watson had arrived at Tim Mercer's home. Once they reported back, they'd make a plan, one in which she hoped no one would get hurt.

Tanya looked in the rearview mirror and noticed a set of headlights bouncing up the driveway. A pickup truck stopped directly behind the squad car. Trygve Hovland jumped out of the truck and walked up to the passenger side of the car. Tanya rolled down her window.

"What's up?" she asked, second-guessing her decision to tell the Hovlands where she was headed.

"Just wondering what's happening," Trygve said as he leaned down and spoke through the driver's side window.

"Not much. Like I told you, we're not sure if Beck is here, but we found a list of businessmen in some of his belongings, and we think it might be a hit list, although that's just a guess at this point," Tanya explained.

Sonja appeared at Trygve's side. "Just so you know—there's a gun in the cubbyhole of my car, which Beck may have found by now, so be careful," she said.

Tanya groaned. "Great! Now we've got a mentally unstable perpetrator with a car, a phone, and a gun."

At that moment, the three officers Chief Pedretti had sent up the driveway returned. Tanya stepped out of the cruiser along with Jenny Lasinsky and Chad Hepple. A full moon hung in the night sky, and somewhere in the darkness, an owl hooted a lonely trill. A gentle breeze wafted through the pine trees at the bottom of the road, filling the air with their pine scent.

"Beck's up there, Chief," one of the officers said. "The stolen car is parked under the trees near a pole shed about fifty yards from the house. We crept along the house wall and looked through the living room windows. Beck is having a conversation with Mercer. So far, it seems to be just the two of them. There's no sign of other members of his family, although they may be in the house somewhere."

Sonja walked from the outside edge of the group into the center. "I'm very familiar with the house. Tim has been my client for over twenty years. I can draw you a floor plan."

"That'd be great," Tanya said. "Somebody get a pencil and some paper."

While the officers tossed around ideas about capturing Beck within the confines of the large home, Sonja quickly sketched a basic floor plan. "My suggestion is to enter the home from the deck that overlooks the bluff," she explained, pointing to the map. "The family seldom uses that door, especially at this time of night. It's locked, but there's a key on a hook near the door on the deck. Once the officers are in, they could travel down the long hallway that leads to the living room and kitchen area to gain access to the two men in the living room." Sonja used her pencil to trace the route on the map.

Tanya stared at Sonja, amazed again at her natural ability to organize and strategize. "Is there anything you don't do?" she asked.

Sonja reddened with embarrassment. "Well, I'm not sure what you mean…" Her voice sputtered into silence.

Tanya turned back to the group of officers huddled around the hood of the car. She began giving orders. "We'll cover all the house entrances so there's no means of escape. Hepple and Lasinsky, you get on the deck, find that key, and see if you can enter that way. Davis and Smith, you cover the other two entrances. I'll go to the back entrance that leads to the kitchen. I'll ring the bell and see what happens. Once I get inside, you make your way into the house, and we'll surround Beck and Mercer."

"Tanya, you should know that Tim is a certified black belt karate instructor," Sonja said. "He can handle himself in a tense situation."

"So you're telling me we've got a guy who's going to throw people across the room if things get tense? Sounds like a real good time," Tanya replied curtly. "Of course, that won't do him any good if Beck has a gun. Guns trump karate every time."

"Beck isn't going to negotiate. I don't think you'll be able to talk him down. It might go south really fast, so—"

"We'll handle it," Tanya interrupted, her voice sharp with nervousness. "Let's hope no one gets hurt." She met the stares of her team with resolute courage. "Let's move out, people. Be sharp."

The group began climbing the steep driveway in the

moonlight, one person following another. Sonja and Trygve watched the line of law enforcement officers bob their way up the hill toward Tim Mercer's house.

"Tryg, we should probably help—" Sonja began, but Trygve cut her off.

"Don't even go there. We've done enough," Trygve said gruffly. "After all, where would the police be if I hadn't found you at Mabel's and called the chief?"

Sonja held up her hand. "You're right. They'd be nowhere, and Beck Watson would be hightailin' it outta the country in my car."

Despite outwardly agreeing with her husband, it was killing Sonja that she wasn't one of the group climbing the hill toward Tim's, preparing to apprehend Beck Watson and throw him in jail. She was dying to tell Trygve she felt cheated out of the experience of capturing her first criminal—someone who'd created havoc in La Crosse and would now be taken off the streets so he couldn't harm anyone else. The whole situation seemed unfair. She thought back to all the things she'd discovered and shared with the police about the Diangelo murder, and now, in this climactic moment, the experience of ultimate victory was being snatched out of her grasp.

As if he could read her mind, Trygve spoke up. "I know you probably feel you should be in on the apprehension of this jerk, but I'm selfish, and I admit it," Trygve said, leaning toward her in the dark and placing a tender kiss on her cheek. "I want my wife around a little bit longer. Besides, you're not very good at self-defense."

"Hey! Speak for yourself," Sonja whispered harshly. "Who's the one who found Beck—"

"You didn't find him, honey," Trygve interrupted again. "You went looking for Mabel Kimble, and you accidentally stumbled on Beck. I'd say that was pure coincidence—maybe even an act of God. It had nothing to do with skill, sweetheart, yours or mine or anyone else's."

"Well, thanks for the vote of confidence, Tryg," Sonja said sarcastically. "It's always nice to have your husband in your corner rootin' for ya." She wheeled around and stumbled to the pickup, climbed in, and slammed the passenger door loudly.

Trygve sighed. Life would be a little testy for the next few hours, but he was hoping everything would get resolved soon, and Beck Watson would no longer be playing on the movie screen of his mind. He stood in the driveway, watching the house lights glow on the bluff. Then he turned and walked to the pickup.

CHAPTER 31
The House of the Rising Sun

Jenny Lasinsky and Lt. Chad Hepple crouched on the deck of the Mercer mansion that overlooked the Mississippi River, waiting in the shadows, listening to the night sounds that surrounded them. In the moonlight, several hundred feet below them, the river was a long, moonlit trail flowing in a southerly direction wedged between the towering bluffs on either side, calm and peaceful. In any other situation, the river could be considered romantic, the stuff of tales and adventures. But not tonight.

Jenny stood up from her crouched position on the huge deck hanging out over the cliff and tiptoed to the door leading into the home. She fumbled in the dark, searching for the key hanging under the deck railing. Her shaking hands knocked the keys into the gravel next to the steps. Chad briefly flashed his cell phone light, plucked the keys off the ground, and handed them back to Jenny, who quietly inserted them into the lock.

Meanwhile, inside the house, Beck Watson and Tim Mercer were engaged in a hostile exchange.

"You want me to do what?" Tim asked, squinting at Beck, his face slack with amazement.

Beck began ticking off several suggestions. "Renounce your capitalist ways, give half your money to charity, step down from your duties at Allied Gasoline, and sell your house—"

"Have you lost your everlovin' mind?" Tim shouted. He suddenly stood up from the recliner he'd been sitting in and took a few steps toward Watson. "Do you know how hard I've worked to get where I am?" He shook his head in disgust and began wagging his index finger in Beck's direction. "It's obvious you've never held down a job long enough or invested any of your skills and talents in a job you love, or you would never say the crazy things you're saying!"

"Are you calling me crazy?" Beck shouted, suddenly reaching into the pocket of his sweatshirt. Brandishing a small pistol in Tim's face, he shouted again a little louder, "Are you calling me crazy?"

In an instant, Tim made a decision despite the gun barrel pointed up his nose. *Who did this guy think he was, anyway?* Tim thought. He realized he might regret his decision to challenge Watson. It's never a good idea to stand up to someone who was waving a gun in your face, but he couldn't ignore or rationalize what this young man had done by forcing his way into his home and discrediting everything he'd worked so hard to achieve. "Well, try this on for size, buddy. You may not be crazy, but you're definitely misinformed, and it's obvious you know nothing about how our economic system works!"

"This is your final warning! Renounce or die!" Beck

shouted. He pointed the pistol at the ceiling and squeezed the trigger. The blast of the bullet blew a small hole in the cathedral ceiling.

"Well, that's just great!" Tim shouted, flailing his arms. "Now look what you've done. You've not only insulted me for the work I've done and the success I've had, but you've blasted a hole in my teak ceiling. What in the hell is the matter with you?"

"It's the system!" Beck yelled back. "Don't you get it? The capitalistic system is corrupt and favors those who crave power and wealth."

At the sound of the gunshot, Tanya Pedretti and two officers rushed through the kitchen and headed into the living room, their guns drawn.

"What's going on in here?" Tanya asked.

Beck Watson and Tim Mercer turned at the sound of the police chief's voice and stared. "Who're you?" Beck asked, the pistol hanging limply at his side.

"Police Chief Tanya Pedretti. I'd recommend that you hand over the pistol so we can resolve whatever conflicts you're having here," she said, moving slowly and carefully toward Watson. At that moment, Jenny and Chad walked into the living room from the back hallway. Beck nervously surveyed the people who surrounded him on several sides. Tim held up his hands in a gesture of surrender.

"This guy forced his way into my house and started lecturing me on the evils of capitalism," Tim explained.

"We know all about it," Chief Pedretti said, still advancing slowly toward Beck.

"You do?" Beck said, backing up a few steps.

"Yep. We found a note in the pocket of Dr. Diangelo's

suit coat that said, 'Death to the Capitalists,'" Pedretti said. "Plus we found books in your bedroom that you've been reading about the evils of capitalism and a list of business entrepreneurs you targeted. We put two and two together." She leaned in and grabbed the small pistol Beck held in his hand with a quick, deft movement.

"What's that supposed to mean?" Beck asked. "You think I had something to do with Diangelo's death?"

At the mention of Diangelo, Tim Mercer stared at Beck Watson with something bordering on incredulity. "Are you the one who killed Dr. Diangelo? I knew him. He fixed my wife's teeth. He did a great job. What was your beef with him?"

"Probably the same thing he has against you," Chad said. "He resents your money, position, and influence, which you earned honestly at Allied."

Beck Watson stared at Chief Pedretti. "You can't prove that I had anything to do with Diangelo's death. For all you know, he could have had a drug problem and taken an overdose of fentanyl. That has nothing to do with me."

"Would you like to revise that statement?" Pedretti asked.

"Why would I?" Beck spat viciously.

"It's not public knowledge how Dr. Diangelo died, so why did you say he died of a fentanyl overdose? Only someone involved in his murder would know that," Pedretti said. She walked cautiously toward Watson and slipped a pair of handcuffs around his wrists. "Beck Watson, I am arresting you for the murder of Dr. Tony Diangelo and the shooting of Lt. Hank Brousard. You have the right to remain silent…"

CHAPTER 32 • SONJA
I Wanna Hold Your Hand

I've never been one to dwell in sentimentality. I'm more of a hard-headed realist, but the capture of Beck Watson without incident blew through every misconception I had of criminal apprehension. Where was the gunfire and the blood and guts capitulation of a desperate criminal? Had I read too many thriller novels? I knew I should have been thankful and elated that no one was hurt during the manhunt and confrontation at Tim Mercer's mansion, but frankly, part of me was disappointed. I expected Watson to put up a fight, but when it came down to it, he seemed to be a toothless lion—all bark and no bite!

"So, you're telling me he willingly handed over my pistol without any kind of struggle or resistance?" I asked Tanya over the phone on Saturday morning. I was sitting at the island in my sun-drenched kitchen drinking a cup of coffee and eating a blueberry muffin, watching Sonny and Cher munching on a haybale in the barnyard. Coco lay sleeping in the sun by the patio door. I had made a harried trip down to the police station earlier in the morning to fetch my Subaru that Watson had stolen and driven to Tim's residence the night before.

"That's what I'm telling you, Sonja," Tanya explained, "although he did shoot a hole in Mercer's very expensive living room ceiling. During our discussion, Watson knew things about Diangelo that could only be known by someone intimately involved in his murder. He blew his cover when he claimed Diangelo might have a drug problem and had taken a fentanyl overdose.

"Further questioning downtown revealed other tidbits Watson knew about Dr. Diangelo, like his penchant for expensive clothes. Watson obviously did his homework and played on the dentist's sympathy by faking a problem with his tooth that needed the doc's immediate care. The doc, being an empathetic professional, agreed to meet him at his office at the ungodly hour of five-thirty to examine the tooth. Beck was supposed to meet him at the back entrance, but he borrowed his brother Sam's ID and got into the building, where he rode the elevator to the second floor. Apparently, Diangelo didn't question Beck on how he gained entrance to the building. Plus, the labwork came in on the stocking. Watson's DNA was all over the stocking. Once we'd finished the interrogation, I knew we had him. He remained mute and docile while I read him the Miranda rights. Later downtown at the jail, he walked peacefully back to his cell after he spilled his guts."

"There's one thing I was hoping he'd admit," I said.

"Oh, yeah, what's that?" Tanya asked.

"How did he give Diangelo the big injection? It doesn't

seem like anyone would knuckle under to that."

"Beck told us he distracted him with a long, involved discussion about eliminating the penny from our monetary system, and while Diangelo was jabbering about the reasons it would never work, Beck poked him with the needle and shot the fentanyl into his mid-section."

"Really?"

"That's his story, and he seems to be stickin' to it," Tanya said.

"One other thing I wondered about was how Beck got out of the building unnoticed. He wasn't seen leaving on the CCTV camera," Sonja said.

"He admitted he hid in the laundry cart under some dirty linens and rode in the cart to the Suds and Duds facility, where he eventually escaped unnoticed. Clever, huh?"

"I'd say. Trygve will be glad to hear he was right about that."

"Before I forget, thanks for all the help with the case. You have an incredible network throughout the city, and I still think you'd make a great detective."

"That might be true, but I don't think Trygve would put up with that, especially when it comes to an exchange of gunfire. Just look at what happened last night. Trygve and I were waiting at the end of River View Lane listening for the shots we felt sure would happen. But it didn't, so we finally drove home. Are you sure your charges are going to stick?"

"We have to get our legal ducks in a row, but yes, I'm confident we've charged the individual responsible for the death of Dr. Tony Diangelo, and we have enough hard evidence that it will hold up in court. I'd love to find the syringe and needle Beck used on Diangelo to deliver the dose of fentanyl, but that may never happen. As for the shooting of Hatchet, the body camera confirms that Beck shot him and then fled the scene," Pedretti said. "That's a done deal."

"I'm glad you finally discovered how Beck escaped from the Midwest building the morning of the murder," I said. That conundrum had bothered me from the beginning of this affair when I'd discovered the expired dentist in his chair and heard the ding of the elevator.

"We're hoping to find out more about that when Lt. Hepple and I interview Beck again about the details of the crime. Sam, his brother, has been encouraging him to cooperate fully with the police, and I'm hoping, for once, he takes his brother's advice," Tanya said.

"He's not prone to insights of wisdom and maturity, but maybe you'll luck out. I hope you succeed, but first you're going to have to convince him our government and elected officials are not the blatant capitalistic crooks and miscreants he thinks they are," I said.

"Well, truthfully, some of them probably are crooks, but we'll never convince him that some of them are also honest public servants, so I'm not even going to go there," Tanya said with resignation.

I talked to the police chief for a few more minutes, wished her luck with the follow-up interview, and hung up. I cleaned up my breakfast dishes, grabbed my lightweight jacket from the hook in the back hallway, and walked toward the barnyard, where I knew Trygve was completing his morning chores.

Walking into the barn, the smell of clean straw and fragrant sweet hay overwhelmed me. My chickens were pecking happily at my feet, and Coco barked at them as if I needed his protection. I chuckled at his silly antics, but as I leaned against the gate, I realized the familiar surroundings were just what I needed to regain my sense of normalcy in my life. The week's chaotic events had upended my optimism and hope and left me gasping for some kind of anchor. I guess that's what happens to your sense of security when you're trussed up like a turkey and thrown in someone's basement to rot. I shouldn't have been surprised at the feelings I was having in the aftermath of the trauma I'd endured. As I stood and watched Trygve fluff the straw in the mules' corral, tears suddenly formed in my eyes and spilled onto my cheeks. *Where would I be without Tryg?* I thought. Feelings of gratitude and thankfulness flooded my heart when I thought of his desperate search and dogged determination to find me.

As if Trygve had read my mind, he walked toward me with a smile. "Wondering if you're ready to head down to the cabin for an overnight?" he asked. "We could take a couple of steaks, a bottle of wine, and our sleeping bags. Whaddya think?" He gazed at me and wiped the tears from my cheeks with his thumb.

"Don't let me forget the dark chocolate-covered caramels," I reminded him. "The ones with the sea salt sprinkled over the top."

"And the cinnamon rolls I bought this morning at the bakery," he said. "They're on the kitchen counter. Ready in an hour?" He leaned over and kissed me on the lips.

"Yep. I'll get packing while you finish your chores down here," I answered enthusiastically. I turned and headed for the house, where I packed a cooler of food and a duffle bag of clothes and toiletries. It would be cool in the valley by the Kickapoo River, so I tossed a couple of warm sweatshirts in the back of my Subaru along with our sleeping bags.

An hour later, Trygve and I were driving along U.S. Highway 14. When we came to 131, we drove south to the little village of Soldier's Grove, then continued down the road for several miles. Arriving at the intersection of County B, we drove to our small cabin just south of Towerville. The one-room cabin was a hand-built structure that sat above the Kickapoo River on a limestone outcropping. Trygve had inherited ten acres of land where the cabin sat from his eccentric Norwegian bachelor uncle, and we'd constructed the cabin about five years ago from recycled timbers and pine boards salvaged from a sagging barn standing on the property. We had a lot of sweat equity in the place, but more importantly, a part of our soul was in this structure. We'd built it after the death of my parents and the loss of our three babies. At the time, it provided some much-needed physical therapy, but more importantly, we both felt a natural affinity in our soul for the land and the sky and the river that bubbled lazily through the unglaciated hills surrounding the cabin. The wildlife we'd seen and the fish we'd caught and fried over our campfire were memories no one could take from us.

Trygve parked my Subaru next to the river, and we began unloading our gear from the car. We walked across the footbridge that led to the cabin, breathing in the fresh air and listening to the water bubbling over the rocks beneath our feet. It was music to my soul, and I felt myself relax and a deep contentment filled my heart as I walked up the hill to the level ground in front of the cabin. We organized the inside of the cabin and built a fire from our stash of split wood stacked along the cabin wall. Then we broke open a bottle of wine and sat next to the crackling logs, soaking in the peace and calm that comes from nature. No cell phones, no television, no traffic. Just wide open spaces, the sound of crickets chirping in the high grass, and the crackle of the fire at our feet.

"Wow! This is great, honey," I said, grasping Trygve's hand and taking a sip of wine. "It's a beautiful spring day."

"Yes, it is," Trygve responded. He leaned back in his chair and studied the clouds floating in the azure sky above. "I love this place … and I love you."

"I'd say you really came through the other night when you found us in Mabel's basement," I said. "That was like a ten on a ten-point scale. When I heard you clomping around upstairs yelling my name … well, that was the best thing that's ever happened to me, babe."

"Wow! I guess I hit it out of the park, huh?"

"Yeah, Tryg. You definitely hit a homer on that one. One other thing—you were right about Beck hiding in the laundry cart and escaping to Suds and Duds. That's why he wasn't on the CCTV camera."

"Wow! I really hit a homer, huh?"

"You might say that." I smiled at him.

"Did Chief Pedretti tell you about the meeting inside Tim Mercer's house?" Trygve asked.

I filled Trygve in on the details of Beck Watson's bumbling confessions. It seemed surreal that one person was dead, and another police officer was lying in the hospital with serious injuries simply because someone disagreed with the economic system in our country. But nowadays, with political disagreements at an all-time high, I wasn't really surprised.

Trygve listened carefully while I expressed my thoughts about the investigation into the mysterious murder of Dr. Tony Diangelo.

"You know, sometimes in life you meet someone, and you just know you're going to be lifelong friends. When I met Tanya at the Midwest building, I knew we'd hit it off. And we did. I do have to admit, though, I was worried when Beck threw us in the basement and took off with my car. I still don't understand why he didn't just whack us and be done with it."

"Well, I'm glad he didn't, and I hope you got all this out of your system once and for all," Trygve said, staring into the embers of the fire. "Maybe now we can get back to some kind of normal life."

After several moments of silent reflection, I waded back into the conversation.

"You know, to be totally honest, I feel really good about helping the police. I know it sent you into left field for a few days, but I'm proud that the information I discovered helped Pedretti and her crew in their search for Dr. Diangelo's killer. I won't apologize for my involvement, Tryg," I explained, "and my people made me proud. They came through at every turn with vital clues and facts that helped the police get a handle on this thing."

"Does that mean you're going to continue to stick your nose in police investigations in the future?" Trygve asked brusquely.

"By invite only," I said coolly.

Trygve groaned. "You know what that means, don't you?" he asked.

"Nope."

"Where you go, I go," Trygve said.

"Sounds good to me," I said. I smiled and sipped some more wine.

THE END

ABOUT THE AUTHOR

Sue Berg is a Wisconsin native and a cheerleader for the Midwestern way of life. The beauty of Wisconsin, the authenticity of its people, and the rural way of life are all ideals she incorporates into her novels. Since retiring from a teaching career that spanned thirty-two years, Sue has pursued writing full-time and has completed six novels in the award-winning Jim Higgins Driftless Mystery Series set in the coulees and bluffs of La Crosse, Wisconsin and *Death at the Dentist*, the first novel in The Dirty Business Mystery Series, which features housecleaner, Sonja Hovland and her blue-collar cohorts.

Sue resides in the beautiful Driftless Area near Viroqua, Wisconsin with her husband, Alan. She enjoys gardening, quilting, writing, and camping on the Mississippi River with her family.

ENJOYED DEATH AT THE DENTIST?

We think you'll also like the Jim Higgins
Driftless Mystery Series!

The Driftless Mystery Series set in the beautiful Driftless region of the Upper Midwest does not disappoint. With complex characters, intriguing plots, and surprising twists and turns, this series will delight you with its ability to entertain while upholding the values we all treasure; love, faith, loyalty, and family. It is destined to become a beloved and enduring legacy to the people and culture in this unique part of the country.

Printed in the United States
by Baker & Taylor Publisher Services